THE PRISONER

Denicalis Dragon Chronicles – Book Two

By

MJ ALLAIRE

Bookateer Publishing
www.bookateerpublishing.com

Layout and design by Ryan Twomey

ISBN: 978-0-9819368-4-0
Library of Congress Control Number: 2010934829

Dedication

First and foremost, I would like to thank my children, Nick, Mic, and Toni, for their many sacrifices during our continuing journey called life. From the things we've experienced the past year, and those we have yet to experience, I believe you now know that life is full of challenges. Sometimes all we can do is take it a day at a time.

Mic, there aren't enough words to describe how thankful I am for your humor and support. I love when you accompany me on book signings and events! It always makes me smile when people say, "I love how he says, 'I'm a fictional character!'" You are a character, indeed!

Toni, every day I watch proudly as you continue to blossom into the beautiful young woman I know you are going to be. Remember that no matter how old you are, or how big you get, you'll always be "mommy's baby girl."

Nick, you've done a wonderful job of supporting me in our daily lives, and I know you know how much I depend on you. Thank you for being the young man you have become, and know that I'm very proud of you.

Carl, my proofreader-on-demand and IPSI brother, thank you for bringing fresh eyes to the heart of my imagination. It seems like only yesterday we were sitting in the back of science class being silly! I owe you big time!

And to the rest of my friends and family, thank you for believing in me!

Warmest regards,

MJ Allaire

The Prisoner

The Girls

"Aahhhh, yessss! I can smell you! I can sssee your light!" Muscala triumphantly taunted them as the taste of victory filled his mouth like sweet nectar, while his tongue flicked wildly in the darkness. He had been seeking the amulet for so long, and soon it would be his! Those meddling children would live just long enough to regret the fact that they had angered him before he would mercilessly end their worthless lives!

With the knowledge that they had a very angry snake hot on their heels, who was, by the sound of it, just a few short seconds away from them, Diam, Tonia, and Kaileen held hands as they prepared to step into the bright rainbow light that filled the portal before them. If they wanted to survive, they simply had no choice but to step into the unknown.

The light from the glowing stones generated an intense humming noise that had quickly filled the cave. Tonia ignored the loud droning and closed her eyes as she took a hesitant step into the magical rainbow. She held her breath gripping one of Kaileen's hands in her left and Diam's in the right. Her throat tightened and she could feel her moist palms adhering to her companions.

Before she could reconsider her decision, she took the one step that would save her from the immediate danger, but could also lead her into oblivion. A sensation of weightlessness engulfed her body and staring at the inside of her closed eyelids, brilliant flashes of light oscillated reds, greens, yellows, and blues. In spite of this, she kept her last breath locked tightly in her chest and clasped her friend's hands for dear life. Together, they continued to fall, fall, fall, into nowhere. The odd feeling lasted a few seconds, a few minutes, an eternity, it didn't matter. As quickly as it had begun, she realized the weightless feeling was gone.

She finally allowed the now stagnant breath to escape her lips and cautiously inhaled a new one. The first thing Tonia became aware of was the air… fresh, crisp, and much different than the warm, stale air of the cave.

Like Tonia, Kaileen and Diam had also closed their eyes tightly when they stepped into the portal, unsure they really wanted to know what magic was unfolding. Diam held her closest friend's hand in her own so tightly, she thought she might crush the small, feminine fingers that offered her the only sense of solace she could find amongst the chaos. Meanwhile, Kaileen imagined this was it, the end. All the stories she heard as a youngling taught her of the journey into the afterlife, and this was it. When their feet once again felt the comfort of sturdy ground beneath them, Kaileen felt a sense of peace overwhelm her. They both quickly noticed the change in the air surrounding them as each girl replaced their expended breath.

At the same time, all three girls nervously opened their eyes. It didn't make much of a difference, however, because in addition to the fresh air, they also found they were surrounded by a cool, silent darkness. Their torch, though lit when they stepped into the portal, had gone out at some point during their journey to this very unfamiliar place.

Tonia and Diam tried to look around but had to wait for their eyes to adjust to the surrounding darkness. Within a few minutes they could begin to make out just where it was they were… standing in what seemed to be some sort of field. Diam knelt down and ran her hand lightly across the ground.

"It feels like grass," she said happily as she smiled in the darkness, almost afraid to believe they had actually gotten out of the cave. More important than this was the fact that they had managed to escape a certain death from the angry snake they'd left behind.

"The fresh air smells wonderful, doesn't it?" Tonia whispered to her friends. "Girls, we made it!"

After being used to the darkness from the cave, Kaileen's eyes adjusted more quickly to their new surroundings and she looked around in wonder. Was this it? Was this where her family, her people, had gone? No, there was something wrong. It was dark... in all of the stories, there was a light. Where was the light?

"It smells funny," she stated curtly. It was all she could say as her hopes came crashing down around her. Perhaps now, she would never see her people again... not in this world... and not in the next.

Tonia and Diam were confused by this but soon realized this was likely the very first time their new friend had ever been outside the cave she had called home. They both wondered how she would handle her new environment.

"What is this?" the kalevala asked them quietly.

"What is what?" Tonia asked, hearing the unamused wonder in the kalevala's voice. Then she remembered that Kaileen's eyesight in the darkness was better than in the light, and that their new friend should be able to see much more right now than either she or Diam could. "Tell us what you see," she suggested.

"Yes, tell us," Diam agreed. As an afterthought she added, "We could try to re-light our torch, but I think it would be safer to let you lead us instead, because your eyes are used to the darkness." As she said this, she firmly gripped the torch in her left hand and held it tight... a weapon in disguise.

"Kaileen, would you mind?" Tonia asked the kalevala.

"Not at all," Kaileen answered softly, moving on from her initial discontent.

Tonia smiled. She was glad she could help to take the kalevala's mind off of the tragedy that had just occurred in the darkness of the cave. She knew how much Ransa had meant to the gentle kalevala. She also worried that the death of the small reptile might prove to be too much for Kaileen, especially after all the heartache and loss she had already experienced during her young life. Of course, Tonia had no idea of the newly disappointing developments in her small friend's mind.

"Where are we?" Merlia asked, puzzled and bewildered, from the bag on Diam's back.

"We're not sure yet," Tonia answered quietly. "You two sit

3

tight for a minute while we check the place out." Diam and Tonia stood quietly as Kaileen scanned their surroundings.

"We are surrounded by a lot of soft, small… things growing out of the ground?" she said with an air of confusion in her voice.

The others remained silent for a moment as they tried to figure out what Kaileen was referring to.

"Oh!" Diam said excitedly. "Is it grass?" she asked, fairly certain she had figured it out.

"There are other things, off in the distance… bigger things. They look like they may be a good place to find shelter if we need it," Kaileen stated as she continued surveying the area. The others could clearly hear the wonder in her voice.

"Does it look like a good place where we can wait for the boys?" Tonia asked. She couldn't tell what Kaileen was referring to because her eyes were still struggling to adjust to the darkness.

"Yes, over there," Kaileen said, pointing off in the distance.

"Okay, let's work our way towards it. I'm not comfortable at all about our being out in the open like this," Diam was quick to add, and Tonia nodded.

Kaileen took the lead as she carefully led them to an area of dense trees. By the time they got there, everyone's eyes had adjusted as well as could be expected.

A cluster of trees stood hauntingly in front of them, thick and dark. The scent of the air had changed again slightly, which quickly reminded both Tonia and Diam of the Orneo Forest near their home.

Diam was very relieved to be out of the dark, stuffy cave. Looking skyward, she could just begin to make out a few scattered stars far above her, where they sparkled in an endless blanket of darkness. The moon, surprisingly, was nowhere to be seen.

"Moonlight would sure make it easier for us to see where we are," she thought, "but it would also make it easier for other creatures to see us, too.

"Why don't we rest there while we wait for the boys?" She suggested as she pointed at the nearby trees.

"Sounds good," Tonia answered. She was still cautious about their new situation and kept her hand close to her sword. She was hopeful the boys would arrive quickly, but had not forgotten the creature that was hot on their tails just minutes earlier.

They made their way over to a large tree with an extremely wide trunk and after gently setting their backpacks on the ground, all sat down. Kaileen kept a guarded watch as she sat between the girls. Once they were settled, Tonia and Diam removed the turtles from their respective bags. As they set the hard-shelled creatures down next to each other in the cool grass, Merlia suddenly began to cry.

"This… this… is something I had convinced myself… I would never see again," she said happily.

The gloomy darkness around them still made it somewhat difficult to see, and they were barely able to make out the shapes of the turtles. As the girls quietly watched them, Celio began to nuzzle Merlia with his extended head. Happiness was evident in Merlia's voice in spite of her tears as she talked softly to her son, reassuring him they would be all right now.

As a comfortable silence fell upon their little group, Tonia gently caressed the younger turtle's smooth, hard shell.

"Celio, welcome to the outside world," she said.

"Yes, welcome!" Diam whispered as she smiled.

They sat silently in the darkness as Celio began trilling softly. The sound comforted the children immensely. They finally allowed their minds and bodies to relax after a long and exhausting day.

As they dazedly stared off into the night, it was Diam that finally brought them back to reality.

"Tonia? I'm worried about the boys. They should have come through by now."

Tonia had been fighting back the same thought in her head and decided to remain silent for the moment and keep on fighting it.

Back in the cave, Muscala sounded like he was right on them before they stepped through the portal. She couldn't help but consider the possibility that perhaps the boys hadn't made it out of the cave after all.

"I know," Tonia finally replied, startling her friend who thought she hadn't heard her and was about to say it again. Tonia tried her best to conceal her worry, but her voice was tight and anxious. "Let's just try our best to be patient. Hopefully they'll be here soon."

They sat quietly, listening to Celio's serenade. It was good to see him happy.

"Why don't we rest here a while?" Kaileen suggested. "It's safer than where we were before and we can wait for the boys."

The others agreed.

"Besides," she continued, "We're all tired after the long day and could use the rest. Why don't you two sleep for a bit while I keep watch? We can take turns."

"Yea, I am pretty tired." Looking at her best friend, Diam added, "I'm sure you are too, Tonia."

Tonia looked at Kaileen and asked, "Are you sure you don't mind taking the first watch?"

Kaileen shook her head. "No, I don't mind."

"All right," Tonia said.

She looked at the turtles. Quiet now, they were audibly enjoying their meal of fresh, green grass.

"Wake me in a few hours... I'll take the next watch," Tonia offered as she stretched before settling down close to the tree.

"I'll do that," Kaileen said.

"I'll take third watch," Diam said as she yawned. She lay down close to Tonia and before she could count ten mud puppies, she was sound asleep.

Two

The rest of the night passed uneventfully and before they knew it, the sun was once again rising in the eastern sky. Chirping birds noisily welcomed the day from the nearby trees and the chill had just about worn off the land.

Tonia sat up and stretched. She was somewhat rested but felt as though she could sleep for days given the chance. She looked around and saw Diam a short distance away, standing quietly in the grass. After glancing over at the sleeping kalevala, Tonia got up and walked softly through the cool, dew-covered grass to join her friend.

Sensing someone behind her, Diam quickly turned and looked at Tonia. Tonia noticed the tears that were welling in her friend's eyes. She reached out gave Diam a long, tight hug. No words were necessary… Tonia and Diam had been best friends forever, it seemed, and they often shared similar thoughts. Sometimes, when they looked into each other's eyes, it was as if they were looking into the heart of a sister, even though neither had a sister. As they stood in the morning sunshine with tears in their eyes, the sadness weighing on their hearts was easily reflected within. In that moment, they both came to a deeper understanding of the phrase 'the eyes are the doorway to the soul'…

"Tonia, I'm afraid that the boys didn't make it," Diam said with a sniffle, her voice filling with sadness. She didn't want to upset her friend, but felt compelled to share her concerns. Although they were not related, Diam loved the boys as if they were her own brothers. She could not bear the thought of life

7

without them, and knew without a doubt that Tonia felt the same way.

Lost in emotion, the girls were caught off guard when they heard a noise behind them. Quickly, they turned to see Kaileen walking up to join them. Her eyes were filled with the same sadness, yet she remained silent. She struggled to keep them open as the sun fell like needles into the black abyss at the center, which had never been showered in such searing light.

"Diam, remember what my dad used to say?" Tonia asked, almost in a whisper.

Diam looked at her friend with a questioning frown.

"Which time?" she asked.

Tonia absently wiped at a tear which was slowly making its way down her cheek as she continued.

"He would tell us all the time that whenever we found ourselves in a situation where things looked tough, we shouldn't let it get us down. Instead of getting upset and thinking negatively about everything, it just meant we would have to work a little harder to find the positive things," Tonia said, trying to convince herself as much as her friend.

Diam's face lit up with a smile as she remembered Tonia's father.

"Yes," she said. "I do remember him telling us there is always a positive side to any situation."

"That's right!" Tonia said, glad her friend was riding the same mental dragon as she was.

Kaileen stood next to them, listening quietly.

"So here we are, in a tough situation, right?" Tonia asked with a coy yet mischievous smile.

Diam and Kaileen both nodded.

"Okay, then, let's put our problems into perspective.

"The boys are missing, that's a fact. We went through the portal before they did and managed to stay together, which is good. We also successfully escaped from the cave, which is even better!" she said as she tried to encourage them to think positively.

While she tried to think of something else encouraging to say, another thought suddenly occurred to her.

"Hey! Didn't the bat go through before we did?" She frowned as she tried to remember.

"Yes, yes, it did! It went through the portal right after telling us we needed to hurry up and go through, too." Kaileen recalled.

"That's right!" Tonia said excitedly. Her mind was gently washing away the fear and anxiety she felt with the hope of something that could actually help them in their troubled situation.

"And…?" Diam asked, wondering where her friend was going with this. As usual, Tonia was busy being Tonia.

"So, if the bat went through first," Tonia said, "then where is it? Where did it go?"

Diam and Kaileen looked at her quizzically. After a few seconds, however, Diam's face lit up again. "Oh, I get it!" she said with a slight smile. "If the bat went through the same portal as we did before we did, then it should be here." She looked at Tonia, somewhat doubtful.

"Right?"

"That's what I'm thinking," Tonia answered her friend.

The girls looked around, hoping to see the bat flying somewhere nearby. Instead they saw nothing but blue sky and sunshine.

Tonia began to giggle.

"We're being silly," she said. "Bats are nocturnal, and only come out at night, so we wouldn't see it flying around now because it's probably hiding in the trees somewhere, getting ready to sleep the coming day away."

Diam chided herself for not thinking about this before.

Dagnabbit!

Just when she thought she was onto something…

"But here's my take on this," Tonia began again, unknowingly interrupting her friend's thoughts.

"If the bat went through the portal first and it isn't here now, then maybe the boys won't be coming here either," she reasoned.

"What are you talking about?" Diam asked, confused.

Tonia sighed as she wished for once that Diam could get into her head. Sometimes they knew each other's thoughts without even trying, but at other times…

"I'm thinking," she continued, "that the boys did go through the portal, but ended up somewhere else."

"Hmm," Kaileen said, "That makes very good sense.

"A while ago back in the cave, Ransa and I had a discussion one day about different ways of traveling. She told me she'd heard stories of creatures that had traveled through a magical vortex. Apparently, not all of the creatures ended up together on the other side." As the kalevala explained this, Diam and Tonia became more interested.

"Okay, so if we say that the boys did make it through the portal but are now somewhere else, how in the world are we supposed to find them?" Diam asked.

It seemed that, although they were gaining ground in their understanding of things, they were not getting any closer to the answers they were really looking for.

"I don't know." The words fell from Tonia's lips like a cold rain.

She could no longer ignore the utter desperation of their seemingly hopeless situation. As the weight of their predicament slammed into her like a lightning bolt, she sat down in the grass and began to cry with a heart-wrenching sob.

"Don't cry," Kaileen said as she tried to comfort her new friend. She wrapped her arms around Tonia, holding her as she caved to the despair. The young girl's emotions spilled like a tidal wave over the edge of her soul. Diam knelt down and wrapped her arms around them both as her own tears joined Tonia's in the grass at their feet.

When Tonia felt her friends surround her with their love and kindness, it only made her cry more. They remained huddled together for a little while as they shared hugs and tears, wishing for easy answers to their difficult questions.

They didn't find them.

After a while, the tears stopped and they stood up, still arm in arm. With bloodshot eyes and stuffy noses, they slowly made their way back to the tree where the turtles were waiting. Unaware of the emotional moments the girls had shared, the turtles barely noticed their return as they continued to enjoy the abundance of fresh, green grass that surrounded them.

Once the girls were settled beneath the tree, Kaileen again decided to share something that was on her mind.

"I have this feeling," she began hesitantly, but stopped. As doubts overtook her, she looked nervously at Diam and Tonia.

"What is it?" Diam asked, hoping the kalevala trusted them enough to share whatever was on her mind.

Kaileen looked nervously at the eastern horizon. The pink hues in the glorious sunrise would gradually change into blue skies and white clouds as the sun continued its journey west. It was going to be a beautiful day.

"It's hard to explain," she said without looking at them.

Diam and Tonia could tell by the tone of Kaileen's voice that she was struggling to find the words for whatever it was she was trying to say.

Kaileen took a deep breath before turning to look back at her friends.

"It's kind of silly, actually," she began. With a loud sigh, she continued. "I have a feeling about which way we should go when we continue our journey."

The others looked at her with question, but not doubt, and waited patiently for her to continue.

"It's just a feeling, but I think we should head east," she said shyly as she dropped her eyes slightly, unsure of how they would take her suggestion.

Diam and Tonia listened quietly as a breeze brushed gently past them, whispering in the leaves of the trees above.

"I'm not sure if you are experiencing the same sensation that I am, but it feels like we're being pulled in that direction. Can you feel it?" Kaileen asked, hopeful her friends in some way felt a little bit of what she felt… and that they wouldn't think she was crazy.

Diam shook her head no.

"I don't think so," she said.

Tonia cocked her head to the side as she considered Kaileen's question.

"I do think I feel a little bit of something, Kaileen, but I'm not quite sure what it is. Perhaps Micah is in the east somewhere, and he's using his magical stones to summon us?" she suggested.

11

"Maybe," Kaileen said. "I just feel like… there's a tarza vine… tied somewhere deep in my belly, somehow tugging me that way." The short, gray kalevala pointed eastward, looking off toward the rising sun. "And as time goes on, it feels like the tension on it gets stronger and stronger, like I have to go." She sighed.

"We should head east," she said in a serious tone. It wasn't a question.

She looked down at the ground, afraid she would make enemies of her new friends if they thought she was being too demanding. She was a kalevala, however, and when kalevalas feel strongly about something, they make it known regardless of the consequences.

In the grass near the girls, the turtles remained quiet. It was not necessary to explain anything to them about what was happening, for both of the smaller creatures in their group understood it all too well. As they talked, the girls relaxed near the tree eating chickleberries. They were silently trying to postpone the inevitable… that they would soon have to continue on without the boys.

After discussing it for a while longer, they finally made a decision.

"Since you feel so strongly about it, Kaileen, we'll head east," Tonia said. She gave Kaileen a quick hug, and the timid kalevala hugged her back with a relieved smile.

After they had finished their snack, Diam's thoughts began drifting back to the ring they'd found on the skeleton in the cave. Curious about it, she asked Tonia to let her see it. Without question Tonia pulled the bag with the ring from her pocket and handed it to her friend.

"Wouldn't it be great if we found some dragons here?" Tonia asked dreamily. "After all the stories we've heard, I would love to see a real flesh and blood beastie!"

Diam looked at her friend and smiled. Tonia… always the dreamer.

"And it would need to be a nice one, of course," Tonia added with a wink.

Diam slowly removed the small piece of jewelry from the

bag, and then began turning it this way and that as she closely examined it. She found it much easier to see the detail on the ring in the sunlight than when they were back in the cave, where the only light source came from the flickering torches.

After seeing what had happened with the magical stones in the cave, Diam had no desire to put the ring on her finger. It was a beautiful piece of jewelry, there was no question about that, but her fear of the unknown was stronger than the beauty held by it. For the moment, she was quite content just looking at it.

The ring itself was small, with a green gem held securely in its center. Diam watched to see if it would cloud up again like it did in the cave, and was surprised to find she was disappointed when it didn't. As she examined it more closely, she could see how it appeared to be encased by the same type of metal as the amulet they'd found in the cave. She had never seen the likes of such a craftsman that could fashion metal so smooth, so shiny.

She wished Nicho were here, remembering what he said when they had first showed him the ring in the cave. His friend Zatona was a jewelry maker and collector. After all the time Nicho had spent with the charm-maker, he was sure she would know, or at least have some idea, of just what the ring was really made from.

In spite of her hesitation just mere seconds before, she found herself tempted to slide the ring onto her finger. Since they weren't sure where it came from or to whom it belonged, however, she thought twice, and decided against it yet again.

Diam smiled as a funny thought struck her. Tonia loved frogs, but she didn't think her friend would be very happy if she put the ring on her finger and suddenly turned into one! Who knew what kind of spells might be tied into this seemingly harmless piece of jewelry!

She chuckled quietly and looked at her friend.

"What?" Tonia asked.

"Nothing."

Tonia gave her friend an unamused look but said no more.

"Let's go," Kaileen offered, anxious to continue their journey.

After another brief glance at the ring, Diam gently returned it to the bag. Since she wanted to inspect it further once the sun was fully in the sky, she tied the bag to her waistband. She had no way of knowing how soon she would come to regret this.

Without a word, the girls worked together to pack up their things. When they were finished, Tonia walked over to the turtles where they were silently resting. She knelt down so she wouldn't tower over them.

"Celio… Merlia… I guess this is goodbye," she said as Kaileen and Diam joined her.

"You said you wanted to be released outside of the cave, to give your son a chance at a new life… and this looks like a wonderful place for you to do just that," Tonia continued as she looked at Merlia.

The mother turtle took a few small steps towards Tonia before the girl reached out and picked her up. Celio followed suit and Tonia lifted him off the ground as well. She gently hugged them both close to her as Celio began softly trilling again. There was no mistaking that the turtles enjoyed life outside the cold, dark cave.

"Thank you for all of your help," Merlia whispered. "I will forever be indebted to you for your kindness.

"When you find your brothers, and I know you will, please thank them for me from the bottom of my heart. I know they did not think it was a good idea to take us with you, but because you did, my son will have a chance at a good life now," Merlia said, tearing as the goodbye came closer and closer.

"You're very welcome," Tonia answered as she handed the turtles off to Diam. After also hugging them, Diam handed them to Kaileen, who did the same before placing them gently in the grass.

"May you have a good life, my turtle friends," Tonia said. She nodded at Diam and Kaileen and added, "I'm ready to go whenever you are."

"And may you, as well," Merlia answered in return. "You will find your brothers, Tonia! I believe that with all of my heart. Once you do, may you also be successful in fulfilling all of your dreams!"

With a final wave goodbye, the girls headed off towards the rising sun, leaving the turtles behind forever.

THREE

The girls walked eastward, heading towards a dense line of trees. As they trudged along, Diam wondered what they would eat once the chickleberries were gone. They'd finished the chickenbird meat already, and she regretted that they hadn't brought more. They still had a few handfuls of chickleberries left, but the fruit, which had been bright red and fresh just the previous day, now looked bruised and old. The small berries had definitely seen better days. Diam thought she would be able to catch and cook a hare if it came down to it, but she wasn't sure how Tonia would handle that. Her friend was an animal lover from the top of her head to the ends of her toes, and would probably give Diam a hard time about killing and cooking anything, even if it meant she wouldn't eat. Diam knew that, for the most part, Tonia would eat cooked meat, but she didn't think her friend ever had to see the meat while it was alive, just before it ended up as dinner.

No, Diam was almost certain if it came to that, it would likely not be very pretty.

They made their way quietly through the trees and tried not to draw attention to themselves. Who knew what lurked in the woods of this unknown place? After a while, the grove of trees they traveled through began to slowly thin out.

"This is creepy," Tonia whispered to the others.

When they had first entered the woods, trees had been everywhere around them… tall, healthy, and magnificent. They were covered in green leaves and provided shade and shelter to

15

the surrounding plant and animal life. Now, however, the trees looked exactly the opposite. Their weathered branches were quite barren, with only a leaf or two remaining on them. Instead of being clustered together in a forest, they were now few and far between.

"What's up with these trees?" Diam asked the others. "It's odd how the place where we just were was crisp and green, and now things look so... dry and desolate."

"Yeah," Tonia agreed in a hushed tone. She looked back at Kaileen who was following them quietly. The kalevala could not compare the scenery to anything from the dark cave she'd come from. It was all still very new to her. Luckily, her eyes had quickly acclimated to her new surroundings.

"It is strange how only one tree, here and there, looks healthy, while the rest of the landscape looks totally... yuck," Tonia finally replied.

After a few more minutes, Kaileen suddenly stopped, and the others turned to see what she was doing. Unaware they were watching her, the kalevala was looking eastward again with an oddly vacant stare, as if listening to something.

"Kaileen? Are you okay?" Diam asked.

The kalevala blinked and looked at Diam as if it was her first time seeing her. She nodded slightly before answering.

"Yes, I think so."

"What is it?" Tonia asked worriedly.

"I'm okay," Kaileen answered. "You know... that vine..."

Tonia and Diam nodded quietly. No further explanation was necessary. Whatever was in the east that was drawing the kalevala was obviously still affecting her. After a short time, they approached one of the rare, healthier trees. It was covered with large, lush, green leaves and looked very out of place among the predominantly brown and gray landscape.

As they got closer, Diam suddenly recognized the large, red orbs that littered the tree's branches.

"Fruit!" she called out as she ran over to it.

The tree was completely covered with ripe, red apples and was one of the largest in the vicinity. Now that they were closer, the fruit were quite noticeable against the background of full,

16

green leaves.

Within seconds, Diam stood before the tree, her mouth watering. Just as she reached out to pick an apple from one of the lower branches, a voice startled her from within the depths of the tree.

"You must ask before you partake in the fruit of this tree!" the voice reprimanded. It was nasally, scolding, and unwelcoming.

As if being burned, she immediately pulled her hand back. The voice had come from somewhere within the trees upper branches, but the source was obscured behind thick layers of sticks with flittering adornments. All they could see were the red and green of fruit and leaves.

Tonia and Kaileen swiftly moved to Diam's side, and it was Tonia who first drew her sword.

"Who are you?" Diam called out nervously. Silence filled the air. They were sure the mysterious voice came from somewhere within the tree, but the dense layer of leaves provided excellent cover and they were unable to see the orator.

Diam decided to do as the voice had suggested. "We are only passing through and our food supply is almost gone. May we please take a few apples from this tree?" she asked politely.

A split second after she finished her question, a sudden rustling erupted from deep within the branches. It was as if the tree itself had suddenly come to life. Diam kept a shaky hand on her sword but had not yet drawn it. Without a word, she took a defensive step away from the tree.

As abruptly as the leaves began to shake, they stopped. This was followed by an eerie silence. A solemn leaf fell through the air and it was so quiet, you could hear it scrape against each and every branch it brushed on its way to the ground. As the girls watched the tree warily, Diam suddenly spotted a small pair of eyes peering at them from a gap between the leaves. If the eyes were any indication of the size of the creature, it was a small one, indeed.

"Hello," she said softly as she nodded a cautious greeting.

Until now, Tonia and Kaileen had not seen anything besides leaves and apples among tree branches, but when Diam greeted the pair of eyes, they followed her gaze and could just barely

17

make out what Diam was looking at. As soon as the creature realized its hiding place had been discovered, it slowly pushed its head through the leaves.

They couldn't see its entire body, but it appeared to be a small tree monkey.

Kaileen frowned and tilted her head slightly. With obvious uncertainty, she also took a slight step back. Tonia guessed that, after spending her life in a dark cave, the kalevala had probably never seen anything quite like the monkey before.

Looking at Kaileen, she whispered, "It's okay. It's called a 'monkey' and lives in trees. They're usually harmless."

Unconvinced, Kaileen glanced at Tonia with a look of skepticism, mouthing the word 'usually', and then looked back at the monkey. It remained partially hidden in the thick cluster of leaves. Regardless of what her new friend said, the kalevala decided to keep her distance.

"What would you require from us so that we may have some of your apples?" Diam asked the creature. "We are low on food and only ask for a few pieces, then we'll happily go on our way."

The monkey looked from her to Tonia before its silent stare lingered on Kaileen.

"You," the monkey suddenly said to the kalevala. "From where do you come?"

Kaileen remained where she was but did not hesitate with her answer.

"I come from a cave."

"A cave?" the monkey asked, doubt evident in its squeaky voice. "There are no caves around here." It turned its beady, brown eyes back to Diam and Tonia before trying again.

"From where do you come?" it repeated suspiciously, turning to stare at Kaileen again.

"I come from a cave in a place far from here," Kaileen answered.

"We are travelers, merely passing through on our journey east," Diam said.

The monkey turned its attention to the darker skinned girl and said, "East? What is there for you… in the east?"

"We are searching for my brothers," Tonia offered.

The monkey shifted a bit as it thought about this. As the branches settled around the monkey, it seemed mindful that they could see the top half of its body. The short fur covering its head was light brown, almost tan, and slightly mottled. Its eyes were a darker brown and surrounded by thin circles of white, while its ears were small and pointy, laid back almost flush with the sides of its head.

As the small animal emerged more from the leaves, the girls noticed how the torso was colored differently than the head. The front half of the creature's body fur was a mixture of gray and black, which was all they could see. For now, the rest of the body remained hidden by the leaves.

"You are traveling east, looking for brothers…" the monkey repeated almost dreamily, "and you come from a cave far away from here?" Its dark eyes darted back to Kaileen, filled with suspicion.

"Yes, we are looking for the boys who were part of our group, and yes, I come from a cave far from here," she declared, unmoved by the monkey's glaring eyes.

"I see," the creature mumbled as it turned its stare skyward. After a few seconds of contemplation, his focus returned to the girls.

"Have you found anything of interest during your travels?"

Diam looked at the small creature, confused by its pointless questions. Questions filled her head like, "Why would this monkey care where Kaileen had come from?" and "Why was it interested in them when all they wanted to do was pick a few apples and be on their way?"

"Why are you asking us these questions?" she blurted out at the inquisitive, yet short and hairy primate. "Where we came from and where we are going is no concern of yours. We bring you no harm. We only wanted a few apples to take with us on our journey."

After a few seconds, she added, "If you do not want to share your tree, it's quite alright. I'm sure we can find another one as we continue on our way."

Tired of his games, she looked quickly at Tonia and Kaileen and said, "Come on, girls."

Without waiting to see if the others would follow, she turned away from the tree and began to head eastward. Tonia and Kaileen followed silently.

"Wait, wait, wait!" the monkey called out springing from the tree. It landed to the sound of crunching twigs on the ground and began to follow them.

"You must answer my questions!" it yelled in a demanding voice, quickly closing the distance between them.

Tonia spun around, her sword still drawn.

"Keep your distance, primate!" she called out defensively. "We are tired and hungry and will continue on our way. We neither want, nor do we need, any trouble from the likes of you!"

Diam stopped and turned back towards the creature, anger now unmistakable on her tanned face.

"Why should we talk to you when you will not share a few pieces of fruit with us?" she asked. "Why should we answer your questions?"

They watched the monkey, nervously awaiting its answer. It returned their gaze in silence as its eyes darted from Kaileen to Tonia, then settling intently on Diam. It wasn't so drawn to look her in the eyes, however. For some reason it was focused on her waist...

Tonia realized too late exactly what held the monkey's attention so intently.

Without warning, the apple-hoarding creature jumped up and grabbed the small bag from where it hung, momentarily forgotten, from Diam's waistband. The mischievous creature was too quick and agile for them as it expertly used the element of surprise to its advantage. By the time any of the girls could think about reacting, the creature had grabbed the bag and hopped away, back to the safety of the tree.

"Hey!" Diam shouted angrily. "Give that back!"

Tonia silently chided herself for not being more cautious of the monkey's selfish intentions. She frowned as it all began to make sense.

"I think the little thief saw the bag hanging from Diam's waistband when it first confronted us, and that's why it was asking so many odd questions about where we had been and where we were going," she whispered to her friends.

Diam nodded as she quickly followed the monkey back to the apple tree.

"Give me back that bag, you little thief!" she shouted, her sword now drawn. If there was one thing that she totally despised, it was a thief!

As they neared the tree, they could both hear and see a great rustling among its branches. In addition to this, they soon began hearing an odd chittering noise. From the sounds of it, there were more creatures in the tree than just the one that stole their bag.

"You go around that way," Tonia whispered to Diam as she pointed to the right, "and I'll go around this way. Let's see if we can find an opening somewhere. I want to see these creatures we're dealing with."

She looked at Kaileen and said, "Stay here in case it comes back."

Kaileen nodded as Diam began to walk around the tree in a counter-clockwise direction. She couldn't believe that she'd been foolish enough to leave the bag hanging on the outside of her pants. She should have been more careful about it and put it in her pocket instead!

She sighed.

It was too late now to worry about what led up to the monkey taking the bag and she knew it. Right now, the most important thing was for them to get the bag back and be on their way.

The two girls walked silently around the tree, and after a few seconds, Diam found just what she was looking for – an opening.

"Tonia, over here."

Tonia walked quickly around the tree until she found Diam. Sure enough, her friend had successfully located a place where the branches had grown apart on the northeastern side of the tree. They looked through it together and could now easily see just where the monkeys were hiding.

The first thing they noticed about the interior of the tree was the many vines that were hung hidden among the branches. Some were tied from branch to branch, while others were tied from one branch and left hanging perpendicular to the ground.

The next thing they noticed was the number of monkeys

hanging from both the vines and tree branches. The sizes and colorings of these creatures were different from the monkey who had stolen their bag. Both large and small, their single fur coloring was eye-catching, ranging from the darkest brown to the palest gray. Looking at these creatures, Tonia noticed that the only monkey to be multi-colored was the one who had stolen the bag.

Some of the monkeys remained motionless as they cautiously watched the girls who were looking in on them within their hidden home. The rest, however, appeared to not be bothered by the uninvited guests. The latter kept themselves busy, swinging actively from branch to branch, interested only in which branch or vine they would swing to next. Some of the creatures were even hanging from tree branches or vines by their tails.

"Hey!" Diam shouted into the shadows of the tree.

The swinging monkeys stopped their antics before turning to stare at her with cool curiosity. Both girls canvassed the crowd with their eyes as they tried desperately to find the one who had stolen their bag. After a few seconds, Tonia spotted the thief in the center of the tree where it sat comfortably on one of the topmost branches.

Neither of the girls liked what they now saw – not one bit.

At first, the girls believed the thieving monkey was in some sort of trance. Its dark eyes stared off into the nearby branches without focus or apparent cause. The eyes gave away its intentions, though. Its fingers were furiously working to open the bag.

"We have done nothing to you to deserve this!" Tonia shouted directly at the monkey.

The monkey ignored her as it worked diligently on the vine which held the bag securely closed. After a few more seconds, it had successfully untied the vine and began to dig into the bag for treasure.

The girls watched helplessly as it first withdrew a rock sparker from the bag. It looked at the item curiously, unsure of what it had found. The creature turned the stone over and over, intrigued by the flecks of shiny material that littered its surface. Without warning, the monkey suddenly raised the rock sparker to its mouth and tried to bite it.

"What's it doing?" Tonia asked quietly.

"Apparently it doesn't know that the sparker isn't food," Diam answered, almost giggling at the monkey's stupidity.

Kaileen heard the girls on the opposite side of the tree and quietly made her way over to them.

Diam turned to look at her and saw the expression on Kaileen's face change from one of curiosity to one of surprise. She shrugged at the kalevala, silently gesturing to her that she had no explanation for the monkey's actions with the rock sparker. One thing was sure, however... the number of monkeys living in the shadows of this tree was truly amazing. Diam silently wondered if they would have ever known that any creatures even lived here if they had decided to walk past it and not stop for some apples. Probably not...

Her attention was drawn back to the monkey with the rock sparker as it quickly lost interest in the stone and threw it carelessly to the ground. Seeing this, some of the other monkeys started to swing on the vines wildly, while others jumped up and down among the branches with obvious agitation.

The rock sparker flew through the air and landed close to Tonia. As she was about to pick it up, the monkey excitedly reached back into the bag and pulled out a second rock sparker.

Disappointment quickly clouded its hairy, brown face when it found the new item was identical to the old one. With almost no hesitation, it threw this stone down to the ground as well, again nearly hitting Tonia in the process.

"Hey!" she shouted up at it, but, not surprisingly, the thieving monkey continued to ignore her. She picked up the second rock sparker as the monkey once again reached into the bag. This time, it removed one of the gold coins.

The other monkeys suddenly stopped moving and complete silence filled the air. They looked in awe at the new item in the thieving monkey's small, hairy hand, mesmerized by miniature rays of sunlight reflecting off the face in all directions. The silence only lasted for a few seconds, however, and the large group soon began to make another sound altogether.

As the girls listened, Tonia and Diam recognized the sound. It

23

was very similar to the sound made by a flock of morning doves as they welcomed the new day's sunshine into their small village of Uncava. This time, however, it was a group of wild monkeys that was creating the cooing sound from within the wide, arcing branches of an apple tree.

The odd-sounding monkeys' cooing continued as they watched the first monkey, their gazes fixated on the coin that still lay in its open, hairless palm. When the lead monkey turned the coin over, a glint of light flitted across some of the other monkeys as the midday sun reflected off the coin. As if electrified, the monkeys began erratically jumping up and down on the branches.

The first monkey seemed oblivious to the reaction of its fellow creatures, and it didn't take long for it to lose interest in the coin. In a matter of seconds, it closed its hand around the circle of gold briefly before casting it away. Instead of tossing it down on the ground, this time the creature threw it towards a group of monkeys where they sat on a branch toward the far side of the tree.

The coin flew through the air for a few short seconds before it was quickly snatched up by one of the larger monkeys. The triumphant creature let out a loud screech of victory. The other monkeys voiced their dismay with loud screeches of their own, and many began swinging wildly from the vines. The losers were obviously very agitated that they were not the successful catchers of the coin.

The first monkey reached into the bag yet again, which reminded Tonia of the antics of some of the village's most mischievous young children. When it withdrew its hand from the bag this time, it held all of the remaining coins. Just as it did with the second rock sparker, the multi-colored monkey did not waste any time looking at these other coins before immediately tossing them in different directions at the other monkeys.

The monkeys became frenzied as they snatched up the tossed coins and it was soon obvious who the winners and losers were. The unlucky monkeys did not hesitate to show their unhappiness with the results. Similar to the way a small child will throw a temper tantrum when they don't get their way, the losing monkeys began to act defiantly. They screeched loudly and swung frantically through the branches, completely dissatisfied with the results of the coin toss.

The girls watched this from the ground in nervous silence, each of them aware of the remaining item in the bag. Frustrated with fate, they could do nothing but watch as the inevitable happened.

The curious monkey hesitated for just a moment before reaching into the bag one last time. It found the final item with no difficulty at all, and quietly removed it from the satchel. The other creatures in the tree caught sight of this and silenced immediately as the glistening green stone shone brightly in its setting.

With the ring in hand, the monkey dropped the bag, no longer interested in the empty sack. Silence surrounded them as the bag cascaded downward through the air, untouched by the other monkeys as it fell gently through the tree branches and vines. In seconds, it landed abruptly on one of the lower branches close to the ground, draped across it, meaningless and forgotten.

The rest of the monkeys focused their complete attention on their leader, silently staring at the ring as if in a trance of their own. One at a time, the previously lucky creatures who had managed to gain possession of a coin now dropped the gold circles without a second thought and moved closer to their leader. Like the bag, the coins fell downward and bounced off the branches, unnoticed and no longer desired by any of the little beasts. The coins landed softly in the dirt around the base of the tree with a soft poof, unimportant and already forgotten.

Within seconds, lead monkey was completely surrounded by his companions. They were eerily silent, their eyes glued to the shiny piece of jewelry. None of them tried to take it… it was as if they knew better.

Diam was the first to break the thick silence.

"Please give us back our ring. You had no right to take it! Give it back to us and we'll be on our way."

Their concentration interrupted, many of the other monkeys broke out in rebellious screeches. They turned and looked with piercing, hateful eyes at the girls, who were now standing beneath them in the tree.

The girls kept their weapons close as they watched the tree

creatures nervously. The agitated monkeys continued to loudly voice their opinions but remained protectively close to their leader. Some of them, instead of swinging through the tree, began to jump frantically up and down on the branches. As a result, a few of the ripe apples fell to the ground with a couple narrowly missing the girls.

The monkey with the ring seemed oblivious to the outrageous actions of the other monkeys and stood up. When the other tree creatures saw this, they quickly fell silent and ended their antics.

Their leader held the ring tightly in one hand as it jumped quickly through the tree branches, using its one free hand and its tail to navigate. Before the girls knew it, the creature appeared on the branch directly in front of them, looking at them intently with its mischievous brown eyes.

"Where did you get this ring?" it asked in a demanding tone, a serious look on its hairy face.

"Give it back to us!" Diam spoke with sudden authority as she avoided the creature's question.

"NO!" the monkey shouted back as it stood its ground, agitation now quite evident in its voice.

The outburst from the leader caused some of the other tree residents to screech in agitation once again. This time the sound was so loud that the girls had to cover their ears.

Without making eye contact with the rest of its clan, the leader raised its empty hand above its head for a few seconds. As if on cue, the screeches from the other creatures stopped immediately and the air was filled with welcome silence.

"From where did you gain possession of this ring? This you must tell me," the monkey demanded as it took the time to glare at each girl individually.

Tonia held her sword firmly in her hand and said quietly, "We found the ring in the cave that we recently came from. It was not found here, in this world, so it should mean nothing to you. Please give it back to us so we can be on our way."

The monkey shook its head defiantly as it sighed with exasperation.

"You don't understand," the hairy creature said as it held the ring in its opened palm for every creature to see. At the same time, it made sure it kept enough distance between them so the girls couldn't try to take it back. The 'tricker' had no desire to become the 'trickee'.

"This ring has been missing for many years," the monkey said in a low voice as its eyes softened.

"You are wrong, stranger," it said in a haunted whisper as it turned and looked directly at Tonia. "This ring is of this world."

"But how can that be?" Tonia asked, confused. "How can it be of this world when we found it in the cave near our village, which is on the other side of a portal? How can it be of this world? Explain this to me!" she said, the confusion in her voice unmistakable.

Diam looked at her friend sympathetically. Her mind raced as she frantically tried to come up with a plan. Instead of making demands of this creepy, demanding creature, which obviously wasn't working, she decided it might be better to get the monkey to think of them as friends. She began by expanding on her best friend's last question.

"If this ring is of this world," Diam said, "then tell us this… who did it belong to, where is it from, and why is it so important to you?"

The monkey looked at her quietly, and within a few seconds, its face lit up with a small, stiff smile. Now that it had the attention of the strangers, perhaps they would listen?

"The ring disappeared a long time ago, and it used to belong to Amandalin. After Lotor took his place as one of the powerful sorcerers of this world, however, the ring was thought to be gone forever," the monkey explained, with a larger, more relaxed smile.

"Who is Amandalin?" Tonia asked curiously.

"Ah, yes… Amandalin. I knew you would soon begin to ask the right questions!" the monkey exclaimed with another smile.

"I knew it was really just a matter of time… and patience!" it crooned happily.

The creature paused for a moment as it focused its gaze upon the ring. The other monkeys quietly watched and observed the scene as they moved here and there among the tree branches, never far from their leader. Diam was sure it wouldn't take much to get them riled up again. The girls had to be careful now, because they were highly outnumbered.

"What of this Amandalin?" Tonia asked, prodding the monkey for more information.

The creature with the ring looked at her for a few seconds as it absently played with the trinket.

"Amandalin is one of our world's smaller creatures. She came through here many moons ago bearing this ring. And if this ring was found in another world, it shall not return there. This ring is of this world, and will remain in this world," the monkey said matter-of-factly before falling silent again, lost in thought.

Tonia's patience was starting to run thin. She was tired, she was hungry, and she didn't particularly care for how this stupid monkey was wasting their time with its riddles and pointless stories. She was anxious to get the ring back and move on. More importantly, however, she wanted to find her brothers. She kept these thoughts to herself, however, as she struggled to maintain her fragile line of patience. It was difficult, but she knew she must allow the monkey to continue.

She sighed.

If it wanted to tell them a story… so be it. She would indulge the creature for as long as she possibly could by letting it say whatever it wanted to say. Once it was storied out, then they could get the ring back. Tonia also made a mental note that they should do their best to retrieve all of the coins that were scattered in the dirt around the base of the tree. The rock sparkers they didn't need, but the coins they may need at some point during their journey. Once they got the coins and the ring, they could continue on their way without so much as a passing glance back…

A sudden movement from the corner of her eye caught her attention. She smiled when she saw what it was.

As if reading her mind, Diam was moving around the base of the tree, silently picking up some of the coins. Following Diam's example, Kaileen did the same while she cautiously watched the creatures in the branches above her.

The monkey surprised them when it suddenly moved back a few branches. As it settled into its new location, it again held the ring out in its opened palm. As before, the rest of the creatures in the tree fell silent. They watched their leader as it held the ring, still mesmerized by the small piece of jewelry.

The monkey looked at the girls below with a gleam in its beady little eyes.

"You want this ring back?" it asked them teasingly.

"Yes!" Diam answered from where she now stood next to Tonia. The coins she had retrieved were safe in her pocket.

"Please give the ring back to us!" she said in a frustrated voice.

The monkey protectively closed its hand over the ring, and after a few seconds, it brought the closed hand up to its chest in a possessive gesture.

"What will you give me for it?" it asked them. The rest of the creatures in the tree remained silent, yet fidgety, as though they could sense something in the air.

The girls looked at each other as they tried to think some item, of any item, in their possession they could use to barter with. They had no food, except for some bruised, old chickleberries… the gold coins they had retrieved from the dirt beneath the tree were obviously worthless to the creature… and relinquishing their weapons was absolutely not an option.

"We have nothing to trade, except for this," Diam said.

She pulled her bag off her back, set it on the ground and began going through it. In a few seconds she withdrew a pia bottle which was half filled with water. She held this out to the monkey.

"Bah!" the monkey shouted, obviously unimpressed with her offering. "I have no use for that!

"You should go and continue on your way now," it said disgustedly. With that, the monkey turned slightly to his right. Its left side now faced the girls as it looked with pretend interest at an apple hanging near its right arm. At the same time, the other monkeys in the tree began to screech and jump wildly on the branches. They carried on this way for several seconds before eventually settling down, yet still anxious for the next chapter of the story to play out before them.

"What?" Tonia asked, not understanding. "We need the ring. Just give it back to us and we'll be on our way."

"Ah, young stranger, but you have nothing which to trade for it," the monkey gloated before continuing. "I will, however, make you an offer."

The girls listened nervously, unable to entertain the idea that they might not get the ring back.

"Since you have so generously given me this small item, I will reward you by allowing you to take some of the fruit of my home," it continued proudly, waving its hand in a wide arc displaying the expanse of the tree. "You may take whatever apples have fallen to the ground. Once that is done, you may leave without any more trouble from me or my clan."

"We're not leaving without the ring!" Diam shouted up at the arrogant monkey.

She gestured towards the creature in a stabbing motion with her sword fervently wishing one of the boys had given them a bow with some arrows. If they had, Diam knew without a doubt she could take this crazy creature out with one shot! As it was, however, they only had their swords, not to mention the fact that they were highly outnumbered.

She looked at Tonia, discouraged and unsure of what they should do. As she did, the creature above them teasingly opened its hand, mercilessly reminding them who had possession of the ring.

Diam took a few steps under the tree. She moved to be under the monkey, her sword held firmly out in front of her.

Without warning, the monkey suddenly tossed the ring to its free hand. At first, Tonia thought it wanted to get a closer look at the green gemstone, but she soon realized it had other intentions.

The monkey smirked down toward them as it triumphantly held the ring in the air. Without a word it brought the ring closer to its face as a mischievous smile curled the corners of its mouth.

"No!" Diam called out, afraid the crazy creature would try to do the same thing it had done with the rock sparkers. Would the monkey be stupid enough to try to eat the ring?

The monkey, however, had something better in mind. With a sparkle in its hungry, brown eyes, the monkey smiled down at the ground audience again, proud it had the complete attention of every creature both in and under the tree.

As they looked helplessly on, the creature took the ring, and, in once swift motion, began to gently ease the piece of jewelry onto one of its hairy fingers.

"No!" Diam yelled at the creature. Once again, it ignored her.

The other monkeys sensed the sudden increase of tension in the air and fell back into their high-pitched screeching. They watched their leader as it displayed the ring, now securely on one of its fingers, for all to see. It turned the ring this way and that, obviously proud to bear the green gem on its finger.

The girls watched helplessly as the monkey smirked down at them in triumphant silence. Each of them realized there was no chance at all to get the ring back.

"If the boys were here, I could take that monkey out with one shot," Diam whispered to Tonia.

"Yea, but they're not here, and there's nothing else we can do, Diam. We're outnumbered and the monkey would be too fast for us even if we could manage to get it out of the tree.

"Come on, girls. Let's go," she said. She hated to give up so easily, but really, what else could they do?

As she prepared to step away from the tree, she glanced back at the lead monkey one last time. What she saw stopped her in her tracks.

The thieving creature's face had clouded over, and its expression changed from one of triumph to one of wonder. As they watched their leader from the surrounding branches, the rest of the clan fell silent.

Like earlier in the cave, the colors in the center of the green gem began to swirl, slowly changing from a dull green to a foggy white and back again. This startled the ring bearing primate so much that it let out a surprised screech. The other monkeys watched in shocked silence, confused by their leader's reaction.

Without warning, the expression on the monkey's face suddenly changed again, this time from wonder to fear.

Surprised, the girls watched from the ground as the lead monkey tried frantically to remove the ring from its finger. No matter how hard it tried, however, the piece of jewelry simply would not budge.

The other monkeys in the tree watched, thoroughly confused, as their leader became more frantic. With fear-filled eyes, the once proud, once arrogant, primate continued to shake its hand wildly in the air in a futile attempt to free its finger from the questionable piece of jewelry.

Still, the ring would not budge.

The next time the lead monkey screeched, it was with obvious pain. The rest of the monkeys did the same, but their noises were from fear and confusion at what was happening to their leader.

"Is the ring cutting off the poor, little, innocent monkey's circulation?" Diam thought sarcastically.

She had no sympathy for the selfish monkey. If it could be mean enough to take something that didn't belong to it, then it should be tough enough to handle a little bit of pain from the ring being too tight.

It didn't take long, however, before she had a chance to regret those thoughts.

As they watched in silence, the monkey's screeches of pain intensified. When it did, the rest of the clan's reaction quickly hit the brink of mayhem.

While they listened helplessly to the monkey's howls of pain, their noses suddenly picked up a very odd and unappealing odor. They looked around as they tried to figure out what was causing the unpleasant smell.

After a few seconds, however, Kaileen whispered to the others, "Look!"

Tonia and Diam looked at the place where Kaileen pointed and realized in disgust what was causing the horrific smell. As they did, Diam had a chance to lament her sarcastic thoughts from mere seconds before.

The ring-bearing monkey held onto one of the tree branches with its free hand as it let loose a tortured cry. Even though it did no good, the monkey continued to shake its hand wildly through the air. The appendage flailed up and down, then left and right, as if it had a mind of its own.

No matter what it tried, the leader could not remove the ring.

The frightened monkey suddenly began to howl in pain. Totally upset and confused with what was happening to one of their own, the other tree residents began jumping wildly through the tree branches. Leaves fall from the branches like rain as the group scatters in total chaos, bumping into each other and screeching loudly. Some of them looked pleadingly at the girls, but there was nothing that could be done.

The visitors watched in amazement, unable to believe the sight before them. Smoke began to rise upward from the monkey's hand into the treetops. As the hand continued to flail, the smoke followed it in a wispy path.

Tonia looked at Diam. In her friend's brown eyes, she saw her own fear reflected back at her.

"What in the world?" Tonia began, but an ear-piercing, human-like scream interrupted her thoughts. Her focus turned immediately back to the tree, not surprised to discover the scream was coming from the monkey with the ring.

As the scream died on its quivering lips, the lead monkey became as still as stone. Tears dampened its fur-covered face. With terror-filled eyes, it slowly looked at the hand with the ring, watching in disbelief as smoke now billowed upwards into the tree branches above. The smell coming from the burning fur and flesh was almost unbearable.

The girls watched quietly as their eyes began to tear up in reaction to the enveloping stench. Diam lifted her hand and placed it over her mouth and nose in an effort to keep out the smell. Tonia and Kaileen did the same, but in the end it didn't make much of a difference.

The girls looked at each other with their hands covering their noses as the monkey with the ring suddenly raised its eyes to the top of the tree and let out the most gut-wrenching cry of pain any of them had ever heard. As if in slow motion, the monkey's scream faded and its entire body quickly disintegrated into nothing but ashes. The outline of the creature's body remained frozen in midair for a split second as the girls watched in silence. Before any of them could begin to question whether or not the outline was really there, the ashes lost their shape and began cascading towards the ground. As it did, the ring fell and landed with a gentle thud at Diam's feet, well before the ashes.

The other monkeys fell silent in a daze, unable to comprehend what just happened to their leader. For a moment, they seemed to forget the girls were even there.

"Diam, grab the ring and let's go!" Tonia whispered quietly.

Her voice was muffled behind the hand that still partially covered her face. Before the words left Tonia's lips, Diam had already reached down to pick up the ring. As soon as her fingers were able to grasp it out of the dirt, she quickly headed back to her friends.

Just as she reached them, reality set in for the remaining monkeys. Fear and understanding filled their eyes and they immediately began to screech erratically. As they swung wildly through the branches and among the vines of the apple tree, the last remnants of wispy smoke lingered at the top of the tree before disappearing into the shaking leaves. For the moment, the monkeys were oblivious to the girls. Meanwhile, the girls did not hesitate to use the chaotic scene before them to their advantage.

Without a word, Kaileen and Tonia picked up a few pieces of fallen fruit from the ground. They quickly placed them in Diam's bag, which was still open from her attempts at bartering with the monkey, and Diam haphazardly put the bag back on her back. As stealthily as they could, the girls ran away from the tree and continued eastward. They ran in silence for a few moments in an attempt to put as much distance between them and the highly upset monkey clan as they could before the pining creatures realized they were gone.

The girls had no way of knowing they had nothing to worry about. The loss of their leader was too much for the large monkey clan, and the despairing creatures had no clue that the girls had disappeared for quite a while. When the monkeys finally did look for the girls, it was too late.

They were well on their way east.

Nicho

ONE

Standing next to Micah, Nicho watched with amazed fascination as the girls stepped into the brilliant rainbow of light and silently disappeared. He looked hesitantly at Micah. They both could hear Muscala ranting and raving in the tunnels behind them as the angry snake closed the distance between them.

Nicho looked at the younger boy with nervous hesitation.

"Go," Micah said. "If I go first, the portal will disappear."

Sensing that the serpent was very close now, Nicho took a step towards the portal as he looked back one last time at his younger brother.

"I'll find you," Micah said encouragingly, "Now go!"

After giving Micah a quick hug, Nicho followed his sister and her companions into the rainbow. Like the girls before him, he silently disappeared.

As he stepped into the rainbow of colors, Nicho automatically closed his eyes. He was surprised at the weightlessness of his body. It almost felt as though he was floating in a dream.

The brightness in front of his closed eyes was quickly replaced by darkness. Afraid he would find himself back in the tunnel with the angry snake, his eyes shot open and he placed his hand on his sword as he prepared for the unknown.

The first thing he noticed was the complete darkness that surrounded him.

"That's odd," he thought.

He had gone from extreme light to extreme darkness in mere seconds, which left him virtually blind. He stayed where he was for a few moments to give his eyes time to adjust to this drastic change in illumination. He didn't want to find himself in another snake pit, especially now that he was apparently alone. As he waited for his eyes to adjust, the next thing that grabbed his attention was the difference in the air around him. The air here, wherever he was, smelled nothing like in the cave. It was fresher and at the same time… almost salty.

Salty?

"Tonia?" he called out nervously. "Kaileen? Diam?"

No answer.

He thought it odd that the girls weren't answering. They only went through the portal a minute or two before him, so they couldn't have gone far. Maybe they couldn't hear him? He sighed. He didn't want to call for them too loudly and risk drawing attention to himself.

"Micah?"

Still no answer.

He waited for a few minutes to see if his brother would follow him through the portal, but it was so dark here that Nicho couldn't make out much. Regardless of that, his brother should be here by now…

Shouldn't he?

"Guys? Where are you?"

The hush of a gentle breeze, cool against his skin, was the only sound that answered him.

Perhaps Micah hadn't stepped through the portal yet? He waited patiently for a few more minutes for his eyes to adjust. Once they did, he didn't recognize anything, and as time went on, he became more nervous about where he was.

Nicho was trying so hard to make out where he was that he failed to notice the small pair of eyes as they watched him silently from within the darkness above.

Two

The minutes ticked slowly by as Nicho waited for his brother to come through the portal. When there were still no signs of Micah or the girls after far too long, Nicho reluctantly allowed himself to believe that they just weren't coming. Once he admitted this to himself, like any other sibling, Nicho's heart sank in his chest.

He looked off into the distance and thought he could see the dark silhouette of a line of tall trees. He strained his ears and slightly cocked his head to the side like a mud puppy, listening for any telltale sounds, hoping to get a better idea of where he was. The only thing he could hear now, however, was the quiet silence that completely surrounded him. Even the insects were silent, he noticed… if there are even any insects here, he thought.

He sighed as another thought nagged at him…

Where had the girls gone?

They had stepped into the portal only a minute or so before he had, yet there were no signs that they had even been here. As he pondered this, the possibility of a time difference struck him which didn't make him feel any better. Even if there was a difference in time, he should still be able to see some signs of them having been here… like footprints in the sand. He searched as well as he could in the darkness, but found nothing.

He called out quietly for them a few more times without any response.

After a while, it appeared his only option was to give up and accept the crazy idea that the others may have gone through the portal to a different location. He didn't like this thought very much, but it was better than the others that now coursed like a raging river through his mind.

Disappointed and not willing to give up just yet, he began to walk in search of some place he could hold up until morning. As he walked toward the distant trees, his mind continued to run through different scenarios.

Was it possible that he was the only one to make it through the portal?

As he walked through the silent darkness he found himself thinking about happier times back in the village. He reminisced about the times when they would do things as a family... before their father had disappeared without a trace.

He smiled with his memories...

Once, when they were out hunting for valley duck in the marshes close to the river, one of the mud puppies they brought with them had run ahead of them, helter-skelter through the reeds, and scared off the ducks before they were ready to shoot. Not surprisingly, they had gone home empty handed.

Another time they'd hiked all the way out to the ocean with one of their wooden rafts to fish. Micah fell into the crystal blue water after his plan to push their dad in had backfired.

As his mind was filled with memories, Nicho stopped to take a deep breath. Sometimes it was difficult to fight the tears, but this time he managed it... barely. Many other times over the past year, he had not been so lucky.

He closed his eyes for a few moments as he tried to get control of his emotions, and then continued on. Unsure of which way to go, he turned to the night sky for guidance. Above him, many stars in the black blanket overhead twinkled like miniature jewels. One star in particular shone very brightly in the eastern sky, just as it did every night. They called this star Aquilo. Over the course of his young life, Nicho had seen this star quite often, and now he would use it as his guide, just like his father had taught him.

He smiled in remembrance once again. After the last two days, his father's teachings seemed like a distant memory when in reality it had only been a few years... a few long, tough years.

Still, he found comfort in knowing he was still under the same blanket of night that he had been his whole life. He only wished he was under the blanket on his bed!

He made his way for quite a while across a strange land that was smooth, sandy, and forgiving on his feet. He had been walking for an eternity, with the exception of the short 'rest' he had at the bottom of the abyss.

As he trudged onward, his thoughts drifted to his mother. He knew without a doubt she would be worried out of her mind because they had not returned home before dark the previous night as she had asked them to. He hated the thought of causing her to worry, but he also knew, regretfully, that this was something well beyond his control.

After a short time, he stopped to rest. He removed his pia bottle from his bag and took a slow sip of water, then closed his eyes and tried to reach out to his mother. He was doubtful it would really do any good, but figured it wouldn't hurt to try. Besides, after all the things he had seen in the cave over the last few days, he knew now that anything was possible. He sat where he was for a little while and concentrated, but in the end, and as he suspected, his efforts were fruitless. He opened his eyes and put away his pia bottle. Disappointed, he continued on.

Soon, the eastern horizon began to lighten, and as he looked skyward, Nicho could barely see Aquilo above him – it was a ghost of a star now.

He let out an audible sigh of distress.

Soon, he would have no choice but to rely on his sense of direction and the sun above him to guide the way. Thinking back to his younger days, he found himself thankful for all those times when Uncle Andar had taken him and his siblings out into the forest. There, he had happily taught them everything he knew about tracking creatures and survival. Nicho smiled with the flurry of happy memories as they ran through his mind. He found himself holding onto these moments almost tighter than he would hug his sister, if he could see her now.

As the sun continued to rise, he could clearly make out a dense line of trees in the distance to the northeast. There was also another line farther to the west. Except for those two tree lines, the rest of the landscape surrounding him was fairly plain and unexciting. There were patches of grass here and there intermingled with areas of sand, which was very similar to parts of the valley near his village. He walked for quite a while until suddenly he realized he'd been hearing a sound somewhere in the distance for quite some time, but he hadn't noticed it until just now.

He stopped and listened carefully. It sounded like moving water.

He sniffed the air curiously. It was definitely salty.

Was he near an ocean? He silently admonished himself for not noticing the salty air sooner, which was becoming stronger the closer he got to the trees. Step by step he followed the sounds of the water towards the forest, which was very close now. As he did, the sun continued to climb higher in the sky.

Nicho's path in the valley had been fairly level for quite some time, but a glance back told him that he'd actually been climbing at a slight incline for a while without realizing it. When he faced forward again, he could see where the valley dropped off suddenly a short distance ahead. He approached the drop off slowly, kicking up dust and sand as he did so. When he finally reached it, he peered cautiously over the edge.

A short distance below him, he noticed a stream that was much larger than anything he had seen anywhere near the village. Nicho wiped sweat from his brow as he gazed longingly at the water. Now that the sun was high in the sky, the water that flowed lazily before him looked cool and refreshing in contrast to his sandy perch. Once again, he glanced up toward the sky at the sun above him. It was now almost directly overhead. With a brilliant, cobalt blue, cloudless sky above him, the day was quickly becoming hot.

Cool, refreshing, fresh water…

He looked back down at the stream, mesmerized by it as he listened to the relaxing sounds created by the moving water. It gurgled gently as it flowed from the forest on Nicho's right towards the valley on his left. Looking upstream, the water appeared as though it flowed directly out of the darkness of the nearby forest. Beyond that, he wasn't able to make out much else.

As he looked from one end of the stream to the other, Nicho wondered what kinds of creatures he might find there.

He knew one thing for certain... he was very relieved to not see any spiders or large snakes!

He found himself a little tired and decided now was as good a time as any to take a break. If he stayed out in the direct sun much longer, he was sure his skin would begin to burn. He touched his arm and cringed... it was too late. It looked like he already had sunburn from his morning walk under the fiery orb.

That decided it for him. He definitely needed to get out of the sun... and the sooner the better. Without another thought, he made the decision to follow the water upstream into the cool shade of the nearby forest. Nicho carefully scooted down the sandy dune and made his way towards the stream. When he reached it, he turned right and followed it upstream to the edge the forest. The smell of salt was unmistakable and he guessed he must be very close to the ocean.

Thirsty from his journey, he knelt down at the water's edge and cupped a little bit of the liquid from the stream in his hand. It was cool to the touch and he could just imagine how good it would feel to immerse his entire sunburned body in the refreshing substance. He was very tempted to do just that, but fought against the impulse. Forcibly pulling himself away from the water, he followed it instead into the nearby trees. It would surely be much cooler in the shade. Besides, he reasoned with himself, he didn't want to get his clothes all wet just because he was hot now, only to end up cold once he got into the shade, did he? Before moving on, he brought a bit of the water in his cupped hand up to his nose and tasted just a drop. It was salt water. He was confounded by the fact that it wasn't fresh water flowing downstream but he couldn't quite put his finger on why.

After walking in the cool shadows of the trees for a few moments, he finally understood why the flow of salt water seemed odd to him. His entire life he had only seen fresh water flowing off of a mountain and into the ocean, not vice-versa.

Strange.

Curious now about the source of the salty water, Nicho followed it upstream, which took him deeper and deeper into the forest. The cool shade provided by the dense green trees was definitely a relief to his hot, sunburned skin. Occasionally, when a breeze whispered through the trees, he would get chickenbird bumps rising up. At those times, he was very thankful he had resisted his earlier impulse to drench himself in the flowing stream. He was sure that if he had, he would be quite cold right now. As the cool breezes worked their way through the forest, he was reminded of something that happened when he was just a young boy.

The day had been quite hot and he had gone out into the bay to play with his friends. After being out in the warm summer sun too long, he'd ended up with quite bad sunburn. After his mother scolded him, she'd brought him into their house and put an odd, mushroom-based concoction on his skin. She said it would stop the burn and heal the redness. To this day, Nicho was totally amazed that it had worked.

At the time, he hadn't cared for mushrooms, no matter how his mother cooked them, but after seeing how they'd worked magically on his burned skin that day, he eventually decided to try them again. Surprisingly, he found that he actually liked them…

He never quite understood how that could be.

Nicho smiled as he continued following the stream into the forest. He remembered how he'd hated the thought of the mushroom concoction being on his skin like it was yesterday. When he closed his eyes, he could see it in his mind's eye as if he were living it again. As he walked by an alia leaf, it brushed the side of his arm and he cringed. What he wouldn't give for a nice bowl of that concoction now!

Oh, how he missed his mother, the village, and the rest of the villagers.

His mind continued to wander and he didn't pay much attention to where he was going. When he finally looked up to see what was in front of him, Nicho suddenly stopped, startled.

About twenty feet away and surrounded by the cool shade of tall trees was a beautiful waterfall. The liquid that flowed from it gently cascaded over the top of a large rock. From there, it traveled down a long, straight cluster of black moss, which rippled with the weight of the downward moving water. At the bottom of the fall, the shimmering flow effortlessly joined a pool of water before it headed off downstream, towards both Nicho and the hot, sandy valley, which now lay well behind him. Nicho watched the flow of water, mesmerized by the beautiful sight. He was surprised at how it barely splashed when it met the pool at the bottom of the fall. The moss seemed to be the reason behind this as it provided a smooth entry point for the water, where it then flowed out towards the valley.

Nicho found that he wasn't surprised anymore when he saw things that were different from anything he'd ever seen before. The events that had taken place over the last two days had taught him to try to anticipate things he wouldn't ordinarily expect. He had a feeling this was only the beginning of a lifetime of different and extraordinary experiences.

"Nicho" he suddenly heard a voice whisper.

He jumped, startled again.

In an instant, he pulled his sword from its sheath and stood perfectly still. His eyes scoured the area, looking first at the nearby trees, then the waterfall, for any signs of life.

He could see nothing out of the ordinary. Within a few seconds, heard the whispering voice beckon him yet again. The voice was soft and gentle, almost feminine.

"Nicho, come to me," it said firmly.

He remained motionless for a few more seconds before he offered a nervous reply.

"Who are you?" he asked.

Silence followed his question; not even a forest creature made a sound. Nicho looked around as he tried to determine where the voice was coming from. After a few unsettled seconds, he heard it once again. This time it was louder.

"Come!" the voice demanded ominously.

Nervously, Nicho remained where he was next to the river. He held his sword drawn and ready.

"I can't come if I don't know where you are," he said to the voice as his own shook with doubt. "Where are you?"

Nicho found his gaze drawn to the moss that hung from the rock at the top of the waterfall. In the flash of a firebug, it began to part down the middle, as if by an invisible hand. He watched silently as the gap began at the top of the moss and slowly worked its way downward, which created two sections of the dark substance. As he watched, the flow of water in the waterfall decreased until it was barely a trickle.

Drip, drip, drip…

Suddenly, he heard a hiss. It sounded like it was coming from the direction of the waterfall. He watched in silence, unable to determine what had created it. Unknown to him, however, his earlier experience of being trapped in the abyss had given him a newfound strength, and he would do whatever was necessary to fight for his life.

The hissing noise continued and he could soon see what appeared to be steam escaping through the upper opening in the moss. The steam floated into the treetops above where it quietly disappeared.

He stood still, unsure of what to do.

The moss continued to part, as slowly as a cave snail, for a few more seconds, until it became two separate entities. Once it was fully separated, Nicho heard the voice call out to him again.

"Nicho, come to me. Do not be frightened."

Now it sounded as though the voice was coming from somewhere within the mossy enclosure. Could that be possible? Could a voice come from an inanimate object?

After a few seconds of indecisiveness about what he should do, Nicho finally made up his mind. He was ready to go home… right now. He had been ready for a long time, but not like he was at this very moment. Where, oh where, was Micah with his magical stones? As he thought this, the voice called out to him yet again, still beckoning to him from somewhere around the mossy rock. Nicho took a deep breath then decided to find out once and for all what this was all about.

Without further hesitation, he took a brave step forward and looked up. He was still unable to make out what, if anything lay beyond the moss from where the water had been falling.

Curious as well as nervous, Nicho leaned forward as he tried to see if anything was hidden in the darkness overhead. Learning from his recent experience in the cave the last time he leaned over something unfamiliar, he glanced down at his footing to be sure he would not end up somewhere less than favorable. After reassuring himself that he still stood on solid ground, or what appeared to be solid ground, he took another careful step forward. As he did, Nicho was now able to partially see into the void, and there was definitely something on the underside of the rock. Whatever it was, though, it was still hidden behind the mossy, wet curtain. When the underside of the rock began to move without warning, the boy's mind had difficulty understanding exactly what it was he was seeing.

At first Nicho thought there were two partially white, odd-shaped circles above him, and as he stepped closer to the once enshrouded void, they shifted and rolled towards him. When he saw this he stopped, frozen by fear, with his sword held out in front of him. As his mind tried to make out the object above him, he suddenly realized that it was not just a pair of circles in the darkness above him...

It was a pair of eyes.

"Nicho," the voice whispered again, and he now undoubtedly knew where the voice was coming from.

A mysterious darkness surrounded these eyes, which now held him, frightened and confused, within their gaze. They were hidden high above him on the underside of the rock, surrounded by the dark moss. The eyes continued to beckon him, inviting him to come in, to come to them, to come closer...

"Come... come..." they called to him silently, yet he could somehow still hear them. He was now no longer sure, however, whether the voice he heard was in his mind or real.

Before he knew it, his legs slowly began to take steps towards those eyes on their own, almost as if he was in a trance. The thing in the rock above continued to look down on him as it cast some sort of spell over him. Although he felt like he was in a trance, his subconscious mind tried to fight the motions of his body. He tried to stop walking forward, but found that he was unable to fight it. All he could do now was look helplessly up into those white and black eyes above him, the orbs that called out to him in the darkness...

"Come to meeee," the voice whispered again, almost

soothingly.

When he stepped into the river, he failed to notice the cool, refreshing water when it slowly covered his feet. He took one more step in his dreamlike trance and stood quietly in the pool of liquid. The waterfall itself was no longer falling... it was now merely a trickling which dripped occasionally from the rock above. The intermittent drops of water landed in the pool here and there, and as Nicho found himself beneath them, he was completely unaware when they landed in his hair and on his shoulders. The trance he was in disappeared in the blink of a firebug and the dazed boy was surprised to find himself standing in a pool that was now almost up to the middle of his calves. Held frozen by an invisible force and helpless to move, he looked down at his feet as he tried to understand. As he nervously looked on, the water level that surrounded him slowly receded as it emptied into the river until there was nothing left except for a layer of smooth, damp rocks.

Motion seen out of the corner of his eye caught his attention. Nicho looked up, shaken, as he tried to take another step forward but he still couldn't move. His feet seemed to be stuck in place.

The movement came from the mossy material which hung over the rock. Nicho watched as the moss slowly moved back into its original position, released by the invisible hand that had parted it just moments before.

He nervously brought his attention back to the eyes above him. As he watched them in silence, they began to glow, which created a soft, gentle, green aura all around him. He felt his own eyes being drawn to the glowing orbs, drawn into them, as he heard the voice whisper to him yet again.

"Welcome, Nicho the Traveler."

Although he stood wet and alone beneath the illuminated eyes, Nicho no longer noticed the dampness in his clothes. He had better things to focus on. He watched the eyes warily as they gazed down upon him and it suddenly occurred to him just what it was he was looking at... as the glow brightened he began to see the likeness of a woman's face in the rock above him.

A woman's face... in the rock? How could that be? Was it possible that the mossy material which hung over the edge of the rock above and surrounded him on three sides might not be moss at all?

"Nicho, I am Shia, Oracle of the Green," the voice said softly, the emerald eyes still calmly focused on him.

"Oracle?" Nicho asked quietly, afraid to talk too loud. He had absolutely no understanding of what this oddity was that spoke to him.

"Yes," the voice answered quietly.

"What is an oracle?" Nicho asked quietly.

"I am one who sees past, present, and future. Many come to me for advice, while others only seek answers to their questions," Shia answered.

"A fortune teller?" Nicho asked.

The eyes above him blinked closed for a few seconds, and then slowly reopened.

"No," Shia answered curtly, and then the voice said something that surprised Nicho.

"I have been waiting for you."

As soon as the oracle with the piercing green eyes said this, Nicho felt an odd sensation in his legs. He looked down. There was nothing there, but he discovered he was able to move them again. To be sure, he lifted first one foot off the ground, then the other.

Now that he knew he could move, he felt an almost overwhelming desire to hear more from the luminous eyes that still glowed above him.

"Waiting for me?" he asked, not understanding. "Why are you waiting for me?"

"I have been waiting, young traveler, because I have some very important information to share with you," Shia explained.

Nicho stood quietly where he was as he held his sword at his side. As he stared at the curiosity above him, his mind still struggled to understand just what was in the rock before him.

How was it possible to see a face within a rock?

"I'm sure you have never seen or heard of anything like me before, but you must listen to me now, Nicho. Time is of the essence and I must share some things with you before you continue on your way," the oracle told him sternly, commenting on the confused look on his face.

Nicho nodded as he struggled to focus on the oracle's words.

"You must turn to the east and make your way to the village you will find there. Once you arrive at your destination, you will look for someone who is familiar to you, someone that you have lost. When you find them, you must work together to free Little Draco before it is too late!

"Travel through the Sendau Valley where you will find the small village. There you will find good food and a warm place to sleep. Once you are rested, those who live there will tell you how to get to a castle, the Castle of Tears."

"The Castle of Tears?" Nicho asked, now more confused than before. "Who is Little Draco? I'm sorry, but I just don't..."

"You must listen to me!" Shia interrupted him as her eyes suddenly glowed green with anger. The luminous aura now lit up the entire area where Nicho stood, including the inside of the dark moss that encircled him. It reflected off the rocks that were piled up next to him and glistened like miniature firebugs on the damp stones beneath his feet.

Nicho found himself again trying to rationalize the resemblance of the oracle above him to a woman. He was sure he could make out the wide eyes, the small, soft nose, and the thin lips that surrounded the narrow mouth. The moss that hung from the rock above was tinted with green, and he realized that, if the shape above him was that of a woman, then the moss hanging around the outside of it could be...

Hair?

As he shook his head, Nicho struggled yet again to focus his attention back to the moment. He could feel the oracle becoming angry with him... he knew she thought he wasn't paying attention to the information she was trying to convey to him, even though that was not the case.

"Shia, I can't go off looking for any Castle of Tears! I need to find my brother and sister," he tried explaining to the oracle.

"We all stepped through a magical portal in a cave after being chased by a psychotic snake, but now I don't know where they are, and..."

"Silence!" she yelled, interrupting him. After taking a few

seconds to calm down, the oracle continued.

"Nicho, you must listen to the words I am telling you and follow my instructions explicitly!" she said firmly, although her voice had softened somewhat.

"You must understand that evil forces are converging in this land, and if they are not stopped, men and creatures alike will suffer unexplainable horrors!

"Little Draco MUST be freed before it is too late!"

Shia looked down at the boy with evident desperation in her mysterious emerald eyes. Silence followed, accentuating her point, as the glow emanating from them gradually lessened. The oracle looked at Nicho, quietly imploring him to follow her instructions.

Nicho may not have understood where he was now, or where the others were, but it suddenly became clear to him that this was something he had to do. He returned a silent gaze up to Shia before he slowly nodded his head.

"Can you give me any more information, like directions telling me exactly where I need to go? And how can I find this castle if I don't know where it is, or even if I'm in the right place?" Nicho asked worriedly. He felt he needed to convey the many questions he had as rapidly as they flashed through his mind.

Shia looked down at him. The serious look remained in her eyes, but the anger was now gone. Her voice was soft once again as she spoke.

"Follow the path through the forest to the east. After you enter the Sendau Valley, you will soon come to a small village. Once there, the residents will answer your questions and help you find the castle," Shia explained.

As Nicho listened to the oracle, a thought suddenly struck him.

"Shia, can you tell me where the rest of my group is? My brother? My sister? Our friends?" Nicho asked the oracle hopefully.

"For now they are safe," Shia replied

"I say 'for now' because this world is large, and within it resides much evil and countless darkened hearts."

"But where are they?" he asked hopefully. Perhaps she could

51

tell him where to find them. If he could do that, they could continue on together to this village, wherever it was, before heading on to the castle. That brought another thought into his mind... hadn't someone said just a day or two ago that there was 'safety in numbers'? Funny how that simple phrase was coming back to haunt him...

"I do not have the answer, Young Traveler. And although where they are matters to you, that is secondary to your journey. You must focus all of your attention and concentrate on the task at hand.

"Go now. Head east and find the village. Follow your instincts as you travel and do not forget that evil is a clear and ever-present danger in this world," the oracle warned.

"But what about the others?" Nicho asked.

"NO!" the frustrated oracle shouted at him, its eyes suddenly blazing a fiery, blinding green once again.

"You must understand one very important thing! If you do not find Little Draco and release him from his evil captors, darkness and evil will reign in this world! You MUST understand this!" Shia bellowed at him, causing the ground beneath his feet to tremble.

"If that happens, it will not matter where the others are!" she continued. "Once evil reigns, fire will fall from the heavens, the rivers of the world will dry up, and life as you know it will no longer exist!"

Shia glared at the young boy, her eyes still blazing.

Nicho lowered his head and closed his own eyes in fear, cowering before the obviously angry oracle. After a few seconds of silence, he raised his head and looked up at her remorsefully.

"Forgive me," Nicho apologized. He took a deep breath before continuing. "I will do as you ask."

The boy sheathed his sword and turned to walk away, prepared to begin his new quest. As he did, the oracle stopped him.

"Wait, Nicho."

He stopped and looked back at her, waiting respectfully for her to continue.

"Understand that yes, there is much evil in this world, but

there is also good," Shia said gently. "You and the others are good, and we in this world have been waiting for you."

Her eyes blinked slowly as she gazed down on him with a small smile.

"Go now. Find the village where you can rest and replenish your supplies," Shia said as the green glow in her eyes slowly faded until it disappeared. With a final smile at him, her eyes closed and did not reopen.

Nicho quietly examined the serene face above him. He felt he could somehow trust the oracle, and would do as she had asked.

In the past, he had always been a pretty good judge of character and was generally able to tell if people were decent. Although this was not an actual person in the rock above him, he found himself hoping beyond hope his judgment would prove correct again.

"I will go now," Nicho said. "Farewell, Shia, Oracle of the Green."

As he said this, the curtain of dark moss hanging down from the rock above him silently parted once again. The opening created a makeshift doorway, providing him with an entrance back into the forest.

Without a glance back, Nicho carefully stepped away from the damp rocks, turned left, and headed eastward.

THREE

Nicho walked through the dense forest as he tried his best to continue on an eastward path. The trees overhead were so thick he could see no trace of the sun at times, which made it difficult to tell what direction he was traveling in. He stopped to rest here and there, sitting next to a tree or on a large rock... whatever he happened to find along the way.

Every time he stopped he would close his eyes for a few moments and simply listen in hopes that the birds or insects would give him a clue as to which way he should go. He laughed to himself when he realized his wishful thinking. The day wore on, proving once again that time waits for no one. As the sun neared the end of its daily journey across the sky, Nicho knew darkness would not be far behind. He walked on and soon found himself out of the forest and in a dry, narrow valley. Low, brown mountains on both the north and south sides bordered the valley. With the sun no longer hidden by forest trees, he could easily tell which direction was east. He wanted to cover as much ground as he could before nightfall so he picked up the pace. He needed to find shelter along the path somewhere soon. Clouds crossed the arc of the sun every so often as he continued on, and he found himself thankful for the shade of the forest during the peak of the afternoon sunshine. If he'd had to walk in the valley sun with the sunburn that already seared his skin, he'd be hurting for sure by now.

And his mother was no where around with that fancy, mushroom concoction...

As he trudged onward through the dry, waist high valley grasses, he began to see a thin band of trees up ahead. As he made his way towards it, something suddenly jumped out at him from behind a tall patch of grass. Caught off guard, he nearly fell over as he stumbled on a tree stump.

"Are you the boy who is looking for the others?" the ambushing creature asked as it bounced up and down along the path. Without giving him a chance to answer, it added, "We were told to watch for the boy who was looking for the others... is that you? Is it? Is it?"

As soon as Nicho regained his footing he unsheathed his sword and tried to make out just what this odd creature was. It certainly didn't sound dangerous, but one just never knew.

"Stop!" the boy yelled at the energetic creature as it jumped up and down all around him. "Be still so I can see you!"

Immediately, the lively creature did as it was told and Nicho could finally see it for what it was. A cat!

But it wasn't just any ordinary cat... this was a smiling and mischievous valley cat with a lot of energy to burn. Nicho looked warily at the critter as he fought a smile. The cat was obviously having a difficult time remaining motionless like he had asked. Nicho had no doubt that the feline was doing everything it could to fight the urge to begin bouncing again... for now.

"Who are you?" Nicho asked the cat. He still held his sword in front of him, but was not really afraid of the four-legged feline.

If Shia hadn't told him about the creatures that were waiting for him, he probably would have wet himself when this cat jumped out and startled him. Since leaving the oracle, however, he had learned to expect the unexpected. He smiled slightly, thinking a bouncy feline was not what he'd had in mind to be ready for.

"My name is Netida and we have been waiting for you!" the feline answered excitedly as it began to bounce once again, apparently unaware that it was even doing so.

"This cat has more energy than any mud puppy I have ever seen!" Nicho thought.

"Who is it that sent you?" Nicho asked, hoping this creature was from the village he was looking for.

55

"We were told to be on the lookout for a young boy, traveling alone," the creature said as it eyed him between partial bounces.

"You are him, are you not?" the feline continued. Unable to contain its energy any longer, the creature suddenly began to bounce happily and erratically around Nicho as the question died on its lips.

"I may be," Nicho answered as he tried to make sense of the creature's odd demeanor.

"What is the name of your village?" he repeated. He was still not happy with the little bit of information the cat had provided up to this point.

"Whey-y-y-y-da," the feline answered, using five bounces to say the single word.

"Wheyda?" Nicho asked.

The energetic cat answered with an affirmative nod, and the boy decided to take the question a step further.

"Can you take me there?" Nicho asked. Sure now that this creature would lead him to the village he was looking for, the boy said, "Netida, my name is Nicho and I need to go to your village right away."

"Right-eee-oooo," the cat said happily. "Follow me!"

With that, the feline bounced its way through the tall grass as it led Nicho to the thin tree line in the distance. Beyond that was an open valley. The boy followed quickly behind the energetic animal, not really worried that he would lose sight of it. They continued on this way for some time, stopping here and there for short breaks. As the sun began setting in the west, they soon found themselves at the entrance to a small village. In it were many houses, each one shaped differently than the rest. As Nicho took in the new scenery in the twilight of the afternoon, he did not notice the small pair of eyes that now watched him from a nearby tree.

At first glance, it appeared to him that the village was abandoned. Netida slowly led him down the path which took them through the middle of the settlement. When they neared the end of the path, Nicho glanced behind them. What he saw caught him off guard... the village was suddenly filled with more cats than he could count!

FOUR

Nicho followed Netida, quite surprised at the number of cats that had filled the village. They seemed to be coming from all directions. There were long cats and short cats, and some were tall while some were almost dwarflike. Just like their sizes, their colors also varied greatly.

He looked around to his right as something caught his attention from his periphery. When he finally realized what it was, he was so shocked he was unable to move.

Approaching him from the side of one of the taller houses near the entrance to the village was a cat that was unbelievably different than any other cat he had ever seen. He closed his eyes briefly as he wondered if something might be wrong with his vision. When he reopened them, however, the cat was still there. Speechless, he watched as it walked towards him on only two legs, just as it had been a few seconds prior.

He shook his head and rubbed his eyes, not sure he wanted to believe what he thought he was seeing. He looked back at the agile feline, hoping it was simply a figment of his imagination… hoping it was really walking on four legs like a normal cat was supposed to. It wasn't.

The cat looked at him and nodded as it continued to stroll casually towards him. Could it really be comfortable walking this way?

Nicho took an anxious step back, quite nervous now about this oddity approaching him.

Some of the other cats in the crowd had been silently watching

57

Nicho. When they saw his reaction they began to laugh, which sounded like an odd sort of cat cry. Nicho remained where he was, his hand on his sword as he tried to sort out in his mind the sight before him. He was still having a difficult time accepting the fact that a cat was walking towards him on its hind legs as easily and effortlessly as a person!

"It's quite alright, young Nicho," a soft voice said from behind him. Caught off guard, he whipped around to confront it.

Sitting in the dirt a few steps away was another cat. This one was also different than the rest, however, which he noticed immediately.

Frazzled, Nicho turned his focus back to the walking cat to see where it was, afraid it would try to take advantage of his change of focus. He was relieved to see that it had stopped about ten feet away from him where it stood silently, still on two legs. Balance did not appear to be an issue with the upright feline whatsoever. It listened quietly to the other cat as it began talking to the boy.

"I understand your nervousness, young one, but it is quite uncalled-for. We will not harm you. On the contrary, we are here to help," the soft voice said from behind him.

Now that the two-legged walking cat had stopped its approach, Nicho repositioned himself so he could talk to this other creature while watching them both. He looked around nervously for Netida. The energetic and bouncing creature that he was semi-familiar with in this strange, foreign world was conveniently nowhere to be seen.

Didn't that just figure?

He turned his attention back to the creature with the soft voice and silently waited for an explanation. When it noticed his look of confusion, the talking feline let out a soft laugh and smiled at the boy.

"You are heading east, yes?" she asked.

"Yes, but what...?" he started before he was politely interrupted.

"We are gentle creatures that live, for the most part, simple lives in this world. Right now, however, our very lives are on the verge of oblivion!

"Our main goal right here, right now, is to assist you in your

58

travels," she explained.

Nicho looked around and began to relax somewhat, though his skepticism still nagged at the corners of his comfort. It appeared the village cats were gathered together for some sort of celebration. He wondered why, but didn't feel now was the right time to ask.

"How are you going to assist me?" he asked, both curious and cautious.

"You were sent here by Shia, yes?" she asked.

Surprised, he hesitated before answering her.

"Yes. But how do you know my name?" he asked.

"The ways of this world are different from those of your own," the feline creature answered. "You will find there are many questions which seem to have no answers. That will change, however, and you will find some of those answers as you continue on in your travels.

"We of this village will help you find your way east. There, among other things, you will find those who wait for you. If you are successful with your quest, you will find and free Little Draco," she said.

As she ended her sentence, the other village cats suddenly broke out in a cheer. After they quieted down, she continued.

"We, of course, will do our best to set you out on the correct path, and if you succeed, young traveler, you will be our hero and our world will carry on," she explained. The other cats cried out a yowling cheer once again, although not quite as loud as the previous one.

When the residents of the village settled down, she added with a whisper, "If you do not, however, our world will perish."

The other cats remained eerily silent. It was obvious that no words were necessary.

As Nicho felt the hairs on the back of his neck rise up, he felt confident that this was indeed the village Shia told him to find.

"For now, come sit with us and enjoy our celebration. We'll soon talk and you will then have answers to some of your questions," the cat said.

The other village cats cried out in another cheer, and, as if seeing the wave of an invisible hand, they began their celebration in earnest.

Nicho watched silently as the cat that had been walking towards him on two legs approached him once again with a mischievous smile. As it reached Nicho, the odd creature hooked one of its arms in the boy's own and led him gently into the crowd. Nicho allowed himself to be led as he hoped his instincts, which told him these creatures indeed meant him no harm, were correct.

Micah

ONE

As soon as Micah stepped into the portal, the light became very intense and he suddenly felt as though he was falling. He closed his eyes but it did not make a difference… the rainbow light penetrated through his closed eyelids as if they were wide open. Even squinting his eyes shut as tightly as he could did nothing to dim the brightness. The humming and vibration disappeared as soon as he stepped through the portal, and for a few seconds he felt like his body was weightlessly floating through space. While his eyes were clenched shut, he suddenly remembered the stones in his hand. He closed his fingers tightly around them and held them as close to his body as he could.

"Micah!"

As he transported, he thought he faintly heard a voice call out to him. Wait… it sounded like his sister! Could it really be her or was it only in his head? The light was too bright for him now, and even if he wanted to, he could not have attempted to look for her. He tried to try to call back to her but for some reason he couldn't. No matter how hard he tried, all he could hear was silence.

Had he lost his voice? Was he unconscious? This would be a totally logical reason for why he could not call out to her.

Then, an even worse thought occurred to him… could he be dead?

Micah was incredibly nervous about what was happening. Would he continue on as he was now? Falling/floating through time, never really ending up anywhere? Would he never see trees, the ocean, or valley flowers again? Would the intensely bright light burn his eyes, damaging them so he would not be able to see anything even if he did survive?

Or would the other end of that extreme happen? As he fell through the air not knowing where the portal would take him, Micah suddenly feared he might end up squashed against a rock or smashing into the ground, breaking in two. He felt like a mouse that had been carried into the clouds by the talons of a bird-of-prey, completely helpless and terrified.

All of this happened in a matter of seconds that seemed like years to him. As his mind raced with possibilities of the things that could happen to him, Micah did not immediately notice the darkness as it gradually enveloped him, bringing relief to his eyes as it did so. It didn't take long, however, for him to discover that he no longer squinted. At the same time, he did not feel weightless anymore... in fact, he no longer felt like he was moving at all.

He kept his eyes closed for a few more seconds, afraid of what he might see when he opened them. He took a deep breath and tried to calm down. He quickly noticed that things here were different, wherever here was. After being in the stale, musty air of the cave, the crisp, clean air was a welcomed relief.

He opened his eyes, happy to find himself standing on solid ground and very much alive. He wondered just how his body could feel weightless one second, and then find himself on solid ground the next, without feeling like he'd moved at all. It probably had something to do with the fact that his mind was too busy trying to think of all the ways his current situation could play out.

He shook his head in amazement. Was it possible that the beautiful rainbow created by the magical stones might just be causing him to lose some of his previously stable mind?

As he looked around, he could see he was completely surrounded by darkness. As his eyes adjusted, however, he thought he could make out a stand of nearby trees. Was it possible he had somehow made it back into the Orneo Forest, just outside the cave?

He remembered the stones after having briefly forgotten them, and panicked for a moment because he no longer felt them in his hand. He looked down and discovered that during his journey through the portal he had clenched his hand so tightly around them he had cut off his circulation. As a result, his hand was so numb now he could barely feel it.

"Oh, this is not good," he thought.

Carefully he worked his way through the tingling sensation in his hand and managed to open it, but in the darkness he could not see the precious stones. As the circulation slowly returned to his hand, he was relieved to feel them still there. To be sure, he used his other hand to count them... one, two, three, four stones, and one amulet. Surprisingly, they were all still there.

Whew.

But something was wrong. The stones no longer glowed. They all sat dark in his hand, as dark as the surrounding forest. Did their journey through the portal cause them to lose their magic?

He closed his hand protectively around them and felt the texture of the trim that surrounded the amulet as he did so. Reassured that the special gem was okay, he gently returned all of the small items to his pocket. Where had their magic gone? Why wouldn't they glow anymore for him? Had he done something wrong? As these questions buzzed through his head, a few others joined them. Where was he now? And where were the others?

More importantly, however... were the others okay?

He looked up at the sky and stared at the moon as it slowly emerged from behind a blanket of clouds, a beautiful, brilliant, half-circle of whiteness. He was thankful for it as it bathed his unfamiliar surroundings with a pale, almost glowing light.

He focused his attention back to the area around him. At first, he thought he was standing in a small field, but, now that his eyes had adjusted to the darkness, he could see the shadowy shapes of nearby trees as they surrounded him on all sides.

Different too was the pure silence which now filled the air. The strange humming sound that had followed him through the portal was completely gone. After a few moments, he was glad to hear the familiar sounds of crickets and frogs as they resumed their nightly conversations. He looked around for the others but they were still nowhere to be seen. With a small smile he thought that, at this point, he would even be glad to see the bat.

"Nicho? Tonia? Diam?" he called out quietly. His unfamiliar

voice silenced the nearby insects. This silence was his only answer.

He paused before he added, "Kaileen?"

Again there was nothing but silence.

He waited a few more minutes, hoping the others would soon join him, and as he waited, the night creatures once again began their discussions. After a short time, when the others didn't show up, Micah uncomfortably admitted to himself that they weren't coming.

He sighed nervously.

He knew he couldn't just wait here all night for them to show up, or for the sun to come up for that matter. He was out in a field and would make an easy target for predators once daylight filled the sky. He would have to decide what he was going to do… and soon.

Similar to how his brother had done from his own remote location in this strange new world, Micah looked up at the stars, unsure of which way he should go. He hoped against hope that the twinkling lights above would help guide him in the right direction. After studying them for a few minutes, he decided that, if he had to, he would head east. It seemed only logical to him that it would be safest to head in the direction where the sun would be rising in the morning. For the moment, however, he considered his predicament. Since he couldn't find any of the others, what should he do?

He looked around for anything familiar… trees, mountains, anything, but there was nothing as far as he could tell. He had no idea where he was. All he could see was the nearby trees that surrounded him in the darkness. As he looked to his left, not very far from where he stood, he could just begin to make out what appeared to be the base of a mountain range.

"Nicho?" he called out again, a little louder this time. He just wasn't ready to give up hope that the others were somewhere close.

Silence continued to be the only response this strange new place offered. He decided to rest next to one of the trees a short distance away. Once there, he pulled off his backpack and jacket before he sat down next to the tree, then began waiting patiently for the others.

As he waited, he leaned against the tree and closed his eyes, which he only intended to do for a few minutes, but the stresses of the day quickly left his young body, and before he knew it, he had drifted off to sleep.

Two

Micah only napped for a short time before he got up, anxious to continue his search for the others. The night air was warm, and after putting his jacket in his backpack, he donned the bag once again. Without much thought, he began to walk eastward through the nearby field. He walked in silence as the night creatures resumed their evening discourse. They seemed to be used to his presence now, and he smiled as he listened to them. Field crickets, tree frogs, and other creatures of darkness, sang their melodies, giving the surrounding area a peaceful tranquility. Micah knew better than to take this at face value, however. Just because the area appeared to be harmless and tranquil, it didn't necessarily mean it was. In contrast, the land around him was still quite foreign. Because of this, he remained on guard. He walked along as the moon slowly made its way across the sky. It would be morning soon.

As he continued on, he found the farther east he went, the more the land lost its flatness. Soon he was walking up and down hills and small trees began to litter the valley. He walked on, and after a while he could see a large tree up ahead that looked like a good place to rest.

As he got closer, he noticed the tree had some small, dark, round objects hanging from its long, leafy branches. In the darkness it was difficult to tell what these round shapes were, but he soon discovered they were just what he hoped they would be… fruit! His mouth began to water as he approached a branch filled with the healthy snacks… plumpears!

He picked a large piece of fruit from the branch that hung just over his head and sat down in the grass next to the tree. Hopefully it was ripe… it was hard to tell in the partial moonlight.

Micah pulled his bag off of his back and took out his pia bottle. As he bit into the piece of fruit, a thin trail of juice slowly trickled down his chin. It was definitely ripe! He smiled as he wiped the juice off his chin with the back of his hand. Oh, how his sister would harass him about it if she were here! Sometimes when he ate, he would literally bite off more than he could chew, and someone in the family (his sister, his brother, and even his mom) would comment on how he should take smaller bites. He was sure right now the juice that ran down his chin from the very ripe piece of fruit would be no exception.

As he ate, his thoughts drifted back to the one nagging question in his mind… where were the others? The three of them didn't do things together very often, but they were a family. In spite of all the harassment they gave each other, family love was definitely there. After everything they'd shared in the cave, he found himself missing them now. He was worried they had gotten lost or were trapped somewhere.

With his spare hand, he gently touched the outside of his pocket as he felt the small objects that were hidden there. He was disappointed they had lost their magical glow when he touched them. They seemed to be just plain rocks now, taking up pocket space.

He finished his plumpear and threw the core at another tree a short distance away. It hit the trunk of the tree with a dull splat as pieces flew in different directions. One piece in particular remained stuck on the tree for a few seconds before it finally fell silently to the ground. Micah smiled as a silly thought crossed his mind… perhaps he invented a new snack? Skewered plumpear! Maybe they could take those skewers and hold them over the village fire, to make fried plumpear skewers? Knowing his luck, he'd be the only one to eat them.

Micah pulled the stones out of his pocket and looked at them again, willing them to glow. The stones, however, did nothing but sparkle innocently in the moonlight. He closed his hand around the lifeless stones and held them in his lap. He tried with all his might to concentrate on the others, willing the stones to search his siblings out. Nothing.

He sighed.

Maybe he was trying too hard? Maybe he should try something different?

Still holding the stones in his hand, he thought perhaps if he relaxed enough they would once again take on a life of their own. He closed his eyes once more and focused on nothing but relaxing. And again nothing happened, but he did realize he was quite tired.

He decided he would try to rest for a little while before heading out again. Surrounded by silence, with the moon and the stars shining in the sky above him, he allowed his body to continue to relax. Soon, he was dozing peacefully. His eyes were closed for what felt like only a few seconds when he heard an odd noise. He cracked one eye open and discovered that he was peeking at one of the strangest creatures he'd ever seen.

The creature, cat-like in many ways, yet it wasn't, was standing next to him, to his right. It was close enough that he could reach out and touch it if he wanted to. The mystery creature had the head and body of a small cat, but as he continued to peek at it, he could glimpse its oddly forked tail as it flicked back and forth in the moonlight. The cat creature was roughly the size of a small mud puppy, which didn't appease Micah much. He knew that even the smallest creatures could be dangerous if one made the wrong move.

He nervously watched it now through the cracks in both eyelids. It seemed to be staring at his legs. What was it looking at?

As Micah's mind cleared from his short nap, he remembered he had been holding the stones in his hand as he closed his eyes to rest.

Could that be what had this creature's attention?

Trying to be as subtle as he could, Micah slowly, gently squeezed his closed hand as he tried to determine if the stones were still there.

Yes, they seemed to still be there, concealed in his hand. But if they were safely hidden there then what was this creature staring at so intently?

Micah remained still for another moment as he frantically tried to remember if he had removed his sword. Had he laid it on the ground nearby or was it still sheathed at his waist? As his mind searched for the memory, it suddenly came to him.

Yes!

He had removed it and placed it on the ground in between his bag and his left leg. The question now was, could he grab the weapon quickly enough to defend himself from this odd creature?

The cat's sudden movement caught Micah's attention. As he shifted his peeking eyes to look at its head, he was startled to see that it was looking directly at him now.

"Stranger, I know you are not sleeping," the creature whispered at Micah, startling him. "You may open your eyes and face me, so that we may talk."

Micah noticeably jumped when the cat began talking to him. His eyes quickly flew open and he rolled to his left, the stones clutched tightly in his right hand. In a flash, he grabbed the handle of his sword, rolled over his bag, and somehow managed to unsheathe his weapon as he quickly rose to his feet.

"What do you want?" Micah asked the creature nervously.

Now that his eyes were fully open, Micah could see the creature in the moonlight, although it was difficult to make out many details.

It was definitely some sort of cat. Although he'd seen many cats before, he'd never seen any quite like this. The feline which stood before him was a multi-colored tiger, with black, white, and gray (or maybe tan, it was difficult to tell in the moonlight) stripes that ran horizontally along the creature's body. The ears were very cat-like, but seemed oddly too large for the creature's head.

The cat's tail was definitely much different than any cat's tail he'd ever seen. It was roughly the length of a normal cat's tail, but the rest of it looked very odd. Where the tail attached to the body, it was one piece, which was just like he expected it to look. Micah noticed, however, that as the tail grew away from the body, other tails branched off the main one. In effect, this cat's tail had three tails in total, and each one moved without regard to the others.

71

At the end of each tail was a ball of fur, all relatively the size of urchins they found in the bay near the village.

The creature looked at Micah where he stood with his sword held out in front of him, its yellow-green eyes glowing in the moonlight. Its nose twitched a few times as it tried to determine whether or not the boy was from this world. Except for nose twitches and the movement of its tails flicking this way and that, the cat watched the boy silently, apparently unafraid.

"You are a visitor," the creature said, ignoring him.

Micah looked at the cat and frowned. How did the creature know he was a visitor? He voiced his question to the cat, whose response was immediate.

"Why, it's obvious," the cat said. "You are not dressed as one of us, you don't talk like one of us, and you do not smell like one of us."

The last part of the statement caught Micah off guard and he started to giggle. The cat looked at him with an odd expression as it cocked its head. It obviously didn't understand what was so funny.

When Micah finally stopped giggling, he could see that the cat was waiting for an explanation.

"I'm sorry," he apologized. "It's just that... you said I don't smell like one of you... so tell me then, what do I smell like?"

Without hesitation, the creature answered, "Well, you smell like an outsider."

"How?" the boy asked.

The cat looked at him curiously, the ends of his tail still flicking through the air behind it.

"You just do."

As Micah watched the cat, he remembered how the creature had been looking at something when it thought he was sleeping.

"When I was sleeping, what was it you were so interested in?" Micah asked.

The cat's eyes squinted partially closed for a few seconds as it looked at the boy.

"I was told to guide you to town," it said.

"Town? What town?" Micah asked, but a thought suddenly struck him and he continued before the creature could answer his question.

"Wait a minute," he said. "Are you trying to say that you knew I'd be here?"

"Yes," the cat answered matter-of-factly. "I will take you to town, where you must speak to Katielda."

"Katielda?" Micah asked, but the cat only nodded without offering more information.

"Why must I speak to Katielda?" Micah continued questioning the smaller creature. He needed to know more before he would agree to go anywhere with it.

There was another question that also bothered him... how would the others find him if he went off gallivanting in the woods with some three-tailed cat?

"Are you the keeper of the rainbow?" the creature asked, taking the boy by surprise.

Rainbow... how did this creature know about the rainbow? Now that the cat mentioned this, Micah was certain he knew what it was the feline had been looking at when it thought he was sleeping earlier.

The stones!

Luckily, he had managed to tuck his hand holding the stones back into his pocket while they had been talking, which is where his hand had remained. He tried to inconspicuously feel for the five stones to make sure they were all there.

The cat waited for Micah's answer as the boy counted the stones quietly in his mind. Thankfully, they were all there.

"The keeper of the rainbow?" Micah asked as he removed his hand from his pocket.

"Yes," the cat said. "You know what it is that I refer to, and I know you are the one. It is imperative that you accompany me to Wheyda. You must speak to Katielda right away!"

With that, the cat began to turn away from Micah, expecting him to follow it.

"Wait!" Micah said. "Wait! You're right... I am not from this world, but others in my family are here, somewhere, as well. I need to find them before I can go with you to see this... Katielda. I must find them first."

"No. You must not worry about them right now. I know those

73

of whom you speak, and they will find you. But first, you must speak to Katielda. She has important information for you, and she is waiting for you as we speak," the cat said impatiently.

"You know of the others? Nicho? Tonia? Diam and Kaileen? Do you know where they are? If you do, please tell me! Please tell me what you know!" Micah exclaimed as he took a step towards the cat.

"No!" the feline creature answered as it stepped back away from the boy.

As Micah frowned at the creature, it lowered its head for a moment.

"Please, you must follow me," it said. It raised its head slowly and looked at the boy, its eyes filled with sadness. "Our world is in danger. We were told that if we were to find 'the keeper of the rainbow', we needed to bring that person to Katielda immediately.

"Micah, without the help of the magic you possess, our world is certainly doomed," the creature said sadly with pleading yellow-green eyes.

"Please…"

Micah considered the creature's words for a moment. It had called him 'the keeper of the rainbow', which sounded like it was referring to the rainbow colors back in the cave, back at the portal. How this creature could know about that, he had no idea. It obviously knew more about him than it was saying.

It also spoke of 'the others', but the creature seemed hesitant to say any more about them. Worried about the others, Micah was tempted to try to get more information. His gut instinct, however, told him to trust this creature. Hopefully, if he could gain its trust, it would then help him find his way back to his own family.

He nodded at the creature.

"Alright. I'll follow you," Micah said quietly. The creature lowered itself close to the ground before springing high up into the air.

"Yeeeoooowwww!!!" it cried happily from above him. It landed almost exactly in the same place it had jumped from. It looked back at Micah sheepishly, but with an obvious smile.

"Before I will follow you, however, I must know your name or have something to call you by," Micah said to the feline. "I do not want to call you 'cat', so if you want me to follow you, you must give me a name." Micah looked at the feline. It was no longer jumping as it had been, but it was still somewhat bouncy.

"You may call me Ragoo," the creature answered.

Micah smiled slightly and said, "Well, Ragoo, nice to meet you. You may call me Micah."

He nodded to the creature, who nodded back with a smile, as Micah added, "By the way, what kind of a name is 'Ragoo'?"

The creature looked at the boy for a moment before answering.

"That, young Micah, is a story for another time."

"Another time?" Micah asked.

The cat nodded slightly but would say no more.

"Very well then," Micah said. "Please lead the way."

The cat's low bounces became slightly higher hops as it pranced along the way into the nearby woods. As he followed the obviously excited creature, the boy glanced skyward. He was relieved to see the slight orange glow on the eastern horizon… the beginnings of a beautiful sunrise as the sun once again began its daily journey across the sky. Micah somehow felt better knowing that, in a short period of time, the sun would soon be up, and he wouldn't have to follow this odd creature into a dark, uninviting forest.

No matter how trustworthy Ragoo seemed to be, Micah was almost afraid to put his faith in him, so he kept his hand close to his sword. He didn't really want to follow Ragoo into the unfamiliar forest, but felt as though, just like earlier in the cave with Muscala and his quest, once again he had no choice.

They rustled through the dried leaves and brush that covered the ground beneath them as they walked, passing many trees and bushes along the way. Micah became more comfortable with the feline he followed as time when on, but he forced himself to remain cautious. After the way the cat had practically ambushed him, he was now nervous about being surprised by other creatures. He needn't have worried, however, because none appeared. Well, none that he noticed. His uncle had taught him and his siblings that forest creatures could be sneaky, and was sure there were some in the vicinity. If they were, they would hopefully remain right where they were, watching, yet unseen.

As the sun came up, the forest opened up into yet another field that was small, hilly, and bathed in the early morning sunshine. When they reached the top of a crest, Micah shaded his eyes and looked ahead. There, in the lower valley, he could now see small hut-like houses clustered together. They appeared to be made out of sticks and straw.

"The village residents that lived here can't be very big," he thought as he wondered just what kind of creatures inhabited the houses.

Silently, they made their way into the village. Suddenly, a door on one of the smaller shelters cracked open, and Micah thought he could make out a small pair of yellow eyes peeking out at him. He thought they resembled those belonging to a kitten. He smiled towards the eyes as they cautiously watched them pass by.

He glanced over at Ragoo. The now somewhat familiar feline was watching him in return as they walked side by side. Micah smiled at the cat, hoping to reassure him that he would bring this village no harm. He found he was relieved when Ragoo hesitantly smiled back. It was common knowledge that cats had sharp claws, and if it came down to a fight between the two of them, Micah was sure the cat would rip him to shreds.

The boy turned his attention back to the assorted houses as they walked by, noticing how their sizes and shapes varied, as well as how they were constructed. They ranged from very small to quite large, though none the size of the houses back in Uncava. Some were round and others were long, almost rectangular shaped, and flat. Still others were tall and thin, like small towers. As different as all of the houses were, however, their roofs all looked very similar, seemingly made from tree branches covered in either straw or some of the larger forest leaves. Micah figured either there was a large difference in the sizes of cats living here, or there was some other kind of creature in the village.

The boy sighed quietly. The situation he was in left him with many unknowns and even more questions. He just wasn't sure if he wanted to know the answers. At times, not knowing was far better than knowing.

They had practically walked through the entire village when they stopped before a house that was much different than the others. The first thing Micah noticed was that it stood by itself at the top of a small hill, a lone sentry keeping watch over the village. The location of the residence was not the only thing that made it stand out from the rest, however. It was also quite unique in its appearance.

Made out of square stones, it had no windows in its walls, which Micah thought was very odd. A cluster of small trees grew around the house, seemingly protecting it. Why would anyone want to live in a house without windows? No fresh air? No sun shining inside, warming the floor?

When the seasons changed at home, one thing Micah loved was opening the windows on a warm spring day, letting in the fresh air while at the same time releasing the gloom that had been brought inside by Old Man Winter. Micah followed Ragoo to the door of the house. He watched silently as the feline knocked rapidly three times.

Rap, rap, rap.

Almost immediately, the door opened and Ragoo smiled briefly at Micah. He nodded at the boy, then stepped into the entrance and disappeared around the corner of the door. Micah hesitated a few seconds, questioning whether or not he should follow the feline. Doubtfully, he glanced back the way they had come.

Scattered throughout the village were quite a few catlike creatures in all manner shapes and sizes. They watched the boy silently, curious about this stranger who had entered their small, hidden village. He saw others as they peered at him through windows of houses, around trees, and even from some of the rooftops.

The boy did not feel threatened by them, only very cautious.

Suddenly he heard a noise. He turned quickly back around and faced the open doorway of the house. He breathed a sigh of relief when he realized it was only Ragoo, who was in turn peering at him from around the door. With a questioning look on his face, the cat sighed as he reassured the boy.

"Micah, you must not be afraid," Ragoo said quietly. "Time is precious, young one, for both your friends and my world. Because of this, it is imperative that we attend to a few important things so you can be on your way.

"We of this village would not hurt you! Why would we, when you are the one who has come to help us? Please come quickly so that we may talk," Ragoo said quietly.

Micah glanced briefly one more time at the village creatures, and then nervously followed the feline into the dark interior of the house. Once he stepped into the gloomily lit entryway of the unique residence, the door closed gently behind him. As his eyes became accustomed to the dim lighting within, he was surprised at the scene he now found before him.

The room had none of the amenities that he had in his own house back in the village of Uncava. At first glance, it appeared to be a sparsely furnished, almost uninhabited room, with the exception of the small fire burning cozily in the fireplace along the wall to his right. As he surveyed the room, he saw something that surprised him. Sitting on the mantle of the fireplace was a small, multicolored rat, its long, hairless tail hanging over the edge of the flat, smooth stone. The rodent sat motionless as it quietly watched him, curious, yet apparently unafraid. The boy looked around as he wondered what other creatures could be hidden in the room, but there didn't appear to be any. He didn't see anything else of significance until something new grabbed for his attention. It took him a moment to realize exactly what it was, and when he finally figured it out, he questioned whether or not he was seeing what his mind thought he was seeing. When looking at the house from the outside, it appeared to be small and cozy, not very tall, and certainly not very long. Now that he was inside, however, he felt very deceived by his first assessment of the home. The inside of the house was definitely not very wide, but the length of the room he was in completely amazed him. It appeared to go on and on, easily the size of ten or more houses put together.

But how could that be?

Micah looked at Ragoo, confused. When the feline saw this, he chuckled.

"The house is different than what you first thought, is it not?" the cat asked with a smirk.

"Yes," Micah whispered, "much different!" As he said this, he glanced over at the wall to his left and got an even bigger surprise.

What was going on?

A window was now unmistakably in the brick wall where only seconds before there had been none… of this Micah was sure. The boy took a hesitant step towards the window, thinking his mind was surely deceiving him. He looked through the window, confused and dismayed to see the village outside. Creatures that had been mostly hidden only moments before had begun to emerge from their hiding places. They looked curiously towards the house that contained an as yet unexplained situation.

Micah turned back towards Ragoo, unsure of whether he wanted to pummel the cat with questions or demand answers. Before he could even make eye contact with the feline, however, another surprise completely wiped all questions out of his mind and put new ones in their place.

A new creature was now in the room with them, lying motionless on the hearth in front of the fireplace where the small, cozy fire continued to burn steadily. Micah had no idea how it had gotten there, but the new creature he now saw was another cat. It was curled up in a ball, eyes closed, enjoying the warmth that filled the room. Micah frowned as he observed the new arrival, more confused now than he had been only moments before. He wondered what it was doing there (besides trying to sleep) when the cat suddenly lifted its head and looked lazily at the boy.

"I see you have finally arrrrrrrived," the cat purred, not surprised in the least by the human visitor who was staring at it in awe and surprise.

The cat was beautiful and much different from any other that Micah had ever seen, at least until recently. Narrow gray, white, and black stripes ran vertically along the length of its body, forming paths of sorts. As the creature lifted its head to look at the boy, Micah could see its chest was pure white. Its tail, which had been curled around the front of its body, suddenly rose in a gentle sweeping motion, which enabled Micah to clearly see the appendage. It was decorated with shiny objects that spiraled around it from the base to the tip. The tip, he also saw, was similar in shape to Ragoo's, forked and furry. Micah watched silently as this new creature gently swished the adorned limb back and forth, almost as if it were testing the air for something. On a whim, Micah asked, "Were you waiting for me?"

The cat with the swishing tail squinted its yellow eyes at the boy as it tried to gauge whether or not he was serious. From behind him, Ragoo answered his question.

"News in our world travels fast, Micah. As soon as you held the first stone in your hand, we knew you were coming, and we hoped you would quickly find your way here. Likewise, as soon as you and your group stepped into the portal, so did we also know," the cat said quietly.

Micah looked back at Ragoo in silence and confusion.

"In answer to your question, yes, we have been waiting for you," the female cat with the decorated tail said quietly.

As the boy looked at both cats with a somewhat dazed expression, Ragoo continued.

"Micah, meet Katielda. Katielda, this is Micah."

Micah looked at them uncertainly as Ragoo said, "Katielda is the leader of our clan, which is signified by the string of jewels that is woven around her tail. We of this village are known as yarnie cats."

Micah nodded respectfully to the cat and Katielda nodded back at him in return. This done, she stretched her back upwards, similar to how he'd seen some of their smaller, domestic cats do in the village when they played together. As he silently watched, Katielda suddenly stood up on her back feet and began to walk towards him. Micah looked on nervously, having never seen a cat do this before, even though somewhere in the back of his mind he knew these cats were nothing like any ordinary cat he'd ever known.

Ragoo chuckled beside him quietly.

Micah glanced at the male cat briefly as he wondered why he had to be the one who brought Ragoo so much humor.

He allowed his gaze to return to the mysterious creature with the glittery, forked tail as she fearlessly approached him. Katielda appeared not to notice his hand as it rested on his weapon as a precaution. Micah could not help but keep it there, because he was so confused now that he did not know who he could trust.

"You have come from another place and time, Micah, but your arrival has come at a perfect time for us in this world," Katielda said. "We welcome you."

Saying this, she stopped a few feet away from him, her tail swishing gracefully to and fro. The jewels woven into the appendage shimmered in the soft light, which emanated from the fire that burned softly in the fireplace. Micah watched quietly as Katielda bent her upper body forward in a bowing motion, her forked tail quickly lowering onto the floor behind her in a submissive gesture. Confused, Micah glanced back at Ragoo and saw that he, too, was bowing towards him in a similar fashion.

This didn't make sense… she was the leader of their clan, yet she was bowing to him?

"I don't understand," he began quietly as both cats began to purr loudly with their heads still bowed. Micah's eyes were once again drawn to Katielda's tail, but this time he had reason to look there. The jewels woven around her tail not only glittered in the firelight… they now glowed a beautiful, iridescent yellow.

As Micah watched in fascination, he noticed that the louder the cats purred, the stronger the jewels glowed around her tail.

A sudden noise interrupted his thoughts. He kept his hand on his sword as he turned quickly toward the window. He almost expected to see another surprise creature in the room with them.

What he saw did surprise him, but it was not what he expected… at all.

On the outside of the house, it appeared as though the entire village of cats had congregated on the other side of the window. Like those inside, every one of them now bowed towards the house, low to the ground, as they purred in unison.

Shocked, Micah realized he was the one they were bowing to.

He watched them in silent amazement for a moment before he turned back towards Katielda and Ragoo. They had stopped purring and were now both standing upright, looking at him respectfully. Although the boy couldn't see Ragoo's face very clearly, Micah would almost bet his favorite mud puppy that the feline was smirking at him yet again because of his reaction.

"You are the keeper of the rainbow, are you not?" Katielda asked him curiously, drawing his focus from Ragoo.

Micah was not sure how Katielda could have asked him the exact same question Ragoo had earlier unless they somehow knew about the adventure he'd just had in the cave. He decided to be honest with them about everything. Once again, he almost felt as though he had no choice.

"Yes, I guess you could say that I am the keeper of the rainbow," he answered. "Or I was, but it seems as though there is no longer a rainbow to be made."

Katielda looked at him curiously, the question evident in her eyes before it was spoken.

"Why do you say that?"

"Do you know where I just came from?" Micah asked quietly. He walked towards the fireplace and sat down by the hearth, both wanting and needing the fire to warm him. He had suddenly felt chilled even though the windows and door were closed.

"We know you come from another place," Katielda answered. "You do not smell of this world."

Micah laughed out loud and his hand quickly shot over his mouth. He looked at the cats sheepishly where they both sat now, opposite him but close enough to the fire to also enjoy its warmth.

After the boy's outburst, Ragoo turned to Katielda to offer an explanation.

"I told him earlier that his smells are different from ours, and it was obvious that he was not from here," Ragoo explained.

"Ah," Katielda responded with an understanding smile.

"I'm sorry I laughed, but please understand that I've been through a lot the last few days," Micah said apologetically.

"Tell me your story," Katielda said quietly as she looked at him with caring eyes. Her forked tail no longer glowed, but it continued to swish softly from side to side on the dusty floor.

Needing a friend more than he would have liked to admit, Micah filled them in on his recent adventure, telling them everything he could think of. He described some of the creatures they'd met in the cave, especially the arrogant snake that had been chasing them. He explained how his brother had gotten trapped in the abyss and how they'd had no choice but to help Muscala find the gem in order to save their brother. He told them about Kaileen, the gentle creature who was now a trusted member of their group. He described her own story of tragedy, ending with the death of her friend, Ransa. He told them about the skeletons they'd found, and the mysterious ring the girls had recovered from one in particular.

Finally, with wonder in his eyes, he shared the story of the mysterious amulet, the magical stones, and the portal. He described his unforgettable trip through the door to the unknown, and explained how they had to go through it in order to save themselves from the villainous snake. When he was done sharing the important pieces of everything he knew, Micah looked at the felines silently. They were both gazing intently at the flickering flames of the fire as they thought about what he had described. When they offered nothing in return, he continued.

"Deep in the cave we were lost in, we found a body of water that Ransa called 'Still Water'. When we found it, we didn't know what it was, other than just a motionless body of water in the heart of the cave.

"Later on, when Muscala woke up and was getting ready to chase us, the bat showed us how to get back to it.

"For some reason, the stones would only light up when I held them… they wouldn't light up for anyone else. When we got to the water, Muscala was hot on our trail and I held the stones and the amulet in my hand. I think the one thing he wanted more than the amulet was to make a meal out of all of us," he said.

He looked at the cats, nervous now with the memories that were running through his mind while they listened attentively to his story.

"I don't doubt for a minute that he would have killed us all without a second thought!

"Once the portal was created, everyone else went through, first the girls, then Nicho. Because I was the…" he hesitated and smiled at them before continuing, "…'keeper of the rainbow', the one holding the glowing stones which made the portal possible, I went through last.

"When I came through on the other side, no one was there waiting for me. No Nicho, no girls, not even the bat," he said sadly.

"I was hoping everyone made it through the portal, but now I'm not so sure."

He looked at them with a worried stare.

Katielda's tail flicked in the firelight as she said, "Do not be discouraged, young one. Just because they weren't there waiting for you does not mean they didn't make it through.

"At times, I have a very good sense of things. I do sense your siblings and your friend made it through the portal safely," she continued.

"So, besides, me, four others made it through the portal?" he asked as his face lit up with hope.

She shook her head no.

"What?" he asked not understanding. There had been four others besides him who had stepped into the rainbow of light... Tonia, Diam, Kaileen, and Nicho. If Katielda had such a good sense of things, how could she not know this?

"Why are you shaking your head no?" he asked.

Before she could answer him, he suddenly said, "Ah ha! I know who else you're thinking of!

"The girls each wore a bag on their backs and each one carried a turtle... they were Merlia and Celio. So instead of four others going through the portal with me, you could indeed say that there were six," Micah rationalized, glad he'd thought of it before Katielda had needed to explain.

Still Katielda shook her head no.

"You are correct in saying that six others transported through the portal with you, and this is just one of the important things you must know," she said seriously, her tail no longer moving.

"Besides those who traveled through the portal with you, there are others who have transported since," she explained.

"Others? What do you mean 'others'?" he asked. Before she could reply, he added his new question, "How can that be?"

She looked at him in silence for a moment as she tried to determine the best way to explain it to him. Before she could answer, he stood up and began to pace around the room.

"Katielda, I have the stones!" he explained as his voice shook slightly and he meandered back and forth in front of the fire.

"The stones have been dark, lifeless, and safe in my pocket since I came through the portal! I haven't opened the portal again since I've been here, and, honestly… I don't even know if I would know how to," he said. He stopped pacing and looked at her, his eyes begging an answer.

Katielda looked back at Micah sadly. She knew he was confused by everything that was happening to him. Regardless of this, she knew she must do whatever she had to for him to understand. Many lives were dependent on this very moment. Without his understanding what he needed to do, their world may not exist much longer.

"Micah, you have the stones of the rainbow, yes. You also have special powers deep within you that are yours and yours alone… powers you have unknowingly used to activate those stones.

"But you also must understand there are other points of travel in our world that others may use if they have the knowledge. I speak of these when I tell you that others have traveled since your arrival into our world," Katielda explained.

Micah looked at her with a frown. He was still confused, but felt a need to know more of what she was saying. He sat back down next to the fire cross-legged, his feet curled up underneath him.

"How many others have traveled since my arrival?" he asked. His mental wheels were spinning furiously now. "Can you tell me that?"

Katielda looked at him and nodded her head, yet remained silent.

"Well?" Micah asked after a few seconds. He wanted to know the answer, but more than that, he needed to know it.

"Four others that I know of," she answered quietly.

"Four!" Micah said, not sure he heard her correctly. "How can that be? I just don't understand…" he started, still doubtful about these other traveling points that she spoke of.

"I cannot tell you who they were," Katielda explained, "but I can tell you this… some you know and some you do not."

Micah looked at her, more surprised than before. "Some I know?" he asked.

When he tried to think of what other creatures may have traveled through the portal, the first and obvious one that came to mind was Muscala. Was it possible that the arrogant snake had somehow found a way to open the portal that should have closed after he went through it with the stones? This thought seemed unlikely, so he pushed it out of his mind.

Next, he thought about Nicho and the girls. They had definitely all gone through the same portal and the only one that he knew of… he had witnessed it with his own eyes. Having seen this, he now questioned the possibility that they could have ended up somewhere else. With that in mind, he now opened himself up to another possibility. Maybe, just maybe, something else could have gone through.

But then again, he had the stones…

"Micah, you must forget about the stones for a moment and realize that not everyone needs that kind of magic to get where they want to go. That is the first and most important thing you must understand!

"There are many creatures and many forms of magic in this world. Sometimes, either the creatures, or their magic, or both, can extend into other worlds.

"That, young Micah, is what happened in your world," Katielda explained patiently.

Micah sat silently as he thought about Katielda's words. The fire continued to crackle and burn gently in the fireplace behind him.

"The amulet is something else that we must speak of," Katielda continued quietly.

"First of all, do you know where it came from?"

Micah looked at her for a few seconds, his memories of the past few days rushing over him as a rock rolls down a mountain. He shivered as he recalled how close to death they had all come and how wild Muscala had gotten when the serpent realized they had possession of his precious gem.

"The giant snake that chased us through the cave wanted the amulet… in a bad way," he whispered as his eyebrows furrowed together in a scowl with remembrance.

"Yes, we know of Muscala. His name is known in this world as well as yours," Ragoo said quietly.

"He told us the amulet was stolen from a sorcerer, but I don't remember his name," Micah continued. "Muscala said if he was able to find and return the gem to the sorcerer, he would be in very good standing with him."

"Lotor," Katielda said quietly.

"Yes! That was the sorcerer's name!" Micah said excitedly. When he saw the serious look on the female cat's face, however, his stomach sank. In silence, he waited respectfully for her to continue.

"Lotor is an evil sorcerer," she said as Ragoo nodded. "Very evil. If he gets the amulet back into his possession, we may all be doomed.

"Now, young Micah, tell me what else you know," she encouraged him.

"Not much, really," Micah said.

"Muscala told us where to find the amulet, and we had to go get it for him because he couldn't fit through the narrow tunnels to retrieve it himself. We went where he told us to go, found the gem, and brought it back to him. Before we would give it to him, we made him free my brother from the abyss he had gotten trapped in.

"Once that was done, the snake became angry and demanded we give him the gem. By then, we knew the portal could only be created with the magical stones and the amulet together, though, so we ran for it.

"Before that, though, Ransa, one of the creatures we met in the cave, managed to put him to sleep for a little while. Unfortunately, it didn't take long for him to wake up and realize we'd tricked him and stolen his gem."

"What did you do with it?" Katielda asked quietly.

Micah looked at her and after only a few seconds' hesitation, stood up and removed the stones from his pocket. When he opened his hand to show them, their eyes were drawn quickly to the amulet where it sat in his palm, nestled next to the other colored stones. As they watched, the dark stones all began to glow softly in the firelight… not the brilliant glow they'd had in the cave, but a soft, gentle glow, much like a firebug at the end of its life. The magical stones continued to glow this way for a few seconds before they again faded back to darkness.

Micah looked at Katielda and Ragoo, almost as if to tell them it was real, that the stones did glow for him… and he noticed they were both smiling.

"What?" he asked quietly. He closed his hand protectively around the stones.

"You are the one that we've been waiting for," Katielda said. "You are the one that can help us save our world."

As Micah looked at her considering her odd statement, she posed him with a question he was not expecting.

"May I have a closer look at the stones and amulet?" she asked timidly.

He stood motionless for a moment. He was unsure of her intentions but he also understood he simply could not spend the rest of his life not taking a chance. The cats had not given him any reason to mistrust them, and he was at a complete disadvantage in his current situation. With that in mind, he slowly opened his hand, giving them a better look at the items he felt so compelled to protect.

Almost in unison, the cats both stood up and took a slow, cautious step towards the boy, their eyes fixed on his opened palm. In seconds, Katielda began to purr quietly from deep down in her throat as her tail moved gently through the air behind her. Without hesitation, Ragoo also began quietly purring.

They stopped a short distance from Micah as he watched them cautiously. Within seconds, the stones again began to glow softly from where they rested in his hand. As the cats continued to purr, the stones grew dark again, much like a fire that has been doused by a bucket of water. The felines continued to look at the dark items longingly for a few seconds before they sat back down on the dirt floor.

It took a few more seconds for the obviously flustered Katielda to regain her composure.

"The amulet… do you know what it is called?" she asked Micah quietly.

She was breathing heavily as though she had just run a hard and fast race up the nearby mountain.

"Muscala told us in the cave that it is called 'Dragon's Blood'," he responded. As he said this, Katielda and Ragoo both gasped for breath.

"Why? What does it mean?" he asked as he tried to hide the fact that he'd noticed their audible surprise.

"It is so," Ragoo whispered quietly as Katielda nodded once in silent response.

"It is," she agreed after a few seconds.

"It is what?" Micah asked. He was beginning to get impatient with the unanswered questions and partial statements.

"It is the amulet we've heard so many stories about," Katielda said quietly.

The fire continued to burn as it bathed the room in its warmth and gentle glow. After tucking the stones back into the safety of his pocket, Micah sat down, intent on learning more.

"Let me tell you the story that we know," Katielda began.

Micah nodded respectfully as he silently waited for her to continue.

"Long ago," she reminisced, "there was a large amulet that belonged to the dragons for as long as anyone can remember, since the beginning of time, perhaps. It is said that, for many moons, only the winged beasts understood the true power held by this precious gem. The beasts kept it safe deep in the mountains where they lived, and all was well in all the worlds. By protecting this magical stone, it in turn protected them, and allowed them to multiply and prosper for moons upon moons upon moons."

Katielda paused for a moment, relieved to see the boy was listening intently to her story. He must if he was going to do what was needed to be done…

"The original amulet was large and tri-colored, with each color having its own section. These colors were blue, red, and white, and each had their own meaning. Together, the three colors are what made the amulet so beautiful… so powerful"

"The blue third represented the waters of the worlds, cool and refreshing. It is called 'Dragon's Tear'.

"Similar to the way water is good for our bodies, so is this

89

amulet the same to the worlds. It washes away impurities and helps to maintain goodness. The blue piece of the original gem was the direct opposite of the red.

"The red third represented the fires at the core of the worlds, hot and powerful. It became known as 'Dragon's Blood'.

"Used correctly, fire can be a necessary tool. However, by the same token, used incorrectly it can lead to devastating results. To some, fire is equal to strength, and that is why the dark ones wanted this amulet so badly. If Lotor could take possession of it, his strength as a wizard would be amazing. Combine that with the qualities of the other two amulets, and he would be nearly unstoppable!

"The white third represented everything in between the red and the blue, and provided the necessary neutrality between the two. It is known as 'Dragon's Breath'.

"This amulet is to all the worlds as air is to our bodies. Without this particular piece, the other two would have no way of working together. As a result, there would be no harmony between the worlds," she said as she looked at the boy.

Micah sat silently, totally engrossed in Katielda's words. He had no idea about the amazing history of the amulet, and had no idea it was about to get better.

"As one piece, the amulet was an incredible source of power, providing balance to all the worlds," Ragoo said.

Micah nodded, clinging to every word.

"Now that you know where the amulet came from, let's talk about the dragons," Ragoo said.

"Dragons are some of the most complex creatures that have ever lived, and they range in size from massively large to adorably small," Katielda explained. "Their physical size did not matter, however, for the inner beings of every dragon were as large as large could be. Some of the smallest beasts were seemingly unaware of their smaller stature, while some of the largest dragons were the gentlest of all creatures.

"At times, however, this gentleness was misconceived as a weakness," the female feline explained. She paused for a moment as if going back to a memory of her past.

Micah sat still as he listened to her story, replaying it in his mind, when he suddenly sat upright.

"Yes?" she asked, coming back to the present, anticipating his evident questions.

"Wait a minute. You said 'dragons are complex creatures'…" he said in a half-statement, half-question.

"Yes," she agreed as she nodded, not understanding his statement.

"Dragons are? Not dragons were?" he asked.

"Yes…?" she said again, but this time it was more of a question. "What don't you understand, young Micah?"

His eyes wide, he clarified his question for her, unable to believe that he'd heard what he thought he'd heard.

"Dragons are real? Real, like… right now?" he asked.

"Oh, yes! They are quite real right now, young Micah," Ragoo said suddenly, a serious look on his whisker-lined face.

"Don't you doubt that for a second!" Katielda nodded.

Micah shook his head in denial.

"You're kidding me, right?"

Ragoo snorted a half-purr, half-laugh sound.

"Dragons are real in both the past and the present, and are very complex creatures," Katielda said, not understanding why he still had a confused look on his face. "They always have been, and always will be."

"What do you not understand, young one?" Ragoo asked.

"Do you know much about dragons, Micah?" Katielda continued. She believed she knew the answer but wanted to be sure. She needed the boy to understand the depth of her story. The more she knew of his knowledge, or lack thereof, the more she could fill in the gaps where it was needed.

"No, not really," Micah answered, dumbfounded by the fact that the situation was becoming more confusing than it already was.

"The people of our village have told many stories around the campfire. We've always loved listening to them, too, especially my sister. But none of us know how much of these stories are real or how much are just that, a simple story."

His thoughts briefly turned to Tonia and their constant antics with each other. A small smile faded across his face before he refocused on the cats before him and their amazing revelation.

"My sister has always dreamed of seeing a real dragon, but none of us have ever seen one," he continued. "I guess we ultimately believed the stories we've heard were always just stories, used for entertainment and to give the village children something to dream about. Tonia may have believed in them, but I honestly never believed they were real…"

"Until now?" Katielda asked quietly.

Micah nodded.

Katielda smiled at him with understanding before she continued.

"Dragons have superb eyesight during the day, but at times, when it rains heavily or fog covers the land, they have difficulty with their perception and judgment. As a result of this weakness, if a dragon tries to fly when the weather is bad, it often proves fatal," she said.

"Time went on and soon a previously unknown wizard heard stories about a very powerful amulet hidden somewhere deep in the Dracaenelia Mountains. He was told the gem belonged to the dragons, but that meant nothing to him. This mysterious sorcerer decided he wanted the amulet and he was determined to let nothing stop him from getting it.

"The wizard scoured the countryside until he found creatures that were willing to follow him. Once he acquired his army of these beings who had nothing but the darkness in their hearts, he set out to gain possession of the one item that would give him unimaginable powers.

"This ruler, you may have already guessed, was Lotor.

"He blinded his followers with pride and soon they found themselves on a mission in search of the amulet. Lotor encouraged them by misinforming them that if they could find the gem and gain possession of it, they would share in his power of ruling this world as well as any others they chose. His followers agreed readily and became known as the dark ones.

"The dark ones searched near and far for the amulet. They questioned every creature who crossed their paths about it. They also used bribery with gold, other gems, and food. Eventually they resorted to the sparing of lives to get the information they so desperately wanted and needed.

"Their hard work finally paid off. They soon learned the amulet was being kept safe and protected deep in the Dracaenelia Mountain Range.

"Long before this discovery, others of their kind had been busy learning and practicing magic. These were called minisorcs. With their newly learned skills, the minisorcs used their magic and any resources possible to help search for the hidden gem. When they finally discovered where it was, they began to plan their attack with excitement and fervor. These minisorcs were afraid of nothing, including the loss of their own lives.

"The information the dark ones learned about the location of the amulet led them to an underground cave, which was, in fact, very close to where the dragons lived. On a day when the weather was bad and a storm was making its way towards them, the vile creatures made their move," Katielda said as she paused for a moment.

She looked at Micah. He sat quietly in front of the fire, arms now wrapped around his bent knees as he listened to the story. She then turned and looked at Ragoo. He was lying close to the hearth, enjoying the warmth radiating from the fire. His eyes were closed, but she had no doubt he was listening to every word. After a quick glance back at Micah, she continued.

"You would think they'd have chosen to make their move when the weather was beautiful and the dragons were out in search of food, yes?" she asked.

Micah nodded.

"As did we, but the contrary was true.

"The dark ones knew in order to successfully gain control of the amulet, they would have to kill as many of the winged beasts as they could. They also knew if they failed, chances were they may never have another opportunity such as this.

"It was well-known across the peaks and valleys that dragons are incredibly smart animals. There was no doubt that if the dragons had even an inkling of a notion the dark ones had discovered their hideaway, they would take the amulet immediately from its hidden location and secure it elsewhere.

"As the storm approached, it brought with it darkening clouds and whipping winds. Using the weather to their unfortunate advantage, this is when the dark ones made their move.

"They carried with them many large arrows made from the sharpest stones, and their swords were made from the strongest metal. Stealthily, these evil beings approached the special place where the dragons lived.

"It was a tragedy. When the dark ones found the winged creatures, they showed no mercy.

"Not surprisingly, dragons cannot fight nearly as effectively from the ground as they can from the air. With the storm now raging around them, the evil ones commenced their surprise attack, and the beasts of Dracaenelia found themselves nearly defenseless as they struggled desperately to survive a seemingly hopeless situation.

"As I said a moment ago, dragons are very smart… they are some of the smartest creatures in all the worlds. Instinctively, the dragons knew without question that these evil creatures had come in search of the amulet. They also knew, above all else, the value of the gem in their possession. The dragons would not hesitate to do whatever they must in order to protect it.

"The beasts fought the attacking evil with everything they had in the most important battle of their lives. In spite of this, on that fateful day, the dark ones managed to successfully slaughter many of our world's oldest and largest dragons. Although many dragons were lost, the beasts of the air fought long and hard, and many of the dark ones lost their lives as well.

"With many dragons perishing at the hands of these evil and selfish creatures, one of their kind realized the odds of them successfully protecting the amulet were quickly becoming very small indeed. This winged beast understood the importance of the irreplaceable amulet, and it knew, without a doubt, if the gem were to fall into the wrong hands, the results could, and likely would, be disastrous.

"After fighting next to its family and friends against the enemy, this particular dragon realized they were losing the battle. The winged creature knew there was only one way to protect the amulet. In that moment, without hesitation, it made one of the most selfless decisions of its long and gentle life.

"The exhausted dragon gently picked the amulet up in its massive jaws and began to fly away with it. It was aware of the risk it was taking by flying in stormy weather, but, in order to save the amulet, the creature was determined to fly anyways. Its mind was set… it would do whatever it took to bring the special gem somewhere else… somewhere it would be kept safe, far away from those who wanted to take it. The dragon felt it had no choice and would try its best to defy the odds.

"Fate, however, had other plans…

"The dragon flew upwards as it protectively carried the gem in its mouth, and it did its best to stay close to the mountaintops to avoid detection. All around it, the passing storm was raising as much of a fury in the sky above as the dark ones were on the ground below.

"In the surrounding rain and darkness, the brave dragon's vision was not as keen as it usually was during fairer weather. The pouring rain pelted its face, striking its eyes and making it more difficult to see. The winds whipped through the treetops, which made it difficult for the dragon to fly as well.

"Still it flew on.

"It fought a valiant battle against the wind and the rain. It struggled on and soon began to believe it would successfully carry the gem of the dragons to safety.

"As it flew along the treetops, the beast concentrated so intently on its battle with mother nature that it failed to see the creature that waited patiently ahead, hidden in the top of one of the tall mountain oaks.

"The creature waiting in ambush was another one of Lotor's followers. It was a massive snake, much larger than any snake ever seen before. As the dragon made its way past the tree, the snake sprung forward and upward with all its might. It struck the dragon's underbelly and quickly wrapped itself around the flying creature's tail with its long, muscular body.

"The dragon was caught completely off guard and began to fly erratically. Unable to control the direction of its flight, it quickly headed toward the rocky mountainside that was coming quickly into view. As the dragon struggled to maintain its balance, the snake wrapped itself around the desperate creature's tail even tighter.

"After the intense battle it had just fought with the dark ones, it took all of the dragon's strength and willpower to try to pull itself up. It struggled to fly higher as it tried with all its might to avoid the rocks that loomed closer and closer with each passing second, directly in its path.

"As the airborne creatures struggled in the gusting wind and the pelting rain, it began to look as though the heroic dragon just might succeed in its struggle after all. It began to pull itself and the snake higher and higher into the sky in an attempt to avoid the rocky face of the mountain.

"The snake changed the path of fate, however, as it suddenly bit down on the dragon's tail. As the snake's sharp fangs pierced the dragon's skin, it sent a stabbing jolt of pain straight up the dragon's spine. Instinctively, the dragon turned back and bit at the snake, but after the battle with the dark ones and its flight through the storm, the dragon was exhausted and its attempt to bite the snake failed. Unfortunately, as the dragon did so, it also lost its concentration and the precious amulet dropped from its mouth.

"When it saw this, the snake's face lit up with an evil smirk of success.

"Infuriated, the dragon used the remainder of its failing energy and swung its head back one last time. In one violent bite, it beheaded the snake. The beast was unaware that, as it did so, its flight path took a sudden downward dip. When it spit out the snake's head, the dragon immediately turned its attention back to the amulet it had dropped.

"Remembering how close it was to the mountain, the dragon quickly swerved to the left and downward as it tried its best to avoid the landmass which loomed perilously in its path. The main thing on its mind was the overwhelming need to overtake the falling amulet before it struck the ground. Sadly, the winged beast realized too late just how close the mountain really was.

"Fate had other plans after all.

"Before it could make the full turn, the heroic dragon crashed headfirst into the side of the mountain, which broke its neck and killed it instantly. After its valiant effort to try to save the amulet, the beast was dead mere seconds before the gem crashed to the ground where it broke into three pieces on the damp rocks below.

"Surprisingly, when the amulet broke, it broke cleanly into the three colors I mentioned before… blue, red, and white. Two of the three pieces rolled off the rocks and into the nearby river. Only the red piece remained on one of the damp, mossy rocks. This is where it stayed, unnoticed, for a period of time.

"After a few days, the dark ones, who had been successful in battle but unsuccessful in their efforts to claim ownership of the amulet, made a surprising discovery on their way back to the castle.

"First they found the mangled body of the dragon where it lay at the base of the mountain, the dead and headless snake still wrapped tightly around its tail. When they continued on to the place where they would cross the river, they were quite surprised when they came across the piece of amulet where it still lay on the rock near the flowing water. Right away they understood just what had happened. They all cheered triumphantly at their lucky discovery. Although it was not the whole amulet, at least they would not return to Lotor entirely empty-handed.

"Upon their return home, they gave their leader the broken piece of amulet and explained exactly what had happened. Their master was understandably upset they did not have the entire amulet, but, of the three pieces he had hoped to gain, the red one would give him the best results," Katielda said as she looked at the boy.

"So Lotor got the red amulet," Micah said, totally engrossed in the story now, "but what happened to the other two pieces?"

"The river washed them downstream," Ragoo said as he took up telling the story.

"After the dark ones attacked the dragons' mountain lair, word spread quickly across the land which told of the amulet's disappearance.

"As the word spread that the amulet was missing, creatures both far and wide frantically began searching for it, hoping to locate the gem before Lotor and his minions. Every creature understood the importance of finding the precious amulet, and it was unknown at the time what kind of damage the gem had sustained.

"Luckily, when the dark ones discovered the broken piece of the amulet, there were a few forest creatures, friends of the dragons, who watched from the shadows of the trees. After the dark ones took possession of the gem and headed back to their home with it, word of the broken jewel quickly made its way back to the dragons as well as to other creatures of this world. It soon became evident that the amulet had been broken, and the search began for the other pieces."

"Were those pieces ever found?" Micah asked curiously.

"Not yet," Ragoo said as Katielda's gaze turned toward the dirty floor. "We have been actively searching for them, but have been unsuccessful at finding either."

Both Ragoo and Katielda looked at Micah and he suddenly realized the enormity of the situation. He had in his possession the most sought after piece of the amulet. Without a word he stood up and dug around in his pocket until he found what he was looking for. He knew exactly which piece it was without needing to look at it. He withdrew his hand and opened it, holding the item out for the cats to see once again, this time without hesitation. As they began to purr loudly again, Micah waited a few seconds before interrupting them.

"If this is a fragment of the larger amulet, why is it trimmed in gold?" he asked.

The cats seemed to ignore him as they purred a little while longer before Katielda struggled to stop so she could answer his question. Micah saw her struggling and closed his hand over the gem, but did not return it to his pocket.

It took a few seconds for her to compose herself before she answered him.

"When Lotor took possession of the red amulet, he knew the dragons would search for it, so he decided to try to disguise it. In an effort to keep the dragons from recognizing the gem if they ever found their way into his residence, the evil wizard had one of his craftsmen first smooth out the sharp edges, then line those edges with a thin strip of the finest white gold. He hoped this would be enough to keep its true identity a secret… and for a while it did."

"But how then did it end up in the cave we came from?" Micah asked as he tried to fill in some of the gaps in the story.

"It was discovered by an unlikely creature in Lotor's castle where he had hidden it behind a stack of books. As I've said, word of the missing amulet pieces spread far and wide across the mountains and valleys. Creatures everywhere, even those within the place where the amulet was hidden, were not exempt from hearing these stories.

"A small rat found the amulet late one night as it searched for food. Believing it might be the missing gem, it quickly took the amulet outside the castle and passed it on to a night fox. The fox, in turn, took the amulet and headed towards the mountains where it heard the dragons now lived. While on its way there, Lotor discovered the amulet was missing and sent his minions out again in search of the missing piece.

"The fox was cunning and soon realized it was now not a hunter, but the hunted. While trying to avoid the minions, it found a small hole hidden behind a rock in the side of the mountain. This hiding place took it into a large cave with many intertwining tunnels. The sly creature managed to keep the amulet from the minions for the time being, but not without a high price.

"The fox is an omnivore and can eat insects and berries, but they much prefer meat. This particular creature ultimately found itself hidden so deeply within the cave that it was undoubtedly lost. Food in the cave was very scarce and without the nutrients its body needed, the fox soon perished. Before it did, however, it carefully placed the amulet in a rock-filled stream.

"There the gem was later found by another unlikely creature... a lifelong cave resident who soon suffered unimaginable tragedies in its life," Katielda finished.

"Kaileen," Micah said quietly. He knew without being told that it was so.

After considering everything the yarnies had just shared with him, the boy opened his hand. He looked at it protectively for a moment. It was clear to him what he must do.

He raised his head and looked at the yarnie cats who were watching him anxiously.

"Well, where do we find us a dragon?" he asked.

THREE

"Fate often has a way of playing games with us, young one, and we can see that you are no exception to this," Katielda continued.

"I don't understand," Micah began as the female cat stood up and began to pace around the room.

"You come here in search of your siblings and your friend, yes?" she asked.

Micah nodded silently.

"You also come here carrying a very special gem…"

He nodded once again.

"I'm sure you understand now just how imperative it is that it be returned to the dragons," Katielda continued.

"Yes, I understand that," he began, but she interrupted him.

"Wait, Micah, and listen to my words," she said. "I will tell you what you must do."

She stopped her pacing and looked at him seriously.

"We have sent for a dragon and it will be here shortly. It is one that we call a Dragon Guard, and it will take the amulet back to where it should be, safe from creatures such as Lotor," she said. "Once this is done, you need to find the others from your group, yes?"

He silently nodded an affirmation then asked, "What is a Dragon Guard?"

She smiled at him, glad that he was willing to learn those things she was more than willing to teach.

"A Dragon Guard is a small dragon who has special powers.

You can think of them as messengers. They are fighters, messengers, and protectors. All dragons are, really, but Dragon Guards are special."

As he nodded, she continued.

"I cannot tell the future, Micah, but I can tell you this. You must continue going east, towards the place where the sun awakens every day. Soon you will come to a large castle." She paused as she looked at him imploringly.

"This is where you will find those who you seek," she finished.

"Nicho, Tonia, and Kaileen are in this castle?" Micah asked. If they were, he wondered how they had gotten there. More importantly, how did this cat know they were there in the first place?

"They are not there yet, but they are on their way," she explained further. "In this castle you will also find others whom you seek."

Micah shook his head in denial. Once again he had no idea what she was talking about. If he found Nicho, Tonia, Diam, and Kaileen, who else would he be looking for? After a few seconds, he remembered what she'd said about others traveling through to this world. Was she referring to Muscala? He wasn't sure what kind of wild mushrooms she'd been snacking on, but he thought perhaps he needed to make it clear to Katielda that he would NOT be searching for the evil serpent anytime soon.

"If it's that crazy, arrogant snake you're referring to," he began, but she interrupted him once again.

"It is not the snake, and that is all I can tell you.

"Come," she said as she began walking towards the door, "the dragon is here to take possession of the amulet."

Ragoo stood up to follow Katielda, but Micah remained where he was near the fireplace. He watched them, wondering how they would get the door opened. A few steps before reaching the door, it began to open on its own. Micah shook his head with a small smile, not really surprised with anything in this world anymore. He stood up and followed them. As he approached the door, he looked through the entryway to see if a creature on the outside was there, holding it open. He didn't really expect to see one. He didn't disappoint himself… no creature outside was anywhere near the door.

"Wait, how did you do that?" he asked curiously as Ragoo turned and smirked at him again.

"In time," was all he said in reply.

Micah stepped through the door into the afternoon sunshine. He squinted his eyes so they could adjust to the light and noticed some of the other creatures that, this time, were no longer hiding.

Many of the village felines stood there before him, in a semi-circle just outside the door, watching him curiously. As he stepped out to join them, they began to part in the middle of their group as if a large, invisible hand were separating them. As they did this, Micah looked through the crowd to where the newly created path led…

There, standing quietly in the late afternoon sunshine, was a dragon.

M icah froze in his tracks.

Was this a real, live dragon standing before him, watching his every move? He looked at it doubtfully when it suddenly blinked.

It was real!

The creature was smaller than he'd imagined, about the size of a large mountain bear, and its body was covered in small, thick green scales. As he looked at it, trying to take in every detail, he was surprised to see it even had scales on its eyelids and eyebrows.

He stifled a chuckle.

As he stood there looking at the dragon, something suddenly shot past him, and it took him a second to realize what it was.

The rat that had been sitting quietly on the mantle of the fireplace when he'd entered Katielda's house scurried right up to the dragon. It stopped just short of the larger creature's sharply clawed feet.

As if it had been waiting for the rat, the green beast reached down and scooped the rodent up in its mouth before swinging its head back and to the left, over its shoulder. As it did so, it opened its jaws and released the furry critter. Micah watched as the small creature flew gracefully through the air before it landed on the dragon's back. Here, it gained its footing before climbing into the valley of the dragon's neck, at the place where the neck meets the back.

It appeared to be unharmed and sat there in silence as if

waiting for something.

The dragon took a gentle step towards the boy. "Greetings, young traveler. Do you have something for me?" the winged beast asked Micah quietly.

Micah remained frozen in disbelief. After a few seconds, he regained his composure and nodded silently. If Tonia were here, he thought, she'd be beside herself with excitement. The thought of his missing siblings and friend made him sad suddenly, but he pushed it away for a few moments in order to deal with the task at hand. He simply could not handle that whole situation until he dealt with this one.

"Yes," he said nervously. "I do have something for you."

The boy took a nervous step toward the green beast as all of the yarnie cats surrounded them in respectful silence. Micah quickly glanced at Katielda and she nodded to him once, encouraging him. With that, he turned back to the dragon and walked to within a step away from it, removing the amulet from his pocket as he did so. He opened his palm to show the dragon the red gem and the crowd of yarnie cats sighed in unison. They had all heard stories of the missing amulet, but none believed they would ever see the beautiful gem in their lifetime. As Micah held the amulet out for the dragon, it suddenly began to glow, brighter now than ever before. In addition to the bright red light that now filled his hand, they could hear a distinct humming sound that began to emanate from the gem.

Micah smiled as he imagined that the gem was calling out to the dragon, asking to be taken home. The yarnie cats, surprised at the gem's reaction to the dragon, backed away from the boy in fear. They had not expected this.

The dragon looked at the glowing amulet as a smile spread across its face.

"You have in your hand an important piece of our past, young Micah. More importantly, however, what you have is our future. Do you understand the enormity of this?" the dragon asked the boy.

"Yes," Micah answered. "I do understand how important the amulet is to you. I know first hand how powerful it is, and I understand why you must take it back," he said as he held it out for the dragon.

Pleased with the boy's selfless decision, the dragon bent its head down as if to take the gem. Instead, the rat ran up the dragon's neck to the top of its head before scampering down its nose. As the dragon's face came down directly next to the boy's hand, the little rodent quickly reached out and grabbed the amulet, which was about half its size. Once it had the stone in its possession, the rodent struggled with the gem back up the dragon's nose and returned to the nape of the creature's neck. When it got there, it situated itself so it wouldn't fall off while holding onto the gem. When the dragon felt that the rodent was positioned safely, it raised its head and looked once again at the boy.

"You have made a good choice, young Micah… the right choice.

"Like the yarnie cats, I also know of your situation and where you came from. I know you need to find your brother, sister, and other friends. Because you have done the right thing by giving up the gem that you felt so strongly to protect, I, in turn, am going to give you something. I, like you, am going to do the right thing." As the dragon said this, all of the yarnie cats lowered themselves and began to bow to both the young man and the beast, a sign of respect and submission. After acknowledging this, the dragon continued.

"Please, Micah, kneel before me."

Micah looked into the dragon's eyes and somehow he knew he could trust it. Without hesitation, he did as the dragon asked. He knelt down on one knee, curious as to what the dragon was about to do.

"Because you have selflessly returned the amulet to me, allowing it to be returned to where it rightfully belongs, I feel that you have earned a reward," the dragon said.

Micah looked at the dragon, surprised. He had not expected anything to be given to him in return; he'd only wanted to do the right thing. A brief thought of his father flashed through his mind and he smiled. He knew if his father were here, he would surely be proud of him.

"That's okay," Micah said quietly to the dragon. "I don't want anything in return. I'm glad to help the amulet get back to where it belongs."

The dragon smiled at him and nodded.

"You are a special young man, Micah," the dragon said. The yarnie cats listened quietly to the boy and the dragon as they continued bowing to them.

"I understand you don't expect anything for your selfless act, but you must understand this. There is something that you need and shall receive in return," the dragon said.

Micah looked questioningly at the gentle green beast as its eyes began to glow with a soft, emerald aura. He remained where he was as he waited for the dragon to continue. A powerful silence fell over the village as the dragon guard suddenly extended its wings out on each side of its muscular body. Micah watched in amazement as the dragon's wingtips slowly began to glow the same color as its eyes.

He looked nervously at the small but mighty beast standing proudly before him.

"Trust me, my son," the dragon said in a soothing voice, and Micah nodded silently.

"Lower your head like the yarnies have and trust in me. Please accept this gift which I am about to give to you," the creature said.

Micah lowered his head obediently.

With his head bowed, the dragon turned to the left and lowered its right wing close to the boy's right side. In the silence surrounding him, Micah began to hear a faint humming sound. It took him a second to realize it was coming from the dragon's glowing wingtip. With complete trust, he closed his eyes. The dragon brought the wingtip down and touched it to Micah's shoulder. As the wing made contact first with his thin shirt, then with his shoulder, the humming sound increased several octaves. As if there was no barrier of thin material between them, Micah felt an intense jolt of energy flow into his upper arm which lasted only a second before the dragon pulled its wing back. Without a word, the beast shifted its position to the right so it could do the same to the boy's other side.

Micah opened his eyes and glanced up at the dragon as

it turned. He caught a glimpse of the rat where it sat on the dragon's neck… it was gripping the amulet tightly with its eyes closed. The small rodent didn't keep his attention for very long, however. His focus quickly turned to the amulet itself.

It was glowing intensely once again, bathing the village and the surrounding yarnies in a deep, red aura. Right here, right now, Micah could no longer deny that he was taking part in something much bigger than he'd ever imagined. With sudden clarity, he finally believed in this magical beast standing majestically before him. The boy again lowered his head and closed his eyes as the dragon's left wingtip began its descent towards his other side.

Like before, the dragon gently touched its glowing wingtip to Micah's left shoulder. Also, just like before, the boy felt the intense surge of energy flow into his body as it touched him.

After completing its task, the dragon drew its wings back towards its body and centered itself in front of the boy.

"You may rise," the Dragon Guard said gently. Micah opened his eyes and raised his head. As he stood up, he looked at the yarnie cats. They were all still bowing, but were now watching the scene before them in silent awe.

The boy turned his attention back to the dragon. The creature effortlessly folded its wings back into place and tucked them in close to its body. The wingtips no longer glowed and the air was now filled with an odd silence. Wondering if the rat was still on the dragon's back, the boy leaned to his left as he tried to see around the beast's neck. The rodent was still there, still sitting in the same place it was in before. The gem was still in its possession, but had fallen dark and lifeless again. Micah looked back at the dragon, waiting for it to continue. He didn't have to wait long.

"When the time comes, my young human, you will understand the gift that I have just given you. When you do, you must make sure that you use it wisely."

The dragon then turned its attention to the yarnie cats.

"My fellow creatures, I thank you from the bottom of my heart for your efforts in helping those of my kind as we continue doing our best to right what has become wrong in this world. I will now return to my home, bringing with me a large piece of the puzzle that is slowly coming back together. I encourage you to continue in your search for the other missing pieces."

The winged creature turned back to Micah one last time.

"To you, young one, I encourage you to continue on as well. I know Katielda has told you the story of the amulet, and you are aware of the other missing pieces.

"Right now, however, you must not think of these. You must instead focus your attention on going to the place where you will find those from your past who are themselves missing. You must find the power of your own amulets. Find it and work with it to fight the evil that is there with them. Along the way, you will do your part to find and return the missing gems... Dragon's Breath and Dragon's Tear. Stay focused on your quest, go to the lake, follow to your destiny.

"In order for this world to continue on, young Micah, you must succeed in stopping the evil that is growing stronger each day. Do everything in your power to find the two remaining gems before it is too late. Although the dragon's now have possession of Dragon's Blood, if the other two gems fall into the wrong hands..."

The dragon did not finish its sentence as it bowed its own head. No other words were necessary. The gentle beast nodded to Micah once before it turned and bowed respectfully to the surrounding yarnie cats one last time. The yarnies bowed in return as the dragon spun around and began to make its way out of the village. As it did, the yarnie cats quickly separated, which created a long, narrow path separating them.

As they all watched in silent wonder, the dragon took a few quick steps down the path before leaping into the air, taking flight as gracefully as a bird. Micah watched in awe as the dragon raised and lowered its muscular wings, carrying itself over the treetops and into the horizon.

"Micah," Katielda said, drawing his attention away from the sky. "Time is ticking away and you must now prepare yourself for your journey."

"But I don't know what I'm supposed to do, where to go, or even how to get there," Micah said in a frustrated voice.

All he knew for certain was that he had to get somewhere, wherever 'somewhere' might be, and he no longer had the amulet to help him get there. He began to doubt his decision to let the amulet go.

"Do not worry about that, young Micah. You will find your way. We will help you get where it is that you need to go. More importantly, do NOT doubt your decision. The amulet first belonged to the dragons, and that is where it should be.

"For now, however, you must rest, for your journey will require you to be in the best mental and physical shape possible. You have already been tested, and you passed those tests by making it here and delivering the amulet to the rightful owner.

"But do not be fooled… you have many more tests to come.

"You will remain with us today and we will provide you with food and rest. Tonight, we will feast in celebration of the return of the 'Dragon's Blood' amulet to the dragons. With a rested body and a full belly, tomorrow you will begin your journey with a few less things to worry about," she said.

With that, the yarnie cats broke out into a cheer. As if hearing a silent command, they scattered in different directions to prepare for the evening's festivities. Micah watched them, surprised at their energy and sudden acceptance of him. He was amazed as he thought back on everything that had happened over the past few days. He definitely felt physically drained.

He turned to Katielda and asked, "I think your suggestion to rest is a great idea. Do you have a place where I can lie down for a little while?"

"Of course," she answered. "A place has already been prepared for you. Follow me."

She turned and headed back to her house. As Micah expected, the door swung gently open before she reached it. He followed her inside and saw something he did not expect.

The inside of her house had changed appearances once again. This time, instead of the room being large like it was earlier, it was now much, much smaller. It was, in fact, exactly what he had expected the last time he came inside.

He glanced from Katielda to Ragoo, who had silently followed them. The male yarnie did not disappoint him. He had a smirk playing around the corners of his mouth and whiskers yet again.

"It is now as you thought it should have been before, yes?"

Ragoo questioned as the smirk turned into a veiled smile.

"Yes, of course it is," Micah answered sarcastically.

"You have seen one variation of magic in your travels, Micah. And now, you have seen another," Katielda explained. "Some of what you have seen here in this room has been real, while some has been an illusion. Which one is which, however, will, for now, remain a mystery.

"Dragons are not the only ones who are capable of special talents," she said with a smile as she winked at him.

Micah turned and looked at the place where the window had appeared earlier after not having been there originally. He chuckled as he saw that the window was no longer there again, but neither was the stone wall. Instead, in the very same place, he now saw a picture, framed in wood and flowers. The picture was a beautiful scene of a waterfall with mountains behind it on the horizon. The entire scene was captured in the glow of a purple and orange sunset.

"How did I know there would be something else there?" he asked, still chuckling. Ragoo just looked at the boy with a silent smile.

Micah looked around. The fire still burned softly in the fireplace, which would relax him for sure. He also saw on the floor against the wall, under the picture of the waterfall, was a freshly laid bed of straw.

"We have made a place for you to rest, young traveler. Lie down and try to sleep for a bit as we continue to prepare for the evening's festivities," Katielda said as she waved one of her cat paws invitingly toward the straw. She nodded at the boy before also nodding at Ragoo, then silently left the house. Ragoo smiled at Micah once again, nodded, and quietly followed her. The door swung gently closed behind them.

Micah was surprised at how exhausted he suddenly felt, but what a story he would have to tell the villagers when they finally returned home!

Home.

He smiled as he thought of the villagers, his friends, his mother.

As he thought of Mom, he suddenly felt sad. He knew how

frantic she must be since they hadn't returned home. He wished there was some way to communicate with her, to let her know he was okay.

He sighed.

The best thing he could do right now was to rest his tired body. Tomorrow, he would head out in search of the others.

He pulled off his backpack and set it next to the bed of straw. Next, he sat down and removed his leggings, glad that he had shorts underneath.

As he got ready to settle himself down for a nap, he noticed a small bowl of water on the floor close to the bed. He picked it up and drank from it.

The cool water flowed refreshingly down his throat.

"Ahhh," he said quietly as he set the bowl down. The water was good, and now he was ready to sleep. He lay down on the bed and closed his eyes. He hoped that, with all the excitement, he would be able to sleep. This should have been the least of his worries. Within minutes, he began to doze off, unaware of the sounds of a distant waterfall as they lulled him to sleep. In the last few seconds before sleep overtook him, he unknowingly whispered one word.

"Shia."

As the sun neared the end of its daily journey, the weary traveler let himself go and fell into a much-needed slumber.

FIVE

Micah slept for a short while before being roused by the sounds of laughing and cheering. He opened his eyes and looked around, at first unable to remember exactly where he was. He sat up and looked at the fire. It still burned softly in the fireplace, the orange embers casting their soft glow across the dirt floor.

Ah, yes, now he remembered. He was in Katielda's house. As he rubbed the sleep out of his eyes, other memories flashed through his mind…

The journey through the cave…

His unsuccessful search for the others…

The conversation with the cat with the forked tail…

And one last thought came to him that brought a smile to his face…

The dragon.

He stretched with a grunt.

Dragons were real!

Now he really couldn't wait to get back to the village so he could tell his story!

He imagined the villagers sitting around the campfire while he told them of his part of the journey! What would they think of the magical stones and his unexplained ability to make them glow? He could only guess how surprised they would be, and how they would prod him for more information!

His smile broadened a bit as he thought of the younger village children. They, more than the adults, would be totally enthralled with his story. He was certain they would be so excited by the things he would tell them that they would definitely not want to go to bed at bedtime! As he daydreamed of these things, a sudden thought in the back of his mind began to silently nag at him. Micah stood up and looked at the picture where it was mounted on the wall above his head. He had a feeling that whatever it was, it had something to do with the picture, but, for the life of him, he could not quite grasp whatever it was. Did it have something to do with the waterfall?

He shook his head and sighed.

He didn't want to stress himself out over something he wasn't even sure was worth the stress. Micah glanced at the window that looked out on the village. The sun had gone down while he slept. He could still hear the yarnies as they enjoyed their celebration outside. As Micah considered this, he was surprised by the feeling that suddenly overtook him… he wanted to join them. He took a few steps towards the door and, not surprisingly, it opened before he got to it.

As he looked outside through the doorway, the first thing he saw was the fire the yarnies had built in the center of the village. It was not a large fire, but it was enough to provide warmth as the chill of the night enveloped them. The second thing he saw was the large crowd of yarnies who mingled around the fire. There were cats everywhere, and as he made his way outside, many of them turned to look at him. As they did, the reflection of the fire from the fireplace inside Katielda's house reflected back at him through their eyes.

When Micah began to walk towards them, the yarnies who had been cheering and laughing only moments ago suddenly quieted. It was almost as if a magical aura overtook the village. This made the boy a bit nervous, but he continued walking towards them nonetheless.

"Ah, there you are," Katielda called out to him from the center of the group of cats. Micah felt the eyes of all the village creatures as they turned to look at him while he made his way towards her.

"Did you have a nice nap?" she asked him with genuine concern in her voice.

Micah could hear subtle whispers as they circulated here and there through the group, but he could not make out what was being said. He had the unmistakable feeling that something was up.

"Yes, I did, actually," he began when he was interrupted.

"Micah?"

He froze in his tracks, thinking that perhaps his mind was playing tricks on him. The voice sounded very familiar, and seemed to come from somewhere near Katielda. He stood motionless, absently listening as whispers continued among the group of cats.

He had an odd sensation, almost like he was sleepwalking. Or perhaps he was still sleeping under the picture of the waterfall? It had to be something other than what it appeared to be, because it seemed highly unlikely that the owner of that voice could really be here. Or could it?

"Nicho?" Micah called out.

At the far edge of the crowd he saw something pop up in the shadows. When he realized what it was, a huge smile spread across his face. There, standing out above the group of still-whispering cats, he could clearly see his brother's head.

"Nicho!" he yelled out excitedly.

The boys made their way towards each other, careful not to trample any of the cats that happened to be in their path. They stopped a step away from each other, neither one able to believe that the other was standing before them, alive and well.

After only a few second's hesitation, they embraced in a tight hug. The crowd of felines watched quietly in the surrounding gloom.

"Where's Tonia? Diam? Kaileen?" Micah asked as he looked around for the girls.

"I don't know where they are," Nicho said sadly as he shook his head.

"For now, the girls are safe," Katielda interrupted as she joined them. "Danger lurks around them, however, as it does both of you. You must be very careful when you again resume your travels!"

"The path leading east is both dangerous and desolate, aye it is," Ragoo added from the shadows of the crowd of cats as he

114

approached the boys.

Nicho and Micah looked at each other, relieved that they'd found each other, while at the same time, a heaviness weighed on each of their hearts.

"Come! Tonight we celebrate your arrival into our world! We will share food and laughter, and then you will sleep like you haven't slept in days!" Katielda said excitedly as the large crowd of yarnies returned to their celebratory preparations. "Tomorrow, you will continue on your journey together… in search of your friends, your sister, and those who wait for you!"

With that, the celebration began in earnest. The boys did their best to enjoy themselves, even though the girls were in the forefront of their minds. They mingled in the crowd, yet remained close enough so they never lost sight of each other. At the end of the evening, they both retired back to Katielda's house.

As the door to her house closed gently behind them, Micah's attention was immediately drawn to the place where he'd rested earlier. It was still there, but now there was enough fresh hay laid out for both boys to sleep on.

"Since you have just found each other, we assumed you would want to sleep near each other. Is that alright?" Ragoo asked the boys.

Micah looked at Nicho and shrugged. "Yes, this is fine, thank you," the older sibling said as Micah giggled.

"Something is funny?" Ragoo asked with a questioning look.

"Sorry, but it just reminds me of when we were little and had to share a bed," Micah said.

"Yeah, you think it's funny," Nicho said. "Watch yourself, little brother!"

Immediately, Ragoo said, "I can set up a separate sleeping area if you'd like…"

"No, no, this is fine, really," Nicho said. He shot Micah a warning look as the younger boy tried his best to conceal a snicker.

"My brother sometimes has issues with… how do I put this? Bodily vapors…" Nicho explained. When he said this, Micah suddenly covered his face and snorted a partial laugh. When he peeked through his fingers at his brother, Nicho noticed with a smirk that Micah's eyes were now teary.

"Don't cry, Micah," Nicho said sarcastically. "You have no idea what it's like to deal with butts like yours!"

Ragoo interrupted them.

"Very well then, if you're sure you're accepting of the accommodations, I will bid you good night," the cat said. He nodded at the boys and Nicho nodded back. Micah nodded but couldn't answer… he was still trying to control his giggles.

"If you should need anything, there will be a yarnie or two just outside the door," Ragoo said as he walked to the door. It opened with a slight creak and the male yarnie stepped through it without another word.

"Behave yourself, Micah," Nicho said. "Enough now, let's get some sleep. Tomorrow will be a busy day, I'm sure." As Nicho prepared for bed, he yawned.

"Nicho," Micah said once the giggles had passed, "I missed you."

Nicho turned and looked at his brother with a smile.

"I missed you too, kiddo," he said.

They wordlessly embraced once more before they settled down for the night. There was no need to talk about what had happened while they had been separated; there would be plenty of time for that tomorrow. For tonight, they were both exhausted, and before long, they were both sound asleep.

Six

Micah woke to the sounds of a rooster in the distance and rolled over. The sun was shining brightly through the window, showering the room in warmth. He allowed his eyes to follow the stream of sunlight to where it fell on the floor, and what he saw there made him smile. Ragoo and Katielda lay back to back on the dirt covered floor, sleeping comfortably in the warm morning sunshine. When Ragoo heard the boy stir, he lifted his head and looked at him. Micah rolled over and tried to go back to sleep, but it was no use. He was up.

The young boy got up and stretched before silently making his way to the door. As it opened, he stepped outside, feeling the need to take a walk in the brisk morning air. He walked around the village in the dew-covered grass and thought about the girls. After a few moments he decided they should get started on their journey, so he headed back to the house. When he got there, he found Nicho, Ragoo, and Katielda also awake. They were busy making preparations for the journey.

"We should get going," Micah said to his brother.

"Yeah, I know," Nicho said. "I feel it too."

"Despite the urgency you feel about heading east and finding your sister and friends, you must be sure to take every precaution as you travel," Katielda warned.

"We will," Nicho said as he finished packing his bag.

Micah looked at the yarnie leader and smiled. "Katielda, thank you for everything," he said. "We will do whatever we can to help you as we travel."

"I know," she said softly. "Now, go."

The boys placed their bags on their backs. With a final wave, they began their journey out of the village, heading confidently into the bright morning sunshine. After a few seconds, Micah heard a noise and looked back, surprised to see Ragoo following them.

"Ragoo, what are you doing?" he asked. They stopped and looked at the cat.

"I'm coming with you," the cat answered matter-of-factly.

"No you're not," Nicho said. "You should stay here in the village… where you belong… where you are safe."

"Yes," Micah agreed. "Stay here, Ragoo."

"My mistress ordered me to accompany you," Ragoo said. "I can either walk with you or follow you, but either way, I am going with you."

Micah looked back at the village with a frown. Katielda was nowhere to be seen.

Nicho looked at Micah, who shrugged. Once again, it appeared they didn't have a choice.

"Okay," Nicho said. "You're sure?"

Without hesitation the cat answered, "Yes."

Micah smiled. He liked the cat and actually felt somewhat relieved to have a creature from this world accompanying them. He looked at his brother, wondering what Nicho's final decision would be.

The older brother didn't disappoint him with his answer. Without another word, Nicho turned east and began walking. Micah smiled again at Ragoo and they both followed Nicho in silence.

Their journey east had begun.

The Traveler

ONE

Blaken was about to embark on the most important mission of his life. He would soon be on his way to a small village with instructions and permission to use whatever means he desired in order to destroy the hamlet and all of its occupants. He could use his strength, innovation, magic, or anything he wanted, in order to successfully accomplish his task, and he was determined to do as The Master asked. He would demolish the village and every living creature he encountered there… leaving nothing but rubble in his wake.

After saving him from certain death during the battle with the yarnie cats many moons ago… those darned dragon-loving felines… Nivri was his hero! The battle was tough, and many of Blaken's family and friends had been lost. Nivri had come along at just the right moment and saved him by using his magic to kill a large yarnie before it had a chance to pounce on him. Blaken had no doubt that the yarnie cat, which was much larger than he, would surely have killed him.

Yes, Nivri was his hero, and Blaken would do anything the creature asked of him…

Anything.

Not long ago, Nivri had called for Blaken from his post at the bottom of the castle, where he was one of numerous castle guards. He had been making his rounds, checking on the various creatures that were being held captive in the prison.

A cross between a bear and a dragon, Blaken was a creature known as a beagon. Those of his kind were enhanced and guided

121

by the strength of a bear with the wiles of a dragon, and the lucky ones could even fly short distances. They made excellent guards, and, in most cases, even better warriors.

Blaken, however, was different. He was smaller than the rest of his kind, and unable to fly. He knew that, if he'd been a normal sized beagon, he would have been able to defeat the evil yarnie that Nivri had saved him from. But he wasn't, and he accepted it.

Other creatures like him were destined to be only castle guards or warriors for the rest of their days. Now, however, his Master was sending him on a mission, and he knew his future would be different from the rest of the beagons. He knew the path of his destiny could, and likely would, be determined by the upcoming events. He had his mind set on making such a difference to the Master that his future would be unlike any other of his kind. Ah, yes, he was on a mission… a search and destroy mission! It seemed as though it would be a fairly simple one as well.

All he had to do was travel through the portal Nivri would create for him, get to the other side, find the village, and destroy it.

How hard could that be?

Once his mission was accomplished, he would return to Nivri and be known as a hero to his hero. He smiled… He would not disappoint his Master. Nivri had endless magical spells and talents, and had painstakingly managed to teach Blaken a few so he could now complete the task that was almost at hand. He was a patient master, watching as Blaken practiced these spells over and over again, day and night, until Nivri agreed he was ready.

Now, the time had come.

Blaken stood quietly in Nivri's throne room, waiting patiently for his Master to arrive. He was a little nervous, but had no doubt he would return successfully to his Master.

Yes, Nivri would be very proud of him.

The doors to the throne room opened silently and Nivri walked in, escorted by Orob. They approached Blaken where he stood waiting for them at the far end of the room. When they were within a few steps of him, Blaken bowed respectfully. He held this pose for a few seconds before he stood upright, awaiting Nivri's command.

"Are you ready, my young guard, to do what is needed in order to serve me well?" Nivri asked from directly in front of the beagon.

"Yes, my Lord," Blaken answered confidently. "I am ready to serve you in any way necessary… any way you desire. Your will be done!"

"Good," Nivri said quietly.

He turned and walked over to the far side of the room where a sheet covered a lumpy object on the floor. He knelt down and whipped the sheet off the item before carelessly casting it aside.

There, on the throne room floor, was a hole. Surrounded by dull, gray rocks, it was a circle of darkness.

"Come here, then, and serve me," Nivri said to Blaken as he turned and gestured for the beagon to approach him. Blaken immediately did as he was ordered, completely willing to serve he who had saved his life. "You remember the spells I have taught you, yes?" Nivri asked quietly.

"Yes, my Lord," Blaken answered without hesitation.

"Good," Nivri said with a small smile. Orob remained where he was, near Nivri's throne, watching them.

"Close your eyes then, Blaken, so that we may begin," Nivri said.

Blaken closed his eyes as he was asked. Nivri turned to stand before the circle of stones and began to chant.

"Humma dorito encanta indu nenuli, washanon ala ipsi!" he called out as he held his hands out in front of him for a brief moment.

Nivri watched the previously dull and lifeless stones with a smile of satisfaction. As he chanted the spell, the stones surrounding the hole in the floor began to glow a dull orange color.

Nivri touched Blaken's arm.

The guard jumped slightly and opened his eyes. He looked at the glowing hole in the floor excitedly. His mission was about to begin!

The portal in the floor now glowed brilliantly before him, alternating between orange and red.

"The portal is now ready for you to transport through, my

young apprentice. Do not worry, for I will know when you have carried out your orders. Once you have, you must return to the same place in which you arrived. When I sense you are there, I will reopen the portal so you may return to me," Nivri explained.

"Yes, my Lord," Blaken said, then waited obediently for the order to step through the colorful doorway to the other world.

"Before you go, Blaken, there is one thing you must know," Nivri said.

Blaken remained silent, his complete attention on his Master as he waited to hear what this one thing was.

"You must succeed in your mission to find the village, and you must find it quickly. Once you're sure you have found it, destroy it and all that lives within it." Nivri paused as Blaken nodded.

"If you do not, I will not reopen the portal and you will not return.

"Do you understand your mission?" Nivri asked.

"Yes, my Lord," Blaken answered.

"When you find the village, it is also of utmost importance that you also find anyone who might be related to the strangers who have now entered our world uninvited.

"Do you know those of whom I speak?" Nivri continued.

"Yes, my Lord. The two boys, their sister, and her friend," Blaken responded confidently.

"That is correct. Anyone whom you even suspect of being related to them... I want you to destroy, any way you can and any way you desire.

"As long as are all destroyed, this is all I ask," Nivri said.

He looked at Blaken as the guard nodded silently.

"Are you now ready to travel? Are you ready to take the most important journey of your life?" Nivri asked the beagon.

"Yes, My Lord... I am ready to serve you in any way that I can. Your will be done!" Blaken called out excitedly.

"Step into the portal when you are ready," Nivri said as he smiled at his young minion. "Go, and do all that I ask! Do this for me and you shall be well-rewarded!"

Blaken smiled, glad to finally be on his way. He bowed to Nivri one last time before he stepped into the portal. As he did, he called out, "Your will be done!"

No sooner did the words leave his mouth than he disappeared. As he did, the stones all blinked brightly once before going out, like a candle being snuffed out by a sudden gust of wind.

Nivri turned and looked at Orob.

"I am determined to teach those young fools a lesson, Orob," Nivri said. "They will soon learn what a grave mistake it was to even think they could challenge me."

"They will regret it, my Lord," Orob replied as he followed Nivri out of the throne room, back through the winding passages of the castle.

Two

Blaken closed his eyes as he stepped into the portal, both scared and excited to be on his way. The weightlessness of his body was an odd feeling, but the Master had explained to him what it would be like, so the beagon knew more or less what to expect.

As he traveled, he suddenly felt a gush of air blow past him, seemingly moving in the other direction. He shrugged, intending to ignore it, when he briefly thought he heard muffled voices somewhere in the distance.

"Hold onto me…"

Was it a voice? Or was it just the wind? He supposed it was possible that his mind was so overwhelmed with what was happening to his body that it was playing tricks on him…

Regardless of this, his eyes remained tightly closed until he no longer felt the weightlessness. He remained this way for a few seconds longer, almost afraid to open them, afraid he might lose his mind if he happened to see he was suspended in mid-air…

When he felt comfortable doing so, Blaken finally allowed his eyes to open.

The air was cool and felt good against his skin. The skies were cloudy, and it was difficult to tell what time of day it was.

He looked to his left and saw the rocky side of a mountain.

Lying parallel to the ground, close to the mountain, was a giant tree. It appeared to have been dead for a while, the leaves having fallen off long ago. The top of the tree was covered in broken spider webs, their inhabitants nowhere to be seen.

Seeing a narrow path over to his right, Blaken followed it into the woods. The path turned here and there, leading to a place unknown. He didn't worry about this however, because it felt right. He believed he would find this village that he so desperately needed to find. After a short time, he came to the edge of the woods which opened up into a small valley. He continued on and at the crest of the hill, he stopped. As he gazed into the distance, he smiled.

Could it really be this easy?

Somehow he thought it could. As he looked at the quiet, unsuspecting village of Uncava where it lay nestled in the valley below, he knew, without a doubt, that it was. Nivri had explained it all to Blaken, exactly what he wanted done and when he wanted it done. He had his Master's blessing to destroy the village any way he chose, but there was one exception. Nivri had made it very clear that he wanted this done once the sun had fallen below the western sky.

As always, the Master had a reason for this… he believed that if the beagon destroyed the village in the dark, the inhabitants would have less chance of survival. Nivri was counting on the idea that they would find escape more difficult if they could not see where they were going. With this in mind, Blaken walked back to the woods, climbed up a tree and waited patiently for the sun to finish its daily journey. It would not take very long… it was well into the mid-afternoon, as far as he could tell. He remained in the tree until dusk, when the sun finally finished its journey along the western horizon. In the last few minutes of sparse daylight, Nivri's minion began his descent out of the tree. He looked forward to the execution of his plan.

Oh yes, the Master would be quite proud…

As dusk began to fall, Blaken walked back to the hilltop where he had first seen the village. From that location, he could clearly see the entire area.

He surveyed every aspect of his location, the nearby woods and the lay of the village. He was right between the mountains and the village, and knew he would definitely need to find another place to be when put his plan into action. He definitely did not want to find himself in the middle of the tragedy that was about to take place! He looked past the village and could see an ocean just to the right of it. Inland of the ocean, a line of trees slowly worked uphill into the mountains behind him where they crested at their highest point.

On the opposite side of the village, the trees on the mountain gradually sloped back downhill, where they smoothed out into a valley before once again meeting the village.

Ah, yes, this was perfect.

Before he could begin, he needed to relocate himself to higher ground.

He looked again at the place where the mountain crested at its highest point. Yes, that would be perfect. From there, he would be able to see the village, yet would be far enough out of the way to remain unharmed.

A beagon's sense of direction was very accurate, and now that he knew exactly where he needed to go, he did so without incident. By the time he stood atop the crest of the mountain, the surrounding land was covered in a blanket of cool darkness.

His eyesight was superb in the darkness, and he had no trouble seeing small flickers of firelight down in the village. The people of Uncava had no idea of the tragedy that was about to strike, of this he was sure.

He sat down on one of the nearby smooth rocks and looked up at the night sky. The stars, partially hidden by clouds, glittered here and there in the darkness above him. This, also, would be perfect for his plan. When things began to happen, they would happen very quickly. Blaken closed his eyes and took a few deep breaths. When he was sufficiently relaxed, he began to do that which he had come here to do.

"Amay boundegar inot fhen wicha," he recited quietly, just as Nivri had taught him, concentrating every ounce of his energy into his spell. He was completely unaware of the clouds as they began to churn in the night sky overhead.

"Amay boundegar inot fhen wicha!" he repeated. He concentrated so intently that he was unaware of the how the winds began to change. After being silent and unmoving just moments before, they now started blowing the trees from side to side.

"Amay boundegar inot fhen wicha kalmanor viatchu!" he

cried. A gust of wind tore through the nearby trees, whipping Blaken's hair across his face as it did so. As he mumbled a few unidentifiable words, the sky opened up, dumping a torrent of rain without warning on the surrounding mountains and valley.

Blaken was oblivious to it all. He continued to concentrate on his spell, wanting only to please his Master. He yearned for the Master to be proud.

"Amay boundegar inot fhen wicha kalmanor viatchu ishtamon cendunugu!"

Blaken's eyes shot open. He looked to the sky, totally aware of the unstable weather around him. The pouring rain pelted him in the face. He was soaked to the bone, yet had no doubt he was safe right where he was. He took a deep breath and held his arms straight out on each side of his body, forming a "t". It would now be just a matter of minutes before his task, his mission, was complete.

The rains continued to fall for the next few minutes, drenching everything in sight. As the winds continued to howl, he closed his eyes and recited the chant one final time.

"Amay boundegar inot fhen wicha kalmanor viatchu ishtamon cendunugu!"

After completing the spell, his eyes shot open again. He watched with pride as the water that had gathered in pools around him, nearly covering half of his body, began to perilously make its way down the mountain as if being propelled by an invisible force. The water flowed at an incredible speed down the slopes, wiping out many of the trees it encountered along the way. It left nothing but a muddy path of destruction in its wake.

Blaken sat quietly meditating in the darkness as the deadly flow of water headed straight towards the village from every part of the nearby mountains. As he meditated, he waited patiently for the torrent of water to converge at the bottom of the mountains before heading full-speed directly into the place he had come to destroy. The villagers did not stand a chance against the overwhelming path of liquid. As it rushed towards them, the unstoppable flow of water carried with it all the things it had gathered on its journey down the mountains... trees, rocks, and unidentifiable objects unlucky enough to be in its path.

When he knew the water was about to reach the village, Blaken decided to have mercy on the villagers. He quietly began to chant another spell.

"Amay indagu vilmu shanta apuáa!"

As he said these words, his hands, which were still held out at his sides, took on a colorful orange aura as they began to glow intensely. He drew his palms together over his head and leaned back as far as he could, before swinging them in a downward motion in front of his body. As they arced downward, a large ball of orange flame flew from his hands and streaked across the mountain and valley. In seconds, it struck the village in an incredible ball of flames, instantly killing many of the unsuspecting villagers. Seconds later, the torrent of water hit the village with an unthinkable force. It wiped out the trees, houses and all that lived there, pushing everything in its path right into the ocean.

Blaken waited quietly for time to take its toll, certain that any of the villagers who survived the ball of fire had not survived the massive wave of water that followed it. While he waited, the sky cleared and the rains stopped. The stars began twinkling once again, oblivious to the devastation that had just occurred.

Blaken stood up and slowly made his way down the mountain, back to the place where he'd arrived through the portal. When he got there, he was not surprised to see that the storm that just caused so much death and devastation had not even come close to this place.

He sat on the dead tree trunk and waited patiently for the Master to create the portal so he could return home. After a few moments, the portal appeared. Blaken smiled as he stepped into it, proud of the fact that the Village of Uncava was no more.

The Prisoner

One

In another world, over valleys and mountains as far as the eye can see, the sun has risen and fallen for eternity. It has never been questioned that the end of each day would be accompanied by darkness. With the arrival of dusk, gloomy shadows appear and slowly creep over the edge of Defigo. With the end of any given day, they converge on the surrounding countryside, bringing with them an end to the oppressive heat which accompanied the day, much to the relief of man and creature alike. The Nimturon Valley is always the first part of the surrounding land that darkness found when it finally arrived. Once the valley was covered by grayness, the shadows would slowly begin to creep up the Nedirian Mountain Range. Here, the sunlight recedes quickly, and soon both the entire valley and mountains are blanketed by cool darkness. The Nimturon Valley lies to the west and the Nedirian Mountain Range lies to the east. Our story now takes us to Defigo, which lies somewhere in between.

The heart of Defigo consists of many intertwining passageways, long ago constructed with hundreds of cold, gray stones. Mounted on the walls which line the depths of these passageways are torches, their miniature flames barely flickering in the surrounding gloom. They struggle to create enough light for one to walk through the underground tunnels confidently and without fear. They are spaced about twenty paces apart, but, in the darkest depths of Defigo, not all of them burn with fire. Some sit there, much like leafless trees scattered throughout the nearby countryside, still and lifeless.

133

Because a majority of these labyrinthine tunnels are located in the bowels of the castle, few travel here. The air that flows through the passageways is cool and damp. It is also seemingly unaffected by the heat which comes with each new day.

In the deepest areas of the castle, the passageways slope down, down, down until they finally open up like a mountain flower into a large, circular room. Here we find many cells that make up a prison where both creatures and men have been held against their will. At a quick glance, it appears that all of these cells are empty. Or are they?

Two

Lazy thoughts, distant memories, faded voices from far away... his daughter laughing in the bright sunshine as she plays jovially with mud puppies... his sons helping with the daily chores as they become strong, proud young men before his very eyes... his wife standing at the window in the moonlight, smiling at him across the room as she begins to walk towards him... He opens his eyes and reality hits him like a hard slap in the face. He remembers where he is as he feels the cool, damp air caressing his bare arms. How long had he been here now? He'd lost track, but it felt like forever. He feels the tears as they begin to pool in his eyes. He misses his house, the fresh air, the smell of a home-cooked meal, a warm bath, and fresh water from the river. More than all of these things, individually or combined, he feels the incredible gaping hole deep down inside, the same one he feels every day. It wasn't there just sometimes... it was there all the time, endlessly eating at him, one piece at a time. It was caused by the intense yearning he felt for his family... for all of those things he now understood that he always had taken for granted.

He often tried to remember how he had gotten here, but his memories of that fateful day were fragmented and unclear.

Silence surrounds him in his dank, dreary cell. This was the way it was most days. He remained there, held captive and alone, cold and hungry. Often, the only things available to keep him company were his thoughts of the future and his memories of the past, which most days was hard to accept, but he was a smart man. Without them, he would have nothing, day in and day out, except for his sheer existence and an overwhelming emptiness in his heart. He looked around his cell in the gloom, just like he'd done so many times before.

Here he had no bed like what he'd had at home, and no fire roaring in the corner of the room. His new home consisted of cold, barren, stone floors, a pia bowl that often only had a few swallows of water at the most, and some dry bread from his previous meal.

Every day, they would bring him fresh water and bread, but that wasn't saying much. The bread was usually old and dry, remnants from earlier meals the "upper" inhabitants of Defigo had either not eaten or not liked. There was a time when he would have never considered eating food that was left unfinished by strangers, but recent events in his life led him to change his way of thinking.

He picked up a piece of stale bread as his stomach rumbled in anticipation. Just as he was about to begin dining on his exquisite meal, he heard footsteps approaching from the main passageway. Sitting quietly on the stone floor, he set the bread back down and waited. The visitor soon came into view in the gloomy tunnel, which was the only entrance into the prison chamber. Without a glance at any of the other cells, the creature walked confidently up to the cell where the man was held captive.

"Get up," the mysterious visitor said gruffly as it stopped in front of the prisoner's cell door. The top half of the visitor's muscular body was covered by armor and he carried a medium-sized battle-axe at his side. His ears were slightly pointed and the small amount of visible skin was covered with hair. He was an odd creature, but one who had become familiar. It was the same creature who had brought the man food and water almost every day since he got here.

The many bars that lined the front of the cell itself were made from a durable, strong material that had been magically melted and shaped. On the outside of the cell was a much larger, stronger bar, laid horizontally across the doorway, which prevented it from being opened. The creature quietly set down his axe. With almost no effort at all, he grabbed the horizontal bar from its resting place and lifted it, eyeing the prisoner suspiciously as it did so. Without taking his eyes off the man, the guard quickly and easily set the bar down on the stone floor and picked up his axe. He accomplished this in one swift movement. He opened the cell door and looked at the prisoner expectantly.

"Where are we going?" the man asked as he stood up.

"You don't need to know," the creature said. "Come." In his given state, the man knew he would be no match for this creature. The food they fed him consisted mostly of bread and water in child-sized portions and his body was in no shape for a physical altercation… with anyone. The creature stepped away from the cell doorway and motioned for the man to follow him towards the only passageway leading to the upper levels of the prison. The prisoner obediently followed the guard through the gloomy tunnels of the castle. As they walked, a thought occurred to him… after all this time, he still did not know this creature's name.

"What do they call you?" he asked it.

The guard looked at him briefly yet remained silent. The man decided that perhaps the creature just didn't like to talk, which was typical of most times the guard came and brought him food. He frequently tried to engage it in conversation, in hopes of finding out exactly where it was he was being held and by whom, but the guard never offered any such information, much to the man's disappointment. Instead, it would only look at him silently before walking away.

The man sighed.

"I am Orob," the creature answered him quietly. The man glanced at the guard, surprised it answered him.

The prisoner was surprised Orob hadn't asked him for his own name, which was just fine with him. He did not want to offer any more information than he had to.

In silence, the guard and his prisoner continued to make their way through the dank passageways.

THREE

After a few moments, the man noticed the passageway was slowly brightening and he had a sense of vújade, which is the feeling you get when you think you've experienced something before. This was because he had been here before. They were getting close to the upper levels of the castle.

The torches that lined the tunnels here were different than they were deeper in the castle. In the lower levels, the walls were lined with many torches, but only a scattered few were lit. This left the passageways very dark and dismal. In the upper levels of the castle, however, the torches all burned brightly with flickering yellow and orange flames. The passageways were not as damp here either. Ah, the amenities of life in the upper floors of the castle.

Soon the man could see other creatures like Orob walking around as they patrolled the passageways. He watched them watching him cautiously as he followed Orob in silence. He had no doubt they all knew exactly who he was.

These other creatures were dressed very similar to Orob (whom he was fondly beginning to think of as "his guard").

Most of them wore only upper body armor, but some also had another kind of armor on their heads as well. Although these armored creatures were residents of this place and quite unlike him, the man was always glad to see other signs of life.

If he used his imagination, he could almost see this trip through the castle as a field trip, even though he never went very far. He could also see it as though he was finally being allowed to go out and play, but the downside was, in actuality, he never really got to play. Instead, the "play" usually turned into some form of punishment. They methodically made their way up through the various levels of the castle, and soon stopped in front of a pair of closed, thick, dark-colored doors.

Standing guard here were two large creatures, heavily armored and standing on their hind legs. At first the man thought they were mountain bears, but then discovered they were somewhat different.

Small, pointy ears protruded from either side of their heads. Their backs were hidden primarily by shadows, but the man thought he could see some sort of appendages extruding from their shoulders. For a brief moment, he thought they might be wings...

Wings?

He didn't think it was safe to stare so he lowered his gaze to the floor as they stopped in front of the guards. The man was certain he had never seen any creatures quite like this before.

Other than the slow movement of their eyes as they watched the new arrivals, the guards remained motionless. They looked at Orob, alert and confident. Each of the guards held a long battle-axe in their left hand, the blade at the top shining brightly in the flickering torchlight. The bottom ends of their weapons rested on the stone floor next to them.

"The Master awaits us," Orob told them gruffly. As if hearing a silent command, the guards simultaneously raised their axe handles up slightly before they quickly dropped them back down, pounding three times on the floor. The pair of guards turned around to face the sealed doors behind them.

In perfect harmony with each other, they both placed a hand on their respective door and pushed. Although the large slabs of wood were each a few inches thick, the doors swung open silently, and with almost no effort at all. As the prisoner glanced at the room beyond the doors, like other times in the past, it took his breath away. Each time he saw it, it was as though he was seeing it for the first time. Cool marble floors inlaid with various colored gemstones shone beneath their bare feet as they made their way toward the far end of the room. Statues of dragons, frozen forever in different poses, lined their path on either side. Some of them sat docilely and appeared to be watching quietly as the visitors walked by, while others had their wings spread wide as if caught in mid-flight.

Sitting in a tall, exquisitely carved wooden chair, an odd creature watched them as they approached the far end of the room. It was encircled by many candelabras, their flames flickering gently. The creature watched them with little emotion.

Since this had become his new home, the prisoner had seen this same male creature quite a few times... always for the same reason. Prior to coming here, however, he had never seen anything quite like it before. The creature in the chair wore black leggings, a black shirt, and had a black fabric wrapped partially around its head. The rest of the fabric trailed casually down its back.

The prisoner immediately noticed something different about the creature that he'd never seen before... there was now some kind of chain hanging around its neck. Scattered sparsely around the odd necklace were a small number of flat, pearl-like objects, which had a green-blue tint to them.

In the center of the necklace hung some sort of large halfmoon shaped object... a bone, perhaps? Or maybe a tooth? It was difficult to tell. When the being in the chair stood up, the item shifted and became partially hidden by its clothing. For a few seconds, the man took a closer look at the creature before him. It could have passed as a human, but the prisoner knew better... it was far from it.

As they reached the macabre creature, Orob stopped and knelt down on one knee, lowering his head in a respectful manner. He held this position silently for a few seconds before he rose back up. As he did, his eyes met the creature's eyes.

"Orob," the creature in black said quietly.

"Yes, My Lord," Orob responded.

"Leave us," the creature said.

"Yes, My Lord," Orob said again. Without another glance at the man, the guard turned and walked towards the entrance to the room.

The man turned briefly and watched Orob go.

"Prisoner," the creature said.

The prisoner turned back and looked at the creature that stood before him.

As the creature looked at the man, its eyes began to glow softly and its fingers began to twitch. The man had a feeling he knew what was coming and knew better than to fight it.

The glow in the creature's eyes turned orange and quickly became brighter. The creature then focused more intensely on the prisoner. As it did so, the man felt a familiar weight as it began to push down on his shoulders. It felt as though a pair of large, strong hands were forcing him down towards the marble floor.

Without resistance, the man knelt down on one knee. Once he had done this, the weight on him remained steady, neither increasing nor decreasing. He knew without question that the creature had brought him here to answer questions, just like it had done in the past.

"Prisoner," the being repeated as it glared down at the man.

"Yes," the man answered quietly with his head bowed. He focused on the creature's clothed feet, the only part of it that he could look at without raising his head.

"Where do the powers come from that are found within members of your family?" the creature asked, its voice relatively calm. As it waited for his answer, it walked around the man where he knelt in the candlelight.

"I know of no powers," the prisoner answered quietly.

"YOU DO!" the creature boomed from above and behind him.

The prisoner dared not move in spite of his fear. He did not know who this creature was, but he knew it had powers, oh yes. Powers that could easily leave him crying like a lost child. The sense of vújade fell over him like a gentle mist once again.

"Do you not love your family?" the creature asked the man in a strangely calm voice. "Do you not want to return to them? To live your life as you once did?"

As it said this, the creature in black returned to its chair and sat down.

"I know of no powers," the man repeated.

Still on his knees, the prisoner looked up at the creature.

Its eyes still glowed with an orange hue. "If you answer my

141

questions satisfactorily, I will release you. You may return to your family... your wife and your children.

"However, if you continue to avoid my questions, you will stay here, with me, in my castle, and ROT IN YOUR CELL!" The creature began this statement calmly, but by the end of the sentence its anger was very obvious.

"What do you want from me?" the man yelled back at the creature.

"You bring me here and ask me questions I don't have the answers to! You barely provide me with enough food and water to survive! I don't even know your name, and you expect me to answer any questions that you have?" the man boldly asked the creature, his own eyes glaring.

The creature sat silently, contemplating the prisoner's outburst. After a few seconds, the orange glow in its eyes began to dull until it disappeared. When the glow was gone, the weight on the man's shoulders lightened until it, too, was entirely gone.

The creature nodded at him.

"You may rise if you wish," it said calmly, as though the creature's previous bout of anger had never happened. The man stood up, watching the darkly clad creature with caution.

"My name is Nivri," the creature added quietly.

The prisoner looked at Nivri, surprised.

Nivri seemed not to notice as he continued.

"You have powers in your family. Either you will tell me about them, or you will die here without ever seeing your family or friends again.

"There are other ways I can get the information I am seeking," Nivri said to the human, an evil sparkle now in his dark eyes.

"There are many ways. I could torture you, if I took a fancy to it. Yes, there are many ways I can get the answers out of you that I am looking for."

The man watched Nivri silently. His heart was filled with a deep sense of dislike for the creature in black standing before him.

"I could go back to your world, as I have done before, very easily. I could find some other means that I'm sure would convince you to tell me just what I want to know. Perhaps by bringing one of your children here... yes, perhaps that would do the trick?" Nivri asked with a sneer. The man continued to remain silent but could not hide the doubt, fear, and anger that now filled his brown eyes.

"One of your children... or perhaps your wife?" Nivri continued. An evil smile began to show at the corners of his mouth.

"There are many hungry creatures who live here in Defigo, creatures that appreciate fresh meat when it is given to them.

"Yes, we have many ways to get what we want here in this castle."

The prisoner understood what Nivri was doing, yet he was determined not to give the creature the pleasure of knowing how it affected him. He stood before Nivri in silence, his eyes glaring with anger. He found himself silently teetering on the borderline of overwhelming anger and pure hatred.

Without another word, Nivri raised his hand and moved it in a waving gesture through the air. Behind him, the man heard a familiar sound and knew without looking that the doors to the room had opened. It seemed as though his quality time with this conniving creature was over.

"Go back to your cell and think over the things we have discussed," Nivri said to the man as a small smile played at the corners of his lips.

"Think long and hard about our discussion, and make the right choices... for your family's sake."

The man felt something brush his arm. He turned and was not surprised to find Orob back at his side. The guard took him by the arm and led him out of the room. Just as they reached the large, wooden doors, Nivri called out to the prisoner.

"Think carefully about your choices, human. Who knows? You are alone now, but it would be very easy to change that. I would be happy to provide you with companionship during your stay here in my humble castle. Yes, you could soon have company..."

As the creature's words faded, the guard and prisoner reached the passageway. Seconds later, the doors closed gently behind them.

The man walked next to Orob while angry blood coursed through his veins like hot poison. He did not have the answers that Nivri was looking for! That single thought ran through his head over and over. How could he make the stubborn creature understand this?

Before coming here, he had lived a simple life with his wife and children in a small, peaceful village. The villagers all worked together, helping each other whenever help was needed. No one who lived there had special powers that he knew of... not anyone.

It wasn't long before they were back in the lower parts of the castle. Once he was back in his cell, Orob closed the door behind the prisoner and laid the large bar back in its place, securing the door.

After a brief glance through the bars at the prisoner, Orob silently turned and headed back to the upper levels of the castle.

FOUR

The prisoner leaned against one of the cool, stone walls as he thought about Nivri's questions.

"You have powers in your family. Either you will tell me about them, or you will die here without ever seeing your family again."

One main thought continued to creep through his mind... he did not have the answers to give to Nivri! This bothered him more than anything else.

He simply didn't have the answers.

Maybe he should make something up just to appease the persistent creature!

As soon as this idea ventured into his thoughts, however, he pushed it back into the depths of his mind. Nivri wanted the information badly, that much was obvious. The prisoner knew with absolute certainty if he tried to be sly and gave the creature in black the wrong answers, punishment would be sure to follow.

No, telling Nivri a lie to satisfy his persistent questions was just not the right answer.

In all of his adult life, he'd never felt so frustrated and alone. As he racked his brain for a solution to his problems, he suddenly felt an odd buzzing, tingling sensation in his head. It only lasted a second before it quickly disappeared.

Confused, he sat upright and rubbed his forehead as he looked around his cell. Nothing was different, nothing had been moved, and no one else was there.

He shook his head, puzzled. Perhaps he had too much on his

mind? He shook his head again. Just when he was about to think his mind was playing tricks on him, the sensation came back. This time it lasted a few seconds longer than it had before.

As soon as he realized it was happening again, he jumped up. He had never experienced anything like this in his life. He had absolutely no idea what was going on.

The buzzing sensation subsided just as quickly as it started. He nervously waited a few minutes, almost afraid to move or even breathe. He felt like a chickenbird anxiously waiting for its eggs to hatch. He waited for the sensation to happen again, but it didn't.

Perplexed, he sat back down, completely unsure now of what to think. What happened next was not something he felt or expected.

Without warning, he heard a soft whimper which sounded as though it was coming from somewhere in the distance. He looked through the cell bars into the gloomy passageway leading to the prison and saw nothing. He also looked around the area immediately outside of his cell… there was nothing there, but the sound continued.

While it sounded as if it was off in the distance, it also sounded very close.

How could this be?

He heard the sound a few more times before it faded away, which left him surrounded again by a quiet, uncomfortable silence.

Believing that whatever was happening earlier was finished for now, he closed his eyes to rest. As his body relaxed, he soon drifted off to sleep.

As he slept, he began to dream.

In his dream, he was there, in his prison cell. He could sense other creatures with him. He could neither see nor hear them in this dream prison, but he somehow knew they were there. He did not doubt their existence for a second.

The little hairs on the nape of his dream-self's neck stood straight up. It was as if a sudden bolt of firebug light shot down from the stormy sky and struck him, painlessly raising every hair on his head.

Creatures, animals, people… in his dream world, they were real and they were close, yet so far. The dream lasted only for a moment. Soon he slept soundly, without dreams.

After what seemed like a few short seconds, the prisoner woke up to the sound of footsteps as they approached his cell. He sat up expectantly. The dream was now a distant memory as his stomach, as if on cue, began to grumble. Did he dare hope for a fresh meal of warm water and stale bread?

In a moment, he began to make out Orob as he walked towards the cell in the flickering torchlight. The prisoner smiled when he saw the tray Orob carried in both hands. He couldn't tell what was on it, but the fact that the guard used both hands was a good thing. Perhaps the castle inhabitants felt pity on the man, and the conversation deficient guard was about to bring him a feast?

As the prisoner considered this outlandish thought, another one crossed his mind. Usually, whatever Orob brought down for him was only carried in one hand – there was no need for a tray. As Orob got closer, the man could see that there was not just one large item on the tray – there were a number of things.

The prisoner's stomach grumbled once again, louder this time.

Orob stopped outside the man's cell and looked at him as though he wanted to say something. Instead, he carefully set the tray down on the stone floor, which allowed the man to see just what was on it.

There were two pia bowls next to each other on the tray, and both contained a steaming substance. Next to these were two pia bottles. The latter probably only contained water, as they usually did. The man doubted Nivri would allow him the pleasure of drinking something else, such as wine or ale.

Orob picked up one of the bottles and handed it to the prisoner. It fit easily between the vertical cell bars, and the man took it without comment. He then slid a bowl smoothly across the floor through the gap under the cell door.

"Compliments of the Master," Orob said quietly to the prisoner as he glanced at him.

Without another word, Orob bent down and picked the tray up off the floor. As he did, the man caught a glimpse of what appeared to be a second bowl, stacked almost invisibly under the first one.

"Why would he have another bowl on the tray?" he thought absently.

"Orob, wait," the prisoner called. The guard turned and glanced back at him questioningly.

Without warning, the aroma from the pia wafted up to the prisoner's nose. His mouth watered and his stomach began to grumble in earnest, and it took everything he could muster to ignore these demands. He wanted to get more information from Orob, and this could be a pivotal moment for him. He couldn't let the thought of food get in the way.

He had to stay focused!

"Can you tell me more about Nivri? Who is he? Is he a sorcerer? A mundunugu? What is he?" The prisoner looked at Orob pleadingly.

"Eat your food," the guard answered matter-of-factly. He then turned and walked towards another cell a few feet away.

"What's he doing over there?" the prisoner thought. "There are no other creatures down here besides me... or are there?"

Remnants of his earlier dream came to him in bits and pieces as his thoughts turned to when he returned from his latest visit with Nivri. He had been so engrossed in protecting his family and coming up with answers to Nivri's questions that it never crossed his mind to look at any of the other cells for new visitors. He didn't have company down here often, but other visitors did show up on occasion. They would also disappear just as mysteriously as they had appeared, without explanation.

As he listened quietly, his curiosity got the best of him.

He could hear Orob on the other side of the room but could no longer see him. How he wished he could see what the guard was doing!

"Orob, please talk to me!" he pleaded as he shook the bars of his cell. "Help me to understand what's happening here!"

Orob apparently had other plans and did not come back to him. Instead, he silently finished whatever he was doing out of the man's sight, and then headed back out of the dungeon the way he had come... without even a glance back.

"Orob!" the prisoner called out to the guard as he shook the bars of his cell, this time even harder. The larger bar held securely, however, and the only answer to his pleas was the all-too-familiar silence.

FIVE

After finishing the food Orob had brought him earlier in the evening, the man fell into a deep sleep. He didn't know exactly what kind of food it was, but it sure hit the spot. It tasted like some kind of stew, probably chickenbird. It was cold by the time he ate it, but he didn't care. Anything, including cold stew, sure beat bread. Now the man lay on his makeshift bed, still groggy after waking up from his nap. As he lay there, his mind was spinning with ideas about his current situation. What could he possibly tell Nivri to make him happy? It would be so much easier if he had the answers to the questions the persistent creature was asking! It would be even easier if he knew why he was asking them. Special powers in his family? The only special quality he knew they possessed was that they were a close-knit family that worked well with the other villagers. Special powers – Bah!

As he lay there on his bed, slowly waking up while pondering these thoughts, a noise outside of his cell suddenly caught his attention.

He listened intently… yes, there it was again! It sounded like something was scuffling around on the stone floor.

He stood up, put his head against the bars, and looked to the right where the sound was coming from. He could see a few of the other prison cells on that side of the room, but not many. A few in between them were out of his view, and he chided himself for not paying more attention when they walked back from visiting Nivri earlier. He heard the scuffling sounds yet again, this time more softly. They were quickly followed by the unmistakable sound of a pia bowl being pushed or pulled gratingly along the stone floor. He was certain now that he was not alone down here in this prison.

"Hello?" he called out towards the other cell. "Hello, who are you?"

The scuffling sound stopped and immediate silence answered him. He waited a few seconds before he tried again.

"I am being held prisoner here, also," he said to the newcomer, more quietly than before. Once again there was only silence.

Just as he was about to give up and sit back down, he heard a different noise.

Was that a snort?

He decided to try one last time.

"Do you have a name?" he asked quietly and was quickly answered with the snort sound again. When had Nivri had time to lock up another creature down here in this dreadful place? Could it be someone like him who was unable to talk? Maybe the guards had bound and gagged the new arrival… his mind was spinning with questions.

"I've been here for countless days, weeks, months…" the man offered, but silence continued to be his only companion.

"Well, if you want to talk, I'm not going anywhere," he said, feeling an intense need to communicate with his new neighbor. He sighed and sat back down. Being locked in his cell didn't allow him much freedom, but one thing it did give him was plenty of time to think. He had no doubt that, given enough time, he could figure out what to do about his situation.

He reached over to the corner where he kept a few dried alia leaves and charcoal. His keepers did not give him much to do, but thankfully they did allow him to draw. Alia leaves were good for this.

Not long ago, he had asked Orob to bring him some supplies to help make his long hours locked up become more bearable. At first Orob seemed to ignore him, never telling him whether or not he would get him the supplies he had asked for. One day, a few weeks ago, however, Orob had a surprise for the lonely prisoner when he was delivering a fancy meal of not-quite-stale bread and warm water. On the tray with his meal, he finally found the things he had requested.

After he got these simple supplies, the man would then sit in his cell, sometimes for hours on end, drawing pictures of his wife and children.

At times, he would draw pictures of the valley or mountains as they were seen from the village. At others, he would draw one of the mountain ranges near his home, which provided a beautiful background to the nearby valley. Occasionally, his artwork would depict a cloud-covered mountain range, reminding him of a blanket wrapped around his children on a cold, snowy night.

With one particular piece of artwork, the background was brown and the color he used to draw with was black, but in his mind's eye he could vividly see the most colorful blue sky that he'd ever seen. He drew all these things, using his fingers to blend the charcoal and shade the areas that needed to be shaded. Without much else to do in his cell, this simple activity was always the highlight of his day.

No one who lived in the castle ever said anything to him about his drawings, which was probably because Orob was pretty much the only creature he saw down here, and the guard didn't seem to have much of an interest in anything. Orob just didn't seem to care… which was a simple and painless philosophy of life.

The man smiled as he thought about his family, and he began to draw a new picture on one of the smaller alia leaves. He had an idea for a jewel he'd recently thought of, and he really wanted to pull it from his thoughts and transform it onto one of the alia leaves. He wasn't sure if he would be able to, but he wouldn't know until he tried. He had a nagging feeling that this was something… something… important.

Besides, what did he have to lose?

He settled into the corner of his cell with a fresh leaf and his charcoal. He closed his eyes and tried to visualize the gem before he began. After a few seconds, he opened his eyes and let the fingers holding the charcoal work their magic as he tried to gently transfer the image from his mind to the leaf.

Just as he began, the buzzing sensation returned unexpectedly within his head. His hand froze where it was, the charcoal resting gently on the leafy canvas. As he nervously waited for the feeling to subside, he closed his eyes and forced himself to stay calm. The sensation felt strange because he still didn't know what it was, but at the same time, it also felt strangely familiar. After what seemed to be only a few seconds, the buzzing subsided and he opened his eyes. He looked around the cell, curious and confused. As before, nothing in his room had changed or been moved.

He sighed and glanced down at the drawing, prepared to resume his artwork. His sigh turned into a gasp of disbelief, however, when he saw the state of the alia leaf in front of him. What had happened to it?

Six

He was shocked at the sight before him. He looked around his cell… it was empty, just as he knew it would be. There had been no one else there with him, yet his mind simply could not understand how this could be? He looked down at his hands. In his right hand he still clutched the piece of charcoal he had been using. He turned his hand so that it was palm up, and then opened his fingers. The charcoal rolled down his fingers before landing gently in the center of his palm.

All of his fingers were dark from the powder, some more than others. It looked as though he'd been sitting there drawing, working the charcoal into the leaf, for hours. He even had some fragments of charcoal under his tattered fingernails, a familiar indication he had been drawing for quite some time.

He looked now at his left hand. It was clean, with no signs of charcoal anywhere on it, just as he expected. This was another typical sign of how he worked. He shook his head again and looked down at the alia leaf, which was now splayed out on the cold, stone floor. Where did the picture drawn on the leaf come from? The alia leaf itself was small, about the size of a pia bowl, and in the center of it was a beautiful drawing that would make any artist proud. The man, however, was not proud. He was more confused now than he'd been since he'd gotten here.

The remnants of charcoal on his right hand told his mind he had done the artwork, but his mind told him otherwise.

He clearly remembered sitting down to work on a picture. He also remembered feeling the tingling sensation in his head as soon as he was about to draw. When he felt this odd feeling, he closed his eyes for two reasons… to help him not overreact to the feeling, and to try to focus on what was really going on.

He was sure he'd only had his eyes closed for a few seconds, and when he had reopened them, the sensation was gone. He was still no closer to understanding it, but he was not as frightened by it anymore.

Only a few seconds…

His gaze returned to the alia leaf, his brown eyes filled with puzzlement and confusion still written on his dark-skinned face.

How in the world could he have drawn this picture in the few short seconds his eyes were closed? In fact, how could he have drawn it at all? His eyes had been closed the entire time he'd been experiencing the odd sensation in his head!

Weren't they?

He knelt down, picked up the alia leaf and looked at the picture more closely for a few seconds. Then he closed his eyes and tried to remember what had happened.

Only a few seconds…

"That's impossible," he thought as his eyes shot open, still overcome with a lack of understanding. He blew gently on the charcoal picture and watched as if in a fog. Dust particles from the charcoal lightly scattered into the air before cascading almost invisibly towards the floor.

Only a few seconds…

The confused prisoner sat down on the stone floor and looked at the drawing. He just didn't understand how he could be seeing what he saw…

Staring back at him from the alia leaf was a perfect drawing of an amulet.

SEVEN

He was a rational man, but in some instances of irrationality, he understood how easy it was to become that which you feel. The prisoner sat on the floor of his cell in a daze as he stared at the drawing of the amulet while he held it in his hand. He did not remember drawing it. His mind's eye remembered only darkness and the odd buzzing sensation.

He remembered nothing except for the odd feeling in his head, which seemed to have lasted just a few short seconds…

Didn't it?

Simply put, he did not know where the picture of the amulet on the alia leaf had come from.

"Prisoner."

Once again, he jumped up, dropping the alia leaf to the floor as he did so.

What was it that kept whispering to him? He looked around, and, like before, did not see anything in his cell out of the ordinary. As he listened for the sound again, he seriously began to question his sanity. This was just great. They begin putting pressure on him and he starts going crazy.

"What kind of man am I?" he chided himself, when something else suddenly struck him.

Could they have drugged him?

It was entirely possible that Nivri believed the only way to get the information out of him that he so desperately wanted was to do it by drugging him. Then he could force him to talk when he wasn't in the right frame of mind! Yes, that made total sense to him!

Eureka!

He thought back to the meal he had consumed not so long ago. At the time, he had thought it was chickenbird stew, but what if it wasn't?

What if it was something else?

The stew was tasty; there was no doubt about that. It was so tasty that they could have easily added a little bit of something extra and he would have never noticed. Because meals around the castle weren't exactly on a regular schedule, he figured this would be one way for them to ensure that whatever food they brought him wouldn't be wasted. Sometimes, like a mud puppy, he wolfed down whatever scraps they brought him without even taking the time to think about what it was. In fact, there were times when he barely even tasted it.

Yes, a little extra something in his evening meal was a distinct possibility. Now what could he do about it? Probably nothing, he mused. It had been quite a while since he had ingested the food, and chances were that whatever drugs they may have added, IF they had added anything at all, were already in his system, and it was too late to try to get them out now.

He decided to lie down and try to sleep it off. He went over to his bed and got comfortable. If he was drugged, he needed to get it out of his system because too many weird things were happening. He was beginning to think it was entirely possible that he might just be losing his mind.

He closed his eyes and focused on his breathing. Just as he totally relaxed, he suddenly heard the voice call out to him once again.

"Human."

"What do you want?" he yelled as he jumped up for the third time.

The only answer he got was silence, which really didn't surprise him.

He chuckled to himself.

The voice in his mind would have totally unnerved him any other day, but not anymore! Oh no! Knowing that his body was trying to deal with whatever had been put into it was a good enough reason for him to laugh this whole situation off. Yelling at the mental voice, although unreasonable, made him feel so much better. With that thought, he chuckled again.

"Human, you must help me," the voice said, a little louder this time.

He froze as the smirk on his face faded away like a river washes a flower downstream. Were conversations with an imaginary voice possible? More importantly, were they reasonable?

"Who are you?" he answered back quietly. Should he even attempt to have a conversation with his drug-induced inner voice?

"I am Drake," the voice answered quietly. The man shook his head with a sigh. It would just take time to let whatever drugs he had coursing through his body wear off. Thank goodness the rest of the prison cells weren't full of creatures. If that was the case, this would be unbearable.

"Drake," he answered quietly. "Here I am, locked in a cell and feeling like I've lost my mind and you want my help?" he asked in a frustrated voice.

"Yes," Drake said in return. "I, too, am being held prisoner, but you are the one who holds the key."

While listening to the voice, he walked over to the cell door and looked out at the other cells. There were quite a few he could see, but he still couldn't see any other forms of life. He stood motionless, replaying the other voice's words in his head.

Drake was being held prisoner. Where... here? Somewhere deep in this castle? Or in his mind?

Drake also said that he was the one who holds the key... what key? He didn't have any key...oh yes, he definitely needed to get some sleep.

"What do you mean, I hold the key?" he asked, but once again, his only answer was silence.

Was Drake talking about the key to the cell? The key to the castle? How could he have the key when he didn't even know where he was?

He waited for the voice to say something more, but the only thing he heard was the sound of footsteps as they approached the prison from the passageway. It looked as though his good friend,

Orob, was coming back to pay him yet another visit.

A shadowy figure soon became visible, and even without seeing it clearly, the man knew it was Orob. He waited quietly to see what brought the guard to him this time. Unlike before, Orob now came empty-handed. He did not carry any food or pia bottles, and, surprisingly, no large battle-axe. The man knew, however, that Orob never came down for a visit without any weapon. He always had at least a small sword sheathed at his side.

"Come with me, prisoner," Orob said as he lifted the bar which blocked the cell door off of its cradle and set it on the floor nearby.

"Nivri would like to talk to you."

The man followed Orob silently. As he made his way away from his cell, he looked back at the other cells near his. They were empty.

He shook his head and followed Orob through the passageways. Not surprisingly, they took the familiar path back to the creatures that stood guard outside the doors leading to Nivri's chamber.

With the usual ritual, the guards dropped their weapon shafts three times down on the stone floor, which simulated the sound of a knock that was done in unison, in an odd sort of way. After the winged bears turned and pushed the large doors open, the prisoner followed Orob past the familiar dragon statues to the front of the room, where the black clad creature was already waiting.

They stopped directly in front of Nivri, who sat quietly watching them. His face showed no emotion.

"Human," Nivri began, "have you used the time I have given you wisely to consider my questions?"

The prisoner looked at him quietly, his mind and heart racing. How should he answer? He hesitated slightly as he gathered his thoughts.

"I know no answers to the questions that you ask. Will you explain to me just what powers you feel my family has? The only powers I am aware of are the powers of love and compassion.

"I am just a simple man, from a simple family, in a simple

village. We have no magic, neither in our family, nor in our village. I'm sorry, but I do not have the answers you seek," the man said as he humbly lowered his eyes to the floor.

As he finished his statement, a loud noise suddenly filled the room around them.

One, two, three... the number of times the guards dropped their weapons on the floor outside of the closed doors. No sooner had the sound ended, one of the doors opened. A small creature, running on its hind legs, came barreling towards them.

"Master! Master!" the new arrival called out as it ambled across the marble tiles.

It was a small mountain monkey, its long brown fur bouncing up and down as it hopped its way past the statues. It was carrying something in one of its hands, waving it frantically in the air.

"Master!" the monkey said again. The monkey's eyes passed fleetingly over Nivri and the guard briefly. When it looked at the man, its gaze lingered, and the mistrust it felt was obvious.

"What is it, Simia?" Nivri asked the new arrival impatiently. "What brought you here? Do you not know you are interrupting a very important meeting?"

Simia stopped at Nivri's side, suddenly nervous that he had made a bad decision in coming to the throne room. It was too late to think that now, however, so he continued.

"Master, forgive me for the interruption, but Crim was down in the prison, making his rounds. He found this in the prisoner's cell!" Simia explained excitedly. With that, he handed Nivri the item he had been waving in the air when he entered the room.

As soon as the prisoner saw what it was, his stomach sank. He knew he would never be able to explain his way out of this one.

Nivri looked carefully at the item. Within seconds, he stood up and made his way directly towards the nervously waiting human.

The man expected Nivri's reaction before he felt it, but in no way could he have anticipated the sudden intensity of it.

In an instant, the prisoner felt the familiar weight as it pushed down on his shoulders from above, forcing him down to the floor. This time was different than the last, and before he had a chance to try to relax, the weight had pushed him completely down onto the cold, marble tiles. As soon as his body was splayed out on the floor, the weight shifted from his shoulders to the middle of his back, which made it very difficult to breathe.

"This drawing… from where did you get it?" Nivri asked the man angrily as he stood over him. The pressure pushing down on him eased up slightly and he took a few seconds to breathe before he answered.

"I don't know," he said.

As soon as the words were out of his mouth, the pressure on his back intensified again and he couldn't help but struggle against it. Although he knew the whole time, in the rational part of his mind, that he shouldn't struggle, he was physically unable to fight his body's natural reaction, and he continued to fight the pressure. Not surprisingly, his efforts remained fruitless.

"That is not a satisfactory answer!" Nivri yelled as he paced around the prisoner. The invisible hands held him firmly in place.

Orob stood silently in the shadows of the room, where he had moved to be out of the way. Simia was next to him. Although the monkey tried to contain himself, he continued to jump up and down obviously excited about seeing a show! Orob, meanwhile, watched the events as they unfolded before him, ready to respond at a moment's notice to his Master.

Nivri stopped in front of the prisoner and glared down at him. The prisoner's physical movements had finally stopped but he still struggled to breathe.

"I will ask you again," Nivri said calmly as he eased the pressure pushing down on the prisoner, allowing him to breathe easier… for the moment.

"From where did you get this drawing? Or, wait! Better yet, did you draw it?" Nivri asked in a demanding tone. The man took several deep breaths before he answered.

"I don't know where the drawing came from, and I don't know if I drew it," he said as he tried to look Nivri in the eyes. If he could make eye contact, maybe he could prove to the sorcerer that he wasn't lying.

In an instant, the weight was completely lifted off of him. In its place, however, the man felt something grab at the back of his shirt before he was lifted roughly off the floor. He cried out as he felt the security of the floor beneath him slip away while he rose involuntarily into the air.

"Put me down!" he called out.

The invisible hands held him suspended in mid-air, very close to the room's high ceiling.

He looked down at Nivri as the sorcerer glared at him. The creature's eyes were glowing a dull orange color once again, much like the embers in the center of a hot fire. The man looked to his left and right over each of his shoulders… there was nothing there but empty space. He had nothing to grab onto.

"The drawing of the amulet… you don't know how it came to be?" Nivri asked the prisoner angrily.

"I told you, I don't know where it came from. I sat down to draw a picture, but then I blacked out. When I woke up, the drawing was already done. I had the charcoal in my hand… but I don't remember drawing it," he explained to Nivri. He was frustrated that the creature below him didn't understand, and just when he thought he would be left suspended in midair forever, he was rapidly lowered back down to the floor. He landed on the tiles and his knees buckled beneath. He crumpled in a heap onto the cold, marble stones. After a few seconds, he rolled over and sat up to face Nivri.

In the blink of an eye, the sorcerer stood before him. He bent down and picked the prisoner up by his shirtfront with one hand as easily as a bag of potatoes. With almost no effort at all, he held the man a few feet above the floor.

The battered human could not avoid looking at the orange glow in the creature's angry eyes. It was almost as though he was being drawn into the swirling colors, deeper and deeper into a sea of amber light. As he stared, mesmerized, he could also see flickers of red buried here and there within the orange sea. There was no mistaking the anger that seethed from the angry sorcerer – from his pores, his hair… from every inch of his entire being.

"This is not good," the man thought nervously.

"You will pay for your disobedience," Nivri hissed at him as a spray of spittle flew from his mouth. The anxious prisoner could smell the stench that was carried to his nostrils from the creature's rancid breath. Just when the man thought he could stand the smell no more, he was thrown roughly across the room. He landed on his back as the wind was knocked out of him. With a grunt, he slid to a stop in front of Orob and Simia, where he tried to catch his breath.

"Take him to the room we have set aside for our very special guests!" Nivri ordered sarcastically. He sneered at the human, then turned and walked angrily back to his chair.

"Yes, my Lord," Orob answered as he lifted the man by the arm. As he got to his feet, the man was thankful to find he wasn't seriously hurt. If he had landed on the floor differently, he could have easily suffered broken bones.

Orob led him through a side door. Still trying to catch his breath, they walked through dark, twisted passageways on a downhill spiral heading into the depths of the castle. After a while, they turned into a gloomy, mid-sized room containing only two dimly lit torches where the man had never been before.

Sitting side by side in this room were numerous rectangular containers like nothing the prisoner had ever seen. The cubes were about half as tall as he was and the same distance wide. Locks hung from each of the containers, some locked and some unlocked. The man couldn't help but wonder just what was in these locked cells. It never occurred to him that he was about to find out.

They stopped in the center of the room, which wasn't saying much. The containers all sat neatly next to each other in a partial circle, which was only broken by the door that entered the room. From where they now stood, the man could take two steps forward and touch the container directly in front of him.

Orob walked over to one of the unlocked containers. He removed the lock, opened the door, and looked back at the waiting prisoner.

"Get in," the guard ordered without emotion.

"What?" the man asked in surprise.

"Get in," Orob growled as he gestured for the prisoner to get into the container.

The man stood there in shocked disbelief. Orob really didn't believe he would willingly get into this... this... box, did he?

"Orob," he started, but the guard quickly interrupted him.

"Master's orders. Get in and hand me the chain that is just inside the door," Orob said firmly. The prisoner took a step towards the container. He could see that there, just inside the opening, a metal chain lay partially hidden in the dark shadows of the box. He sighed. He did not like this at all.

Reluctantly, he did as Orob ordered.

He sat down just inside the container door, picked up the chain, and pulled it towards him. One end stopped abruptly, apparently secured to something inside the container. He pulled the other end of the chain and it moved towards him without resistance. After a few seconds, a large, metal shackle came into view.

Orob held his hand out expectantly and waited for the hapless prisoner to hand him the end of the chain, which the man did without argument. The guard then pulled a key out of his pocket and unlocked the shackle.

"Give me your foot," he said.

"Orob, I have never shown you any resistance in the past, and I will certainly not show you any now. You don't need to chain me to anything," the man said as he tried to change the guard's mind about what he was planning to do.

"Give me your foot… now," Orob said firmly.

The human knew it was no use to put up a fight. He could try to get up and run, but, since he didn't really know his way around the castle, it would only be a matter of time before he was caught again… or even killed. He just couldn't risk it. He didn't want to do anything to jeopardize what little chance he had of being able to see his wife and children.

He sighed again as he held his left foot out to Orob. Without a word, the guard secured the shackle around the prisoner's ankle, and then gestured for him to crawl into the box.

"Get in," Orob said.

The man looked back over his shoulder into the container. It was very dark inside, but, as his eyes adjusted, he could just make out tiny holes in the container at both the far end and along the sides. He was relieved that at least he would have some fresh air. Other than the small holes, the box was filled with darkness.

Reluctantly, the prisoner crawled into his new cell, and his chain rattled and clanked as he dragged it behind him. Once the chain cleared the container door, Orob closed it securely. The man heard a click as the bolt dropped into place.

With his job completed, the guard turned and headed back to the upper levels of the castle, leaving the prisoner alone in the darkness of his new prison.

EIGHT

The inside of the container was as dark as a moonless sky in the dead of night. He sat silently in the box, his back against one of the side walls, deep in thought about his predicament, which had quickly gone from bad to worse. The container itself was tall enough for him to sit comfortably in, but there was definitely not enough room to stand up. From where he now sat, he could stretch his legs out comfortably, his toes just touching the wall on the other side.

His attention turned to the locked door. There were three air holes near the bottom of it, but none were at the top. It would be much more difficult for him to tell if anyone was outside the container, and he hoped he'd still be able to hear footsteps when a visitor entered the room. Like so many other times that day, he sighed in exasperation.

He felt around the dark interior of the container, almost afraid of what he might find.

What was he chained to? Was there anything else in here?

The thought of touching long forgotten bones from another creature (or creatures) suddenly crossed his mind and he shuddered.

He hesitantly ran his hand along the inside of the box.

He felt nothing until he came across the chain attached to his ankle. He followed the chain away from his foot and found the other end where it was connected firmly to a post. He tried to move it, but it wouldn't budge. It was somehow embedded into the bottom of his container. As he finished his exploration of his new home, he was relieved to find nothing else except for the chain. Because he was a tall man, it was also good to know that he could lay down with his head at one end and still have enough room to stretch out completely.

It could be worse, he supposed. They could have locked him up in some small, square box with no room to move at all.

Half full.

One of his good friends in the village would often say that one must look at life's challenges as half full, not half empty. He smiled. His current situation definitely called for half full… and how!

Now that things were apparently settling down, his thoughts drifted back to when he was in his other cell. The alia leaf with the drawing of the amulet… where had the drawing come from?

Although he was shrouded by darkness, the man closed his eyes as he tried to remember drawing the picture. In his memory, all he could see was blackness surrounded by the odd buzzing sensation.

He definitely remembered having the charcoal ready in his hand. That much he was sure of. His next memory was when he looked down at his dark palm once the picture was already drawn. In his mind there was nothing in between. He had no idea how the drawing of the beautiful amulet came to be.

It was no use.

"Hello?" a voice called out from somewhere nearby.

The man's eyes shot open and he again felt that eerily familiar feeling of vújade.

Where did that voice come from? Was it a real voice this time, or was his mind playing tricks on him yet again? He had another thought and didn't know if it was better or worse… was he still experiencing a reaction from being drugged?

"Hello?" the voice repeated itself as if it was a slow echo.

The man scooted over to the container doorway and tried to look through the holes near the bottom of the door. It was difficult to really see anything, but there didn't appear to be anyone there. He also hadn't heard any footsteps…

"Hello," he answered the mystery voice. "Where are you?" the voice asked quietly.

"In one of these containers," the man answered. "Where are you?"

"In a container also," the voice said. "My name is Zacharu. Are you a human?"

"Yes," the man answered without hesitation.

"I thought so," the voice answered. "I heard you come in with Orob."

After a pause, the mysterious voice asked, "Do you know why you're here?"

"Nivri wants answers I do not have," the man answered. He felt an instant bond with this other being, which was apparently in the same situation as he was.

"Why are you here?" the man asked Zacharu.

"For similar reasons."

After a slight pause, Zacharu asked, "Do you know Lotor?"

"Lotor?" the man asked. "No, I don't know that name."

"Lotor is a very powerful wizard. He lives in Immolo, but he is the ruler of Euqinom," Zacharu explained. "Similar to your situation, he wanted answers to questions that I, also, did not have. At times, he chooses to lock me up until I 'remember'. That is why I am here now.

"I have been here, in this castle, for many moons. I hope someday to be returned to my home, to my family and friends, but the chances for that do not look good."

"What is 'Euqinom'?" the man asked curiously.

He heard a chuckle from Zacharu.

"You really do not know about Euqinom?" Zacharu asked, surprised. He thought every creature, large and small, knew about this world.

"No, I know nothing about it. What is it? The name of this place we are in now?" the man asked.

"The name of this castle is Defigo, which means Castle of Spells. It is the home of Nivri. Euqinom is this whole world… the mountains, the valleys, the castles, and the villages on the countryside. It all is a part of Euqinom," Zacharu explained.

After a brief consideration, the man said, "So we are now living in Defigo, which is in the world of Euqinom?"

"Yes," Zacharu answered.

The man had never heard any of the other villagers talk about either of these places, and some of them traveled through the valleys and mountains quite frequently.

"And you are a human?" the mysterious creature asked again.

"Yes," the man answered. "Why?"

Zacharu was silent for a short time, then answered, "I heard a while ago that a human was captured and was being kept somewhere in the castle. It was said this human knew information that both Nivri and Lotor would find as… shall I say, very useful? I had not yet heard whether or not they were able to get that information, however.

"We have few visitors here in the castle, so something tells me that you must be the human they spoke of," Zacharu finished.

The man sat silently for a moment. It didn't take long for him to decide he would try trusting this creature. "Yes, I think I am, too," he answered Zacharu. "Nivri earlier asked me some strange questions about my family… and special powers, but as far as I know, we don't have special powers in my family."

"Yes, that sounds similar to the things I've heard… that the human who was being held captive was not cooperating," Zacharu said.

They both sat silently for a while, each in their own thoughts.

"I have a wife and children back at the village," the man continued. "Nivri says he will bring them here and feed them to hungry creatures if I don't give him the answers he seeks, the answers to the questions that I DO NOT KNOW!"

The man angrily banged his fist on the wall of his container as he yelled this last. He felt helpless that he could not sway the direction his situation was going in.

"Human," Zacharu said quietly. "Calm down and listen to me. I think I may be able to help you with your situation.

"Like you, I also have a family and friends that I would like to get back to. I have been here much longer than you have, however, and I believe I am even more anxious than you to get out of here.

"My situation is different from yours, yet in a way, it is the same.

"My life, as I used to know it, revolved around a world of

darkness. I lived with my family and friends in a dark cave that was located deep in heart of the mountains. We were content living there, in darkness and in peace.

"I used to wander the tunnels of my home, often alone, and often found solitude in the darkness by myself. One day, however, a simple wrong turn changed my life.

"Before I knew it, I found myself lost. I wandered for quite a while, and before I knew it, I found an opening in the darkness that led me into the light, something I had heard about, yet had never seen. This opening led me from the comfort and safety of the only home I'd ever known into a whole new, light-filled, colorful world.

"My new world was filled with trees. I've since learned this is called a forest.

"I was not too concerned with paying attention to where I was going as I explored my new surroundings, because I wasn't planning on going very far. I remember thinking I would surely have no problem finding my way back to the cave, back to my family. I decided to look around in hopes of finding it suitable to bring my people to."

The man listened to the mysterious creature's story in respectful silence. As Zacharu continued, the man closed his eyes and could almost see what was being described.

"Fresh water flowed throughout the cave, and I suspected that, if it flowed within the cave, it must come first from outside the cave," Zacharu continued. "If I could find this water source, we would then only have to find food. From what I could see of this outside world, there would be no problems with that. I saw the opportunity to give my family and friends an entirely new life, one filled with beautiful colors, new smells, and new adventures every day!

"I struggled for quite a while to see where I was going, as my eyes were not used to the brightness that surrounded me. The excitement I felt about where I was got the better of me, and I continued exploring. After wandering through the unfamiliar forest for a while, I became undoubtedly lost, as you may have already guessed.

"I stopped to rest as I tried to figure out just where I was.

Before I knew it, the sun began to set and I was soon surrounded in shadows. This made things much easier on my eyes. Once I could see better, I thought I could make my way back to the cave… back to my family.

"As I headed back the way I thought I'd come, I suddenly found myself surrounded by soldiers on horseback. They all had their swords drawn and their bodies were very muscular and covered by a thick armor. I had never before seen creatures such as these, and had never been more frightened than I was at that moment!"

The man sat in his container, mesmerized by Zacharu's story.

"There was, however, one in the group who was different," Zacharu continued.

"This one was dressed the same as the rest of the group, yet he carried himself much differently, and when he talked, his voice was gentle. Regardless of this, he was with these other menacing creatures, so I did not trust him.

"He told me he and his soldiers were searching for a valuable gem, an amulet. He explained that it was vital that they find this stone, and asked if I had any knowledge of it.

"Of course I did not. My people and I live in complete darkness. What use would we have with an amulet such as he was searching for?

"I explained to him that I had never heard of such a thing, but he did not believe me. He said they received word that some creatures were living in a dark, remote cave that had possession of the missing gem. He asked me to take him to my people, so he might put forth the same questions to them as he had to me. He was confident that someone would know the whereabouts of this amulet.

"In my heart of hearts, I knew not to trust this creature who demanded these answers that, like you, I did not have. I told him the only thing I could think of, the one thing that I hoped would dissuade him from searching for my people."

He paused…

"I told him I had been travelling for a long time, many moons, and I no longer knew where my home was.

"When I said this, he became angry and ordered his soldiers

to take me back to the castle. As soon as he'd given the order, one of the soldiers rode his horse forward and scooped me up, laying me across the very powerful and muscular creature's back. Before I had time to react, we were running with the wind as we headed to the castle."

Zacharu stopped talking for a few moments while the man remained silent in his container, patiently waiting to see if Zacharu was going to continue.

"Not long after my arrival here I was brought before Nivri. He immediately began asking me questions about the amulet. I have no knowledge of any amulet, and have told him this many times, but I don't think he believes me. I have asked him to set me free, so I might enjoy the freedom to explore the surrounding valleys and countryside, but he refuses, saying only that his work with me is not yet finished.

"Since that day long ago when I first found the beauty and warmth of the sun, I have never seen the creature who ordered my capture again.

"If there is one thing you must know, know that evil lives in this castle," Zacharu whispered. "I have not personally experienced it, but there have been a few visitors who have, and the stories are not pretty.

"Also know that Nivri can be very persistent when he wants something, and he will not stop until he gets it. I am not quite sure why he keeps me here, but because of what I know of the evil things that are here in the castle, I will not question it. I know better than to argue with him. As I said, I am treated fairly, and that, for now, I can live with.

"Instead of sitting in a cell, wasting away, I am given menial chores to do around the castle, such as cleaning, errands, and miscellaneous things. Sometimes, having that kind of freedom can get one into trouble, however, as I have found out," Zacharu said quietly with a slight chuckle.

"What kind of trouble?" the prisoner asked, his complete attention focused on the story coming from the unseen creature in the other container.

After a slight hesitation, Zacharu continued. "A few days ago, I was cleaning some of the guest rooms in the upper levels of the castle. Before I knew it, I was on my last room, looking forward to the afternoon meal. This was the way it was… we would be allowed to eat once our chores had been completed for the day.

"While I was making the bed, I noticed something white as it drifted off the covers when I moved them. It fell to the floor on the other side of the bed. Curious, I walked around the bed to see what it was."

When Zacharu fell silent, the man prompted him with, "What was it?"

"It was a note from a sorcerer who goes by the name of Scurio. He lives in another castle some distance away from here. Apparently, one of his favorite dragons disappeared quite a while ago, and Scurio is offering a reward for the dragon's safe return… Eighty-thousand gold pieces."

"A dragon!" the man whispered, not hearing the last part of Zacharu's statement about the reward.

"Yes, quite an offer for such an animal," Zacharu said. After a moment of silence, Zacharu asked, "Are you alright, Sir?"

"I've heard many, many stories about dragons for many, many moons, but I've never heard a story about an actual, modern day dragon! I thought they were a thing of the past!" the prisoner whispered with excitement in his voice. His children, like most children, loved dragon stories most of all. Oh, how he wished they were here to hear this!

NINE

The two prisoners continued talking for quite a while, sharing tales of how they came to be where they now found themselves. As they did, the man learned many things from this mysterious creature.

Zacharu told him what he knew about Scurio and the missing dragon. As Zacharu talked, the man closed his eyes again, and soon he forgot he was chained to a post inside a makeshift prison cell. Instead, he felt as though he was living in the time and world that Zacharu spoke of…

"Long ago," Zacharu narrated quietly, "before the time which is known as the here and now, dragons filled the skies over the mountains and the surrounding valleys. For centuries, these massive and powerful creatures were wild, unharnessed, and untamed. Soon, however, some of them became domesticated and had owners. These dragons were permitted to fly freely in order to hunt or exercise.

"Surprisingly, the feral and domestic dragons got along well, for the most part. They had their occasional squabbles, as did all creatures, yet when they hunted, they did not hunt each other. Instead, they would hunt larger forest and valley creatures that, at the time, were plentiful. Their prey consisted of forest lions, mountain bears, and other large creatures.

"Some of these dragons came from a long line of dragons that were both honored and revered. Tales of these beasts were passed down from generation to generation, telling why they were so special.

"One of the most powerful dragons ever known was Anthonon, an alpha male who lived for hundreds of years. His immensely muscular body and expansive wingspan could be seen frequently canvassing the countryside. He would fly here and there as he searched for food to nourish his body, which provided increasing layers to his muscles and strength to his wings. He also traveled the skies in an endless and tireless search for a mate, a female who would be a lifelong companion.

"It was imperative for him to find the right mate to carry on his family line. This task could not go to just any female... oh no. It had to go to the right one, a very special one. She would have to be cunning enough to survive in a world of many, many dragons, strong enough to fight any creature as necessary, and gentle enough to love the many smaller creatures of the world.

"Anthonon searched for many years for this perfect mate, which was quite an undertaking. Dragons of long ago were plentiful, but many of them were males, and females were few and far between.

"Anthonon continued to search for his perfect mate, day in and day out. Whether he was hunting or just out exercising his wings, it was always at the forefront of his mind that he was looking for her.

"Dragons back then were also very smart, yet were unable to communicate like humans and other smaller creatures. Instead, they learned and perfected a different form of communication by talking through their emotions, which is to say they learned to communicate silently, much like talking through thoughts."

"What?" the man interrupted inquisitively, surprised by this bit of information. "Are you telling me that dragons could communicate with each other through their minds? Without actually speaking?"

"Yes, that is how the story goes," Zacharu answered.

"Why do you ask?"

The man was suddenly lost in his own thoughts, unable to believe what he had just heard.

Dragons of long ago communicated through thoughts?

How could this be?

The man shook his head silently, then said, "I'm sorry,

Zacharu. Please go on."

Zacharu cleared his throat, took a deep breath, and continued with his intriguing story.

"One day, Anthonon was exploring a deep, wide ravine after a long day of hunting. His stomach was full and his muscles taut.

"While trying to find a place to rest, he found an entrance to a shallow cave and decided it looked like a good place to take a nap before he continued making his way back to the mountain range he called home. It wasn't long after he'd settled down in his new resting-place that he sensed the presence of another creature somewhere outside the cave.

"A dragon's eyesight is incredibly good… much better than any other creature's. Not wanting to give himself away to the mysterious creature he knew was very near, Anthonon barely moved. If it was another dragon and it was within eyesight of where he was resting, Anthonon knew the creature would easily see him.

"He barely lifted his massive head and kept his eyes focused on the nearby ravine in front of him. He lay quietly, watching the nearby rocks, and soon saw a dark shadow from a flying beast circling somewhere above where he lay.

"In the mountains and valleys Anthonon called home, he was feared and respected because of his large size and girth. As soon as he knew this creature outside of the cave was another dragon, he changed positions and took a defensive stance. This was not because he was a violent dragon who always looked for a fight or a chance to prove his stature among the other dragons… it was quite the opposite. Anthonon knew he was powerful and respected, and he was not afraid to defend what was his. He was also a kind dragon and did not like conflict unless he was left with no other choice.

"Regardless of this, he did not like the position he now found himself in… with another dragon circling the ravine above him, he was trapped in a shallow cave with nowhere to go. As he realized this, his defenses kicked in and he thoughtlessly prepared to stand his ground.

"He remained frozen where he was in hopes that the other creature would go away so he could continue his nap. His hopes were dashed when the uninvited beast soon landed on the rocks in front of the cave.

"Anthonon sized up this new creature in the blink of a firebug. It was a dragon indeed, smaller than he, but still large enough to inflict damage if a battle were to ensue.

"As the new dragon's large feet touched down on the rocks before him, the expression on its face was one of obvious surprise. Although it had not expected to see another dragon here, the visiting creature remained calm as it looked at Anthonon with respectful curiosity.

"Anthonon remained motionless and examined this creature that was interrupting his much-needed nap, unsure of what he should do. Should he just turn his back to the visitor and curl up into a dragonball, making it loud and clear that he was unaffected by the new dragon's presence? Or should he remain as he was, strong and unmoved, letting the visitor know with his body language alone that this was his napping place first and he would not give it up?

"Because he was an older dragon who had traveled many places, he'd had the opportunity to see many creatures like himself during the course of his lifetime. Dragons came in various colors and sizes. While some were large and menacing, others were very small and innocent. He knew very well, however, perhaps more-so than most, that looks could be deceiving.

"This particular dragon standing before Anthonon was one of the larger dragons; this much was immediately evident. Beyond that, however, Anthonon was surprised to admit there was little else he could perceive about this new creature, which was odd. Usually he could sense the type of personality that other dragons, and other creatures for that matter, had, and whether they had good intentions or otherwise. This dragon proved to be very different though… much different, in fact, than he'd first thought (as he would soon find out). He gave the newcomer a quick once-over and surprisingly, was unable to tell one way or the other just what kind of personality it had.

"The visiting dragon was aware it was being sized up and watched Anthonon silently. It remained still for a moment, but soon it bowed down and lowered its head in a submissive and respectful gesture. Anthonon watched as the visitor silently acknowledged that it was the lesser of the two beings. As Anthonon relaxed a bit and accepted the visiting dragon's gesture, the newcomer suddenly began to communicate with him. This brought with it the most surprising thing of all, and Anthonon chided himself for not figuring out this most important fact from the second he laid eyes on this new creature…

"The whole time he was inspecting this new dragon, he had no idea that it was a female."

TEN

"Female?" the man asked quietly, surprised at where the story was going.

"Yes," Zacharu answered back quietly, glad to keep the interest of the castle's newest guest. Zacharu loved telling stories and it was nice having someone around who was willing to listen. He saw many creatures as he performed his duties in the castle, but they rarely talked to him. As he talked to this stranger, he found he enjoyed the companionship the human offered. Rare times like this helped take his mind off of his family and friends back in the cave.

He missed his family a lot, and it felt like it had been many moons since he'd last seen them. Sometimes he dreamed of the day when he would be released from this castle and returned to his brothers and sisters, his parents, and his friends. For now, however, it was a daily priority to do as he was told, whatever was expected of him, without complaint. He did not cause trouble now, and had not the entire length of his stay here. He was confident that, when the powers-that-be who lived higher up somewhere in the castle were ready, he would be freed. For now, however, he would resume telling his story.

"Anthonon was a beautiful dragon to look at. His body was covered with hundreds of callused, thick scales whose color was quite eye-catching, as blood red as they could be. He was one of the largest dragons that has ever existed.

"His wings were enormous, and when they were fully extended in flight, they seemed to go on forever, as wide as the widest ocean. The skin covering these wings was very thick, and the dark trails of many arteries and veins could be seen as they coursed through the wing structure. These arteries provided much-needed blood from the heart to the wingtips.

"At the center of each wing was a high point where one white, curved, incredibly sharp claw grew. These were used primarily to both catch and eat prey, but they were also used during battle.

"At the other end of his large, muscular body was the dragon's tail. This appendage was covered with scales and thick with muscle, save for one bone, which ran all the way through the tail to the tip. The most important part of the tail lay at the end. Shaped like a large arrowhead, the tip was thick with pointed ends, and was used as a deadly weapon during combat.

"During physical altercations, dragons used their tails frequently. They would whip them around fast and hard as they tried to do the most damage to their opponents. In some cases, one lone, mighty swing could cause their opponents to fly through the air, oftentimes to their deaths. In others, the weapon of muscle would decapitate the enemy, which was most unfortunate for the opponent. In most cases, the result was much the same.

"Margaris, the female dragon who happened upon Anthonon that day in the ravine, was different in almost every way from her male counterpart.

"Light blue in color, her smaller body was also covered in scales, but this is where the similarity between them ended. At a glance, these scales appeared to be just one color, but in the sunlight they would also shimmer with a tint of green. The colors changed much like how a sea pearl shines in the sun after being removed from a salty oyster, and this pearly look to her scales was consistent on her entire body, not just on her backside.

"Her wings were somewhat similar to Anthonon's when it came to the veins and arteries, but because she was a smaller dragon, they also reflected this size difference. It was unnoticeable during flight, however, for she could fly just as fast and hard as Anthonon. They have been seen many times cavorting through the skies as she put him to the test.

"Her tail was similar in that it had an arrow-headed tip to it, but it was much narrower than and not as thick as Anthonon's tail tip. This difference was consistent between male and female dragons."

Zacharu paused for a moment.

"What happened when Margaris surprised Anthonon in the cave?" the man asked, anxious to hear the rest of the story.

"Ah, yes," Zacharu continued. "That is just where I was going to pick up the story…

"Anthonon watched the visitor in silent surprise as he realized she was a female. He then looked more carefully at her and admonished himself for not having realized her gender sooner. After he knew that she was in fact a female dragon, everything else seemed to fit, right down to the size of her tail.

"Size alone would not necessarily dictate a dragon's gender, and neither did its color. More often, it was the same with dragons as it was with most other species… the color of the offspring are a direct result of some myriad of color combinations from the parents.

"As Anthonon began to communicate with Margaris, he soon found himself mesmerized by the pearly, blue-green color of her scales. Looking at his own plain, single-colored red scales on his hind legs, he wondered what her parents must have looked like to create such beauty in one creature.

"Time passed, and it did not take long for Anthonon to admit he had found his dragon-mate. She possessed every quality he wanted in a mate and future mother of his dragonlets. They had many great conversations together and spent hours and hours every day soaring high and low through the nearby valleys and mountain ranges.

"Anthonon came from a long line of strong and powerful dragons, and, as he got to know Margaris better, he soon discovered that her family shared equally important, yet different traits. Her bloodline was one of love and nurturing, and her family line was kind and gentle, not large and overpowering like his. Anthonon recognized early on that this would be an important quality for the survival of the next generation of dragons.

"The pair of dragons became inseparable, and soon, rumors were heard in the hills and valleys both far and wide that the strongest male and the gentlest female were expecting a dragonlet! Creatures everywhere anxiously awaited its arrival. Days turned into weeks, and weeks turned into months, until one day, Margaris bore one single, fragile, white egg deep in the mountain forest.

"Word quickly spread with whispered news of the egg's birth and soon the forest was buzzing with excitement. The hatching of the much awaited dragonlet was just days away!

"After hardening for a few days, the proud parents waited patiently as the egg began to twitch ever so slightly. Eventually, the movements of the unhatched baby dragon became stronger and more frequent, and before long, muffled sounds could be heard coming from the small, white sphere.

"Anthonon and Margaris watched in amazement as a small crack began to appear along one side of the egg. The birth prison that held their offspring continued to twitch slightly, and, as it did, the crack began to grow longer and wider. Soon, other cracks branched off the first, and before they knew it, a small hole appeared on one side of the egg.

"The parents watched in anxious anticipation. Although they hadn't spoken about the birth of their dragonlet, they knew they could not help the young one during its exhausting task. The ways of dragons could be cruel at times, and the birth of a hatchling was no exception. Many generations of dragons had gone through this very same chore, and it was unspoken, yet well known, that this event was a life or death ordeal. It was understood, without discussion or argument, that if a dragon could not survive its own birth, it was not worthy of life.

"As the dragonlet continued struggling to free itself from the egg, the parents, as well as some of the other forest creatures who watched the event, could see occasional glimpses of the youngster. They watched as the small horn on the baby's nose occasionally pried at the hole it had created in the side of the egg.

"After a while, the baby dragon's efforts became less and less, and soon its struggles stopped completely. A silence fell across the forest and between the parents as they patiently waited in hopes that the baby would survive the difficult ordeal.

"As the birthing clock ticked, they soon heard the hatchling as it made more muffled sounds. When she heard this, Margaris quickly tried to communicate to her dragonlet through her thoughts. She encouraged it to be strong and continue working at the opening in the egg. She told her baby that she and Anthonon were waiting for it when it finally broke free.

"After a period of quiet silence, the dragonlet resumed the difficult task of hatching, and, within a few minutes, the baby dragon finally pushed its nose most of the way through the hole it had created! When she saw this, Margaris lowered her upper body so she could be closer to the egg, where she gently licked her baby's nose. As soon as the young one felt its mother's gentle touch, it began squealing with excitement. The egg rocked erratically as it continued struggling to break free from its white prison. With one final burst of energy, the baby pushed with all its might at the interior of the shell, and with a sudden crack, the top half of the egg flew back and landed a few feet away in the grass.

"Anthonon and Margaris began to glow with a happiness only new parents could understand. As the dragonlet sat before them, exhausted and nestled in the remaining bottom half of the egg, one large tear rolled down Margaris' cheek and landed with a *plink* on one of the dragonlet's front feet.

"The baby dragon blinked a few times as it tried to focus on its new surroundings, then turned its attention to the place on its foot where the teardrop landed. It looked at the shattered circle of wetness and cocked its head as if trying to make out exactly what it was looking at. After deciding the teardrop held little interest, the dragonlet raised its eyes and looked around. It quickly located the two larger dragons, where they stood only a step away. The dragonlet looked up at these creatures that were much larger than it in confusion, but it didn't take long for the youngster to realize they were the mother and father who created it.

"With a quiet squeal of happiness, the dragonlet joined them in their circle of love."

ELEVEN

As silence filled the room, the man smiled and encouraged Zacharu to continue with his story.

"There's not much left of the story to tell," Zacharu said quietly. He then paused while his thought gathered.

"Anthonon and Margaris remained busy for years raising their first dragonlet, which was a son. They had other dragonlets over the years, each one special in its own way. None, however, was quite like their firstborn, whom they named Gruffod. Something about this dragon was very special, and even almost odd. Anthonon and Margaris sensed this, yet did not understand exactly what the difference was.

"Gruffod was a beautiful dragon, purple in color, which was a colorful combination from both his mother and father. As he continued to grow, his parents began to see one of the visual differences that Gruffod had over his siblings, which was the color of his scales. Some of his them had the pearly look to them like those of his mother, yet they were subtly different. Sometimes these pearly scales also had a red tint to them, but at other times the tint was blue. This was virtually unheard of in all the history of dragons!" Zacharu took a moment to reflect on the miracle.

"What Margaris and Anthonon did not know was that somewhere in a castle, far, far away, someone with strange and magical powers had received word of the birth of their special dragonlet. This was a sorcerer named Lotor.

"Many years ago, Lotor had gone to see a mundunugu named Sinopa, which was something he had done frequently in the past when he felt the need for a seer's insight.

"One such time, he went to visit Sinopa and was told to watch for a special creature of power, one who was born from both strength and gentleness. For years, Lotor lived in his castle, patiently waiting for the arrival of this special creature, unsure of what it was or where it would be born.

"Because of his power, Lotor had many spies who lived in many places, from the deepest parts of the forests to the depths of the ocean. As time went on, word got back to him about the hatching of a special dragon. This dragon, rumors said, was the product of one of the strongest and most powerful male dragons that ever lived, and one of the most gentle and loving female dragons. When he heard this, Lotor knew in his heart of hearts that this creature was the one he had been waiting for.

"It takes many years for a dragon to reach full size, and as time went on, Anthonon and Margaris realized Gruffod was not growing as quickly as his siblings. The fact that he was the oldest dragonlet had no bearing at all on his size, and before long, he was the smallest dragon in their family. His scales were still beautiful in color, but they were simply smaller than those of other dragons.

"Gruffod's appetite was also smaller than all the other dragons and he did not eat as much. He wasn't unhealthy, however, so the other dragons soon became accustomed to his size. They never thought any more about it.

"After a time, Anthonon and Margaris learned some very disturbing news... there was a powerful sorcerer who was searching for them. This sorcerer was Lotor, and his spies were painstakingly searching for their firstborn son. Margaris and Anthonon knew these spies would not stop until they found what they were looking for."

"Hold on a minute," the man said, interrupting Zacharu.

"Why would Lotor be searching for Gruffod? If he was just a miniature dragon, for whatever reason, why would he be of interest to a powerful sorcerer?"

"You really don't know?" Zacharu asked, surprised the man even asked.

"No," the man answered. "I've only heard stories of dragons

and have never seen one. I never really expected I would ever see one, for that matter. I wasn't sure if the stories I'd heard were just that, stories made up by someone with an active imagination, or if they were real and the dragons of yesterday were gone forever…"

"Oh, no, they are not gone, not by a long shot," Zacharu said candidly. "Dragons are absolutely still alive and real, albeit there are fewer today than there used to be. There is a reason for that, however, which I will explain shortly. First, let me answer your other question.

"I've explained that Gruffod was a special dragon, and there are reasons for that.

"One reason is because of both of his parents… that is, the bloodline in his ancestry. To be born from strength and gentleness, power and fragility, is rare. To have all of those qualities wrapped up into one creature is truly amazing.

"Second and more importantly, is what Gruffod was made of. I've explained that his color was interesting, and it absolutely was. The varieties of purple coloring in his scales were beautiful, but mixed with the pearly hues… that, my friend, made him one of the rarest dragons ever born.

"The combination of both of those qualities, the second more than the first, is what Lotor was searching for," Zacharu explained.

The man considered Zacharu's words but still didn't quite understand.

"But, why?" he asked.

Zacharu sighed. The man heard this and began to worry that the storyteller was getting frustrated with him. Without further hesitation, Zacharu continued.

"Why? Why, because Lotor was, and still is, one of the most powerful sorcerers in all of Euqinom. He knew if he could obtain some of Gruffod's scales, teeth, or claws, he would be able to create some very powerful magic indeed.

"Spells could actually be created by any body part from this miniature dragon, but the scales are what Lotor wanted more than anything. They, more than any other part, held the most power. Not surprisingly, power is an important thing to a sorcerer, especially one such as Lotor," Zacharu explained.

"So, Lotor wanted Gruffod's scales to concoct spells?" the man asked. "That shouldn't have been a problem for Gruffod, seeing how he had the strongest and most cunning parents around."

"True, but you don't know Lotor," Zacharu answered. "He is not one to want something and not get it, no matter what the cost."

"But," Zacharu paused, "There was one small advantage for Gruffod."

"What was that?" the human asked.

"Well, from what I've heard, if a sorcerer wants to use parts from a dragon, the spells created are more effective if they use dragon parts from a mature, full grown dragon. The older and larger the dragon, the more valuable its parts," Zacharu explained further.

"Okay, so Gruffod wasn't finished growing yet, so he wouldn't be of much use to Lotor," the man said, finally beginning to understand.

"You are both right and wrong," Zacharu answered. "Gruffod was indeed not fully grown, but because of his lineage, his body parts were important, just not as important as they would be when he was full grown. Lotor knew this. He also knew he could use parts of the little dragon to create the spells as he so wished, and that those spells would be much more powerful if he waited for a while and allowed Gruffod time to mature.

"Lotor lives far in the east, and he searched near and far for Gruffod. At the same time, however, another sorcerer heard the stories of a magical miniature dragon's birth, and he also began looking for the dragonlet. His name was Scurio, and he lives in the west, so the stories say.

"Both Scurio and Lotor have long been rivals, and I do not believe this fact will change over our lifetime. Lotor wants what's best for Lotor, from spells, to gold, to wild creatures for all parts of Euqinom. Scurio, on the other hand, wants best for all creatures he comes in contact with, and it wasn't long before Scurio sent out his messengers and creatures to look for this special, little dragon.

"When Anthonon and Margaris heard that both Scurio and Lotor were looking for their son, they decided to take a chance and give him to Scurio. They'd heard many stories about both sorcerers, and knew Gruffod would be in good hands if he lived with the kinder one. They also knew that the other choice would be a certain death sentence for their little one.

"Before they knew it, the time came for them to say goodbye to their dragonlet, who was still young but not as young and innocent as he appeared to be. As Gruffod followed the messengers on the way to his new home, he looked back at his parents with a long pause, and then slowly nodded to each one of his siblings. He reassured them he would only be gone for a while, and said they could come visit him in his new home soon.

"Gruffod's family silently watched as the little dragon turned and followed the messenger without another glance back. His family felt secure in their decision to send Gruffod away, believing it was in his best interest. They had no idea it would be the last time they would see him."

"What happened to him?" the man asked Zacharu, totally engrossed in the story.

"I'm not sure," the storyteller answered. "I've heard that Gruffod disappeared many moons ago and that Scurio, to this day, is still looking for him with every resource he has. I've also heard rumors that Lotor found the missing dragon and killed him. The stories say that Lotor, the all-powerful sorcerer that he is, needed Gruffod's scales and claws for many spells he wanted to create, and killing the dragon was a necessity.

"However, there are also rumors of another reason why Lotor would want the young dragon dead…" Zacharu said quietly, his voice fading into silence.

"What's that?" the man asked curiously, not understanding why any creature should be killed for its scales and claws alone. He loved all creatures, great and small, and was proud he had taught his children to do the same. They knew, above all else, that it was not right to kill any creature unless you were either defending yourself, or if you planned on consuming the creature in every way possible. The meat would be eaten, the hide would be dried and used for clothing, and the teeth or claws would be used for tools or weapons. Every possible resource from the creature would be used. It was not acceptable for any creature to be killed for minute body parts and the rest of it left for waste.

Zacharu remained silent with his thoughts for a few seconds before continuing. He was unsure of how much to tell this stranger, but felt as though it was something he must do.

"There are ancient ones who live deep in the mountains that believe Gruffod is the dragon born of a prophecy," Zacharu explained quietly.

"A prophecy?" the man asked.

"Yes, a prophecy which states that a dragon would be born to cleanse the world of evil. It would grow to be known everywhere, across every land, as a hero," Zacharu whispered.

Before the man could say anymore, Zacharu continued.

"It's late, and we must get some rest before tomorrow. You'll soon learn that one never knows what to expect here in the castle of darkness. Rest while you can, and hold onto the thought that tomorrow will be a new and better day," Zacharu added.

As he finished talking, the human could hear the mysterious creature shifting around in his own dark container as he settled down to sleep. He heard Zacharu's chain rattle once, then twice, as he got comfortable, but after that, all he heard was silence.

"Good night, Zacharu," the man whispered quietly.

"Good night," the unseen creature whispered back. The man shifted in his own container as he tried to make himself comfortable. After he made sure his chain was not underneath his legs, he lay down on his side with his head near the entrance to his container. With his arm curled beneath his head, he thought about the stories Zacharu had shared with him.

An evil sorcerer who lived in a mysterious castle… missing dragons, prophesied to cleanse the world of evil… his wife and his children, back in a time and place where he longed to return…

As he drifted off to sleep, his mind filled with the many thoughts from that day's events, and soon he began to dream.

In his dream, from some unknown point high off the ground, he found himself looking down at a land covered in darkness. Through the shadows, white fog swirled like a blanket over the land in patches. Some of these patches almost glowed in the cloud-scattered moonlight. Suddenly, from out of the corner of his eye, he caught movement.

A child emerged from the coverage of the nearby trees and headed into the swirling mist. As it walked through the fog, it turned its head from side to side as if looking for something.

He watched as a cloud suddenly blew across the face of the moon, which darkened the land and made it difficult to see what the child was doing. As the youngster continued in its search, oblivious to the eyes that watched from above, the moon peeked out once again from behind the cloud. As it did, the man could now make out the long hair that gently cascaded down the child's back.

It was a young girl. As he watched, the man looked ahead of her. In the darkness, he could just make out the edge of a cliff that dropped off abruptly, a short distance in front of her. It appeared to border a deep, dark ravine of blackness.

Not realizing he was dreaming, he tried to call out to the child, to warn her, to tell her to watch where she was walking! Surely she couldn't see the edge of the cliff which was shrouded by the ghostly fog!

From where he lay inside of his dark container, the man knew nothing about his voice, which was not really a voice at all. In his dream there was no sound, and his thoughts were just that… his thoughts.

His eyes twitched behind closed lids as he continued trying to reach out to the girl, to get her attention, to prevent her from falling into the pit of blackness. If she did, she would certainly die! But no matter how hard he tried, his voice remained silent and without sound. The innocent girl continued walking closer and closer to the edge of the cliff… to the edge of her life.

As the man watched, helpless and frustrated, with no way of stopping her, the girl abruptly stopped mere inches from the edge of the ravine. She appeared to be listening to something only she could hear. She cocked her head slightly before she carefully peered over the edge of the rocky cliff.

The man could not hear anything. Once he realized she was not going to walk off the edge of the world to an unfortunate death, he peered down through the darkness into the ravine, curious about what had gotten her attention. The moon suddenly seemed brighter, and all thoughts of anything else left the man as he began to make out the shape of something a short distance down the wall of the ravine. He struggled to focus as he strained his dream eyes to decipher the shadows. Soon, he began to see some sort of a barren tree that jutted off the side of the rocky wall. As his eyes focused even more on the tree, he began to see another shape, something he had not expected to see. Hanging from one of the thick, leafless branches of the tree was an object. Soon, his eyes were able to make out that it was a cage with many bars, and was large and almost oval-shaped. It was held suspended from the tree by a long, thick chain, which secured it to one of the large, lower tree branches.

The girl stood looking at the cage as if in a trance. Curious, the man wondered why the cage was there, hanging from a dead tree in a dark ravine.

When a breeze blew across the land below, the fog swirled once again, and the man suddenly realized that the cage was not empty. There appeared to be something there that completely filled it, but the darkness filling the ravine made it difficult to tell what it was.

He turned his attention back to the young girl. He was unable to see her face, but she appeared to be interested in the object in the cage as well.

A stronger gust of wind quietly made its way across the land. It blew the girl's hair out from behind her back, which made it look like invisible hands were holding her dark locks parallel to the ground. She stood motionless as the fog swirled around her, her shadow a dark silhouette against the white mist. The wind died down, but the girl stood still as she continued to look over the edge of the ravine. The man again looked back at the cage, wondering why it still held the girl's attention. The cage remained still and lifeless where it was, suspended in mid-air. Suddenly, he saw something move inside it. A creature was being held captive within the oval prison. In his dream state, the man was surprised the cage held a live creature, but what surprised him even more was the size of the creature within the cage. The prison was much too small for the creature, and he was sure it barely had room to breathe.

Without warning, a pair of glowing, blue-green eyes looked

up at the girl where she still stood at the edge of the cliff. The creature's gaze lingered on her for a few seconds when the man heard a voice whisper in the darkness.

"You must help me," it said sadly.

The man looked from the creature to the girl, but was unable to tell which one, if either, was doing the talking.

"Help you how?" a shy, feminine voice asked in return. The man turned his eyes towards the girl as he tried to see her face, but it was covered mostly by shadows. He looked skyward… passing clouds blocked much of the light from the moon.

He turned his attention again to the girl. He could not see her face, yet, somehow, he was able to see her mouth.

It was not moving.

"You must come to my prison and free me," the first voice said pleadingly.

No matter how hard he tried, the man could not make out where the voice was coming from.

"Free me," the voice continued, "before it is too late."

"Too late for what?" the girl asked.

"Too late for anything… and everything," the voice answered.

Without warning, the swirling fog thickened and quickly filled the entire area below him, completely covering the girl, the cliff, and the cage. In a matter of seconds, everything was helplessly buried in a sea of white.

Silence followed, and in the flash of a firebug, the man slept more deeply than he had in many moons.

TWELVE

The man was awakened abruptly when he heard a loud clanking noise close to his head. Startled from his deep sleep, he sat up quickly and opened his eyes. Surrounded by darkness, he struggled to remember where he was, and sighed when he realized he was still being held prisoner. The clanking continued and was soon accompanied by growling. The man scooted back away from the closed door, curious about what was going on beyond it. After a moment or two, he soon heard a key as it finally turned in a lock.

Click.

At the same time he realized it was the lock on his own container door, the door to his cell of darkness opened. As the light from the room entered the bleak confines of his new home, the man put his hand up to shield his eyes. Only now did he realize just how well they had adjusted to the blackness within. As he struggled against instinct to open them as they winced before the invading light, he found himself wishing for the cool darkness once again.

"Human, come here," a familiar voice greeted him with authority.

The man could not see who or what the figure was that stood just outside of his opened container door, but he knew by his voice that it was his old friend, Orob. Only Orob spoke to him in such a loving way, in a way that almost made his heart beat faster…

Of course, this was not a good thing. When Orob came to

193

see him, unless he was bringing food, it meant they were about to embark on yet another journey to an unknown place, which meant, very likely, that they would end up seeing Nivri.

"Human!" the voice said, angrily this time. "Come with me NOW!"

Although the only light from outside his container came from a few dimly lit torches, the prisoner still squinted as he lowered his hand from his eyes. He was able to see a shape before him now, but he would have to give his eyes more time to adjust before he could make it out clearly. Without a word, he scooted towards the opened door on his backside.

As he got to the edge, Orob spoke again. "Stop!"

The man, now at the entrance to the container, did as he was instructed.

"Give me your foot," the guard ordered. Again, the man did as he was told, and brought his chained foot to the opening of the container. As he did, the creature knelt down in front of him, grabbed his foot roughly, and then turned the shackle which held the chain in order to see the keyhole.

By this time, the man's eyes had adjusted to the light, and he could see that the creature was indeed Orob. He watched the guard as he tried to unlock the shackle, and got a chilling feeling that something was wrong with him… Orob just wasn't acting the way he had so many times in the past.

"Hello, Orob," the man said as he tried to maintain a friendly attitude with his creature.

Orob obviously had things on his mind, and he worked at unlocking the shackle in silence. Once it was removed, Orob glanced at the prisoner, but remained eerily silent. The guard stood back up and motioned for the prisoner to follow him.

Through the dark, gloomy passageways, the man followed Orob until they finally came to an unfamiliar door. The guard opened it and motioned for the prisoner to go through.

As he stepped through the doorway, he instantly recognized the room. They were back in the same room where he'd had his other meetings with Nivri. Was that earlier today? Or was it yesterday? The man had no way of knowing what day it was anymore, so he decided to think of the time he was here as "earlier"… it was easier this way.

Orob again led him to the chair where Nivri was seated, waiting for them. The sorcerer wasn't watching them as they walked towards him, but when the man stopped before him, Nivri looked up.

"So, human, we meet again," Nivri said calmly, but looks could be deceiving. The man trusted nothing about this creature.

"Hello, Nivri," the man answered back quietly. Nervous about seeing the sorcerer again, the prisoner did not see the wooden club as it was swung behind him. In an instant, the club made contact with the back of his legs. The man cried out in pain and surprise as he crumpled to the marble floor.

He had no idea what had just happened! With a look of confusion written all over his face, he turned with a painful grimace to see what had hit him.

Orob stood over him with a club in his hand. His eyes blazed with anger.

"Do not speak to the Master unless he asks you a question!" Orob said through clenched teeth as he glanced from the man, to Nivri, then back to the man. As the prisoner lay on the floor, rubbing the back of his right leg, he grew even more suspicious of the way Orob was acting. Was it fear he saw in the familiar creature's eyes when he glanced at Nivri?

The prisoner remained where he lay on the cool tiles, afraid to move. He waited for instructions from either Nivri or Orob.

"Get up," Nivri said, still seated in his chair. The sorcerer looked at Orob and motioned for the creature to take his place on the side of the room. Orob did as he was instructed without a single word.

The man struggled to stand up for a moment, but soon brought himself, against his aching body's dismay, to rise before Nivri. He remained still and quiet as he waited for whatever would come next.

"Human," Nivri began again, "have you had time to consider the things we talked about yesterday?"

"Yes."

"Goooood," Nivri cooed with a small smile. The creature stood up and began walking in a wide circle around the prisoner.

195

The man did his best to keep his eyes focused on the chair... he did not want to show his nervousness. He was a fast learner, and couldn't help but try to steel himself against another possible blow from behind.

"Very well, then. Since you have thought about our earlier conversation, you certainly must know what kinds of questions I'm going to ask you, should you not?" Nivri asked. He circled the man in a slow, wide arc around the man.

"Ask your questions," the man answered through clenched teeth. He didn't like playing games and was quickly becoming angry that this creature was toying with him.

"Very well," the sorcerer said, stopping in front of him.

"What are the powers that you have in your family?" Nivri asked without emotion.

Without hesitation the man answered him.

"I know of no powers."

As he said this, the prisoner physically prepared himself, as best as he could, for a possible blow, but, surprisingly, none came. Instead, Nivri took a few steps toward him until he was face to face with his prisoner.

"Human," he whispered angrily, no longer trying to hide his emotion. "I will ask you one more time where you get your powers from, and what they are."

The man remained perfectly still and maintained eye contact with Nivri. He had nothing to hide and would not say anything different, no matter what this creature said or did to him.

"You do not understand me, human, so do NOT even try," Nivri continued. "If you do not tell me what I require of you, you will not like the consequences!" With that, Nivri stepped back and began to walk around the man once again as he waited for his answer.

"Nivri, I give you my word that I do not know of any powers in my family. Even if there were any, I do not know where they would come from," the man explained. He struggled to hide his frustration at the sorcerer's questions.

Nivri stopped walking and turned to look at the prisoner. The man was not surprised to see that the sorcerer's eyes were again beginning to glow.

"Very well," Nivri growled in anger.

"You leave me no choice, human, just as I knew you wouldn't! I have already sent a messenger back to your home to look for your family, and he was instructed to bring me any and all of your family members. Do you think having them here with you will help you to remember, you foolish man?"

As he asked this, Nivri smiled evilly.

"What? You know how to get back to my family?" the man asked.

As the prisoner took a step towards Nivri, movement from the side of the room caught his attention. Orob had taken a protective step towards both of them as he quickly drew an arrow and strung it in his bow. The arrow was now pointed directly at the prisoner.

"Nivri, I lie to you not! I know nothing of these powers! Please leave my family alone! They have done nothing to you!" the man pleaded.

Nivri threw his head back and laughed heartily before saying, "Human, I knew what your answer would be long before you answered. Do not underestimate my powers!" With a wave at Orob, Nivri said, "Take him back to his cell of darkness."

"Yes, My Lord," Orob said as he suddenly appeared at the man's side.

"Nivri, please, leave my family alone," the man yelled again. As the words left his mouth, he found himself crumpled to the ground once again after being struck by Orob's club.

Orob looked at him angrily and said, "Get up! Now!"

The man did as instructed, taking a bit longer than he previously had. Orob seemingly held nothing back when swinging at him this last time, the man thought. As he struggled to get to his feet, the man looked at Nivri silently, but this time held his tongue. The creature had gone back to his seat and was now sitting down as if he did not have a bother in the world.

As the man turned to follow Orob back to his container, he glanced back at Nivri... the sorcerer was smirking at him.

Thirteen

The man followed Orob back through the castle passageways in total silence. Had he done something to offend the guard? He could ask him what was wrong, but he knew the creature would likely not answer him. The entire time he'd known the guard, the man had rarely heard him talk. Orob was just not a talkative kind of guy.

They walked in silence through one of the long, dank passageways when Orob suddenly stopped and grabbed the man by his shirt, pushing him roughly against the cold stone wall.

"What...?" the man started, but Orob interrupted him.

"Shh," Orob said quietly. "I want to tell you something very quickly, and I must make it look like I am reprimanding you in order to do so.

"You must understand that I did what I had to do back in Nivri's throne room. He is an evil, cold creature, and I knew I would be punished if I did not do as was expected of me.

"I believe you are a decent creature, human, and if I had a choice, I would bring you no harm. Do you understand this?"

The man looked at Orob as he explained his actions.

"Yes," he answered quietly.

"Good," Orob said.

As he said this, he slightly cocked his head to the side.

The prisoner listened and could also hear what Orob heard... footsteps approaching them in the passageway in the direction they were heading.

Orob maintained a firm grasp on the man's shirt as he lifted

198

him away from the wall, only to roughly push him back up against it once again.

"Do not do that again or I will not hesitate to club you as I did before, prisoner!" Orob yelled at the man angrily. "You test my patience! Now get moving!"

As Orob pushed him forcefully back into the passageway, the prisoner lowered his head in submission. He walked in front of Orob now, head down, as they headed back toward the container room. As the approaching footsteps got closer, he allowed himself to look up briefly at the creature approaching them, both to see who it was, and to watch where he was going. As his eyes finally fell upon the approaching creature, he could see that it was the same kind of creature that stood guard outside of Nivri's room.

The man saw the bear-creature motion to Orob, who then said gruffly, "Stop there, human." The man did as he was told and kept his head down. He looked nonchalantly at the floor while straining his ears to hear their conversation.

"Aseret would like to see you in her chamber when you finish with him," the guard said as he looked at the human in disgust. The man could not see this, but the tone of the creature's voice left no room for doubt about how it felt about him.

"I will go to her as soon as I lock him up," Orob answered.

"Would you like me to do it for you?" the guard asked with a hint of sarcasm.

Orob considered the offer for a moment, and then said, "No, I will do it. It will only take a few minutes."

"Very well," the guard said before turning and walking away.

"Move on," Orob said to the man, nudging him with his club.

The man began walking again in silence, making sure to keep his eyes on the floor. Although he could still hear the bear-creature walking away in the opposite direction, he couldn't shake the feeling that they were still being watched.

Soon, they were back in the container room. Without waiting for instructions, the man immediately sat down in his container and handed the shackle to Orob. With the hint of a smile, Orob silently secured it around the prisoner's ankle. After a brief glance at the guard, the man silently crawled back into his container. Once he was inside, Orob closed the door and manipulated the lock until it latched, then the guard walked away without another word.

"He's probably going to go see Aseret," the man thought.

Now that he was back in his container, the prisoner began to relax a bit. As he stretched out, he noticed right away that both of his legs were quite sore. Although Orob had apologized, the man thought the creature had done quite a number on him with the club. He would not be surprised if he ended up being bruised and sore for weeks. After what Zacharu had told him earlier about the dark stories he'd heard, the man considered himself lucky to be only bruised.

He sat silently in his container as he rubbed his legs and thought about what Nivri had said. There was no doubt in his mind that Nivri was an evil creature, which only added to his worry about his family.

He could feel himself getting upset again, because he didn't know the answers Nivri was looking for. What frustrated him more than anything was wondering how he could get the psychotic sorcerer to understand this, especially now that Nivri had threatened to go after the man's family! As both a husband and father, it was his job to take care of his family. He hated the fact that now, when they needed his protection most, he was unable to fulfill his role and responsibility.

He'd never felt so helpless in his life.

"Human?" his unseen friend in the other container called out to him quietly. "Are you okay?"

The man did not hear Zacharu as he spoke.

Instead, his mind and soul were consumed with anger at his current situation. The more he thought about it, the more thoughts of escaping raced through his mind. The next time Orob came to take him somewhere, would he be able to grab his club and strike him with it? The more he thought about this, however, the less it sounded like a good idea. The main reason for this was because he still had the issue of his body not being able to do the things it used to, due to his lack of food. He was definitely not physically capable to handle much of any kind of encounter with any creature.

Mentally, he was ready for any encounter, but physically?

He would be a fool to challenge the guard.

Another thought suddenly occurred to him.

Even if he did manage to escape, where would he go? Although he had been a prisoner here for quite a while, he was still very unfamiliar with the castle's many dark and winding passageways. Also, his chances were very high that he'd run into any of the number of castle inhabitants as he tried to make his escape.

No… he would have to think of something else. As he racked his brain for other ideas, Zacharu called out to him once again.

"Human?"

"Yes?" the man answered the creature quietly.

"Are you okay?" Zacharu asked worriedly. The man explained to him what had happened as Zacharu listened quietly. When the man finished with his story, neither of them felt like saying much. A short time later, they again heard footsteps approaching. A few seconds after they heard footsteps enter the room, they both heard a loud clank. It sounded as if something heavy was set down, probably on top of a container. This was followed by the rattling of keys, which sounded different than it had earlier that morning.

The man sat quietly as he waited to see if his container door would open. It didn't.

He tried to look through the holes in the lower part of his door to see if their visitor was standing outside of his container. He couldn't see anything other than the floor immediately outside of his new prison.

Keys rattled again before he heard the familiar sound of a lock being unlocked, followed by a faint squeak as a door was opened. It was definitely not his container that was being opened. Since he had not heard of or talked to any other creatures in this room besides Zacharu, he assumed it was Zacharu's container.

The man listened quietly as he heard the scraping noise again. He wondered what was happening when he heard the door squeak again, a little louder this time, followed by keys rattling and a lock being locked. Zacharu remained silent, and the man began to worry about his new friend. He would wait quietly for the footsteps to recede before asking if he was okay.

The footsteps, however, didn't go away. The man heard one footstep, then two. The keys rattled once again, closer this time. Without trying to look through the small holes in the bottom of his container door, the man knew without a doubt that some creature now stood outside of his container. He heard the familiar unlocking sound, then a *clank, clank* as the lock was removed. The prisoner sat back with nervous anticipation as the door to his own cell swung open with a slight squeak, much like the other door had opened just a few seconds before. The man heard the scraping noise repeat again. He couldn't help but squint his eyes closed as the light once again invaded his darkness. He scooted back away from the door, nervous about what he could not yet see. When he finally realized what was happening, he felt somewhat foolish.

Orob stood outside the opened container door. He knelt down and placed a metal tray just inside the container for the prisoner. As he did, the guard looked at him, holding his gaze for a split second before he closed the container door without a word.

The man got a glimpse of what was on the tray... a slice of bread, a pia bottle, and a pia bowl which held something red. Before he could tell what the item was, the door to his container closed and he was again surrounded by darkness.

Now that he knew food was somewhere in front of him, the man's stomach began to grumble with hunger. He scooted towards the tray as he felt carefully for it. Food was so scarce that he didn't want to spill whatever Orob had brought him.

His hand found the tray, then the pia bottle, and finally, the bowl. Curious about what the concave container held, he picked it up and gingerly felt inside it. Berries.

He picked one up and tasted it. Once he determined it was a red fruit, he guessed it might be chickleberries. As the small berry exploded with cool juice over his tongue, he smiled in the darkness.

Chickleberries they were.

Although his stomach continued to growl with hunger, he savored every bite of his meal, right down to the last drop of water in his pia bottle. When he finished, he waited a short time before trying to talk to Zacharu again. He wanted to give his new friend ample time to enjoy his own meal. The man sat quietly in his cell with a smile and an almost full tummy. Like so often in the past, his thoughts soon turned to his wife and children. More than anything, he wanted no harm to come to them. He began to dwell on the fact that he had no way to protect them. His mind raced as he tried to think of a possible story to tell Nivri, but, once again, he knew better. There was much more to Nivri than he had seen, and the man knew it. His better judgment told him he would be worse off if he began to lie to the evil creature.

Footsteps approached them once again, bringing him out of his thoughts, but this time it was different. This time there was more than one visitor. As the man listened, he soon heard the familiar sound of the keys in the lock on his container. Again he scooted back as the door opened and light poured into his cell.

The prisoner squinted as he watched a hand drop down into his container. It grabbed the empty tray that sat by the cell door and removed it. As the man waited for his eyes to adjust to the light in the room, a familiar voice spoke to him.

"Come here, human," Orob ordered.

Not wanting to anger the guard, the man did as he was instructed. He scooted to the entrance of his container, and, with squinting eyes, glanced to his right. There, at the container next to his, was another creature much like Orob. It had unlocked the container door and was in the process of opening it.

The man squinted back at Orob, and, as he expected, the guard motioned for the man's foot once again. The prisoner complied silently.

As Orob worked at unlocking the shackle, the man looked over at the other opened container, curious about the creature he had been talking to.

The Orob-like creature that stood before the second opened container kneeled down, probably to unshackle the other prisoner. The door to his neighbor's container opened to the left just like his did, and it now blocked the man's view of the other mysterious prisoner. Once Orob had freed the man's foot from the shackle, he stood up and said, "Follow me."

The prisoner stood up with a grimace, his legs aching from his earlier punishment. As he did, he looked to the right and was now able to see his neighbor. He gazed curiously at the odd creature and gave it a small smile. In return, the creature nodded slightly. The man believed, without a doubt, that this mysterious creature was Zacharu. Looking at him, however, the man had no idea what kind of creature he was. The man had never seen anything like him before. His neighbor was dark in color, almost as dark as the underside of a mountain mushroom. His eyes also appeared to be dark, probably brown, in color.

As the man watched silently, the other Orob-like creature told Zacharu to stand up. When Zacharu complied, the man could now make out a short, stubby tail on the creature's backside. He figured Zacharu to be about the same height as his daughter… somewhere between the height of a small child and an adult.

"Human!" Orob called out to the prisoner. With one last quick smile at Zacharu, the man turned away and followed Orob.

In silence, they made their way through the castle's passageways, but this time, there were four of them walking instead of two. The man wondered if they were all going back to see Nivri.

Their path eventually took them into a different passageway than they'd taken earlier. Step after step, the various tunnels led them downward into the lower levels of the castle. After a few minutes, the tunnels soon became familiar…

They were heading back to the prison cells that the man had called home for most of his stay here. When they got to the prison level, the man watched as Zacharu was led to the cell just to the right of his old cell. Zacharu stopped outside of the cell, turned to his guard and asked, "Why must I go here?"

Both guards looked at Zacharu, then at the man, then back at Zacharu.

"The Master instructed us to bring you both here. We do as we are told," Orob said.

As Zacharu looked at them, the other guard took his club and pushed Zacharu towards the opened cell.

"I want to know what I've done to deserve this." Zacharu said defiantly as he pushed his weight against the club. "I have done nothing wrong!"

Orob took a few steps towards Zacharu. When he stood mere

inches from his face, he hissed, "What you've done or have not done is not my concern, creature! The Master instructed us to bring you here and lock you up! We do as we are told and do not ask senseless questions.

"Now, if you know what's good for you, you will do as you are instructed. You know as well as we do that there are many forms of punishment here in the castle. You have not personally seen many of them, but it can be arranged…" Orob growled. He waited a moment to let his point sink in.

"Oh, yes it can," the other guard added with a smirk on his face and an evil twinkle in his eye. Zacharu looked at the guards. It was obvious he didn't want to give up so easily but he was smart enough to know it was futile to resist. He definitely did not want to encounter any of the forms of punishment that were used in the castle. Yes, he'd heard stories, and some of them were downright cruel.

Without another word, Zacharu lowered his head in defeat as he entered the cell. He immediately sat down on the floor and refused to look at either of the guards. Once the man knew there would be no trouble, he looked at Orob, who nodded towards the man's earlier cell. Without a word, the prisoner made his way back into his former home. As he walked by Zacharu's cell, he looked at his friend, but Zacharu was looking away. After the man stepped into his old cell, both cell doors were locked. Worried about Zacharu, he watched quietly as Orob and his accomplice headed back towards the tunnel, which led them to the higher points of the castle.

Once they were gone, Zacharu began talking again. "I do not understand what I've done to make them put me here," he said quietly, frustration and anger dripped from his voice.

"Zacharu, I don't think we're supposed to understand any of it, just like the questions Nivri has been asking me. Hopefully, one of these days, we'll have a better understanding of it all," the man said to his friend.

After a few minutes of quiet silence, the man heard a noise.

He looked towards his cell door, but saw nothing in the room outside of his cell. He stood up and walked towards the door and placed his hands around the metal bars. He looked to the right and to the left, but nothing seemed out of sorts.

He waited for the sound again, but it did not repeat itself.

"My friend, are you okay?" the man asked, worried about Zacharu.

"I will be… I have to be," Zacharu replied, his tone one of a defeated man.

"I wish we could find some way to get out of here," the man said, "but even if there were, it would take a miracle to actually pull it off. I don't know about you, but I just don't have the energy and strength I used to. It would be nice if we could get an upgrade from our deluxe meals of stale bread and water."

"I agree," Zacharu said. "It would be nice if we could find a way out of here, but in all my time in this castle, I've never heard of anyone or anything escaping… ever. I have heard rumors of some ill-fated attempts, but as far as I know, no creature has ever been successful.

"Besides that, if we were to escape, neither of us would have any way of knowing how to get back to our families. I think I would rather stay here and have a chance of being set free than take a chance at trying to escape.

"Escape would bring two options… being hunted down and killed, or managing to actually get away, only to have no idea where to go once I'm free.

"No, I think I would rather stay and wait to be freed. That way, I will be returned to my family, and I will not have to worry about being hunted by Nivri's happy henchmen forevermore," Zacharu said with a sigh.

"But Zacharu, what if you are never released? What if this castle is the home of your future, no matter what you thought or wanted? Could you live with that? Could you live with knowing you had a chance to escape and let it slip by you, only to live out the rest of your days here, under Nivri's beck and call?" the man asked quietly. Silence answered his question.

As the man turned to sit back down in his cell, he heard the same sound he'd heard earlier that he had been unable to identify. He turned and looked once again at the area outside of his cell. Still he saw nothing.

Silence.

The man listened patiently as his heart thumped in his chest. Zacharu remained silent, and sure enough, the man soon heard the sound again.

It was coming from one of the cells to his right. He peered around the bars towards the sound as far as he could, which wasn't saying much. He could still see nothing.

As he wondered what it was and where it was coming from, he vaguely remembered the sound he'd heard when he'd been in the cell... hadn't that been just yesterday? It was right before he'd been taken to the blackest confines of the metal square.

He'd been lying on his bed after waking up from a nap when he heard... what? Scraping sounds? The man closed his eyes as he tried to remember the events from the previous day, but it was as if his mind was filled with a dense fog. He knew there was a memory there, somewhere, but it just wouldn't come to him. Like a dragon soaring high above the clouds on a summer day, the memory seemed beyond his reach.

He closed his eyes. After a few minutes of intense concentration, he began to remember the previous day in pieces. He could vaguely see himself lying on his bed, waking up after eating the stew Orob had brought him. Stew... oh, yes, and how scrumptious it had been! After so few decent meals, it was absolutely delicious, and he had thoroughly enjoyed every drop!

Just thinking about it again made his mouth water! At the time, the stew had tasted fine... it never occurred to him that there could be anything wrong with it, but afterwards, he'd had his doubts. He remembered now how he had questioned the possibility that he could have been drugged.

Aha!

His eyes shot open!

Like a torch being lit in his mind, he suddenly remembered the sound. Something being moved around in one of the other cells... a pia bowl!

Yes, he remembered now! There had been another creature down here with him!

He remembered he had tried to talk to his neighbor but had heard only silence. Whatever creature had been in that other cell, it must have been very timid. Could it still be there now? Could that be what was making the sounds he'd heard and was now hearing again?

"Hello?" the man called out quietly.

"Yes?" Zacharu answered.

"No, Zacharu, not you. I think there's something or someone else down here with us," the man explained quietly. "Hang on a minute, okay?"

"Okay," Zacharu answered.

"Hello?" the man called out again.

Still, only silence followed his question. After a moment, however, the man heard another muffled scuffling sound. He was certain now that there was something in one of the cells to his right. As he wondered how else he could get this mysterious creature to communicate, he remembered something else that had happened the last time he'd been here.

Something had talked to him, telling him what? He searched his mind and this time the answer was almost immediate… the voice had told him that he was the key, and that it needed his help…

As he remembered how odd it had felt, he chuckled. How could he, in his current situation, try to help some other creature? Especially when he had no idea where it was? Or what it was, for that matter. He'd heard stories of evil creatures during his lifetime that will cry for help, and when some gullible, trusting soul goes to help them, they wind up dead, or dinner. A creature well known for this exact characteristic was the valley mantis. The man knew he definitely did not want to fall prey to any creature such as that. To be ripped limb from limb and eaten at a leisurely pace…

He cringed at the thought.

Oh yes, evil creatures were certainly out there, and sometimes they found you when you least expected it. His mind raced as he tried to think of something, anything, to tell this mysterious creature to get it to talk to him when something surprising happened. The creature communicated with him… without his help.

"Human, are you ready, now, to help me?" the mysterious creature asked, catching the man completely off guard.

"How can I help you when I myself am locked up?" the man asked the creature quietly. "I am merely a prisoner in a place I know not how to escape from."

As the prisoner waited for an answer from the unseen creature, Zacharu said, "Human, I didn't ask you to help me. What are you talking about?"

The man frowned for a moment before he answered his friend.

"Wait, Zacharu. Let me talk to this creature. Maybe we can all work together to find a way out of here…"

"What?" Zacharu asked in a confused tone. "Talk to the creature? Talk to what creature?"

Although he could not see Zacharu's prison cell, he turned to look for his friend.

"Are you saying you don't hear the whole conversation I'm having with this creature?" the man asked Zacharu quietly, almost afraid to hear his answer.

"I hear nothing but you mumbling to yourself in a broken conversation," Zacharu answered. "Did they bring you wine with your deluxe meal of stale bread?" he asked jokingly.

The man sat down on the cold, stone floor, the reality of his situation hitting him like a hard, thick pia seed. He knew he was talking to the same creature, whatever it was in the cell to his right, just as he'd done the previous day, but it had not occurred to him until this moment that Zacharu could not hear the conversation. It was possible that the other creature was only speaking loud enough for the man to hear, but after what Zacharu just said, he didn't think that was the case.

What he found more difficult to believe, which began to make total sense to him now, was not IF the creature was communicating with him. No, the "if" part was not the issue. The issue was something much different than he would have ever imagined. Everything was definitely beginning to make sense to him now, and he couldn't believe he hadn't realized it before. The real issue before him was not the question of whether or not the creature was communicating with him…

The question was how?

The man smiled briefly. He knew in his heart of hearts that this was the answer to the question he'd been having, but had been unable to figure out. It was the answer to the question of how the creature had been communicating with him.

Like the sun coming out from behind a dark rain cloud, the answer was suddenly there, and now it was almost blinding him. The creature had been communicating to him mentally, not verbally. It had been talking to him inside of his head.

FOURTEEN

Once he realized what was happening, all of Nivri's questions began to make sense. The powers the evil creature wanted to know could very well be what he had just discovered about himself… the fact that he could hear something that not everyone else could hear. At first, he found it difficult to believe, but the evidence was right there in front of him, though not literally. Zacharu was in the cell to his left, this he knew for a fact. The man could hear this other mysterious creature quite well, so either it was talking out loud, in which case Zacharu would have heard at least some of what it was saying, or it was talking to him in his head, which Zacharu could not hear. Zacharu had accused the man of having a conversation with himself, so the only plausible explanation would be that he was hearing this creature in his head… or perhaps he was losing his head altogether.

"Human?" the creature said. The prisoner decided to try to communicate silently back to it.

"What is your name, creature?" the man questioned in his mind.

"My name is not important just yet, human. In time…" the mental voice replied back to him. "First, I must know if you are willing to help me."

"Help you how?" the man asked excitedly, knowing now that he was communicating with this creature solely through his thoughts. This was almost insane!

"We must work together to get out of here, before it's too late," the voice replied.

"Wait a minute," the man said, then turned his attention back to Zacharu.

"Zacharu, do you hear me talking to the creature still?" the man asked. The prisoner was almost afraid that Zacharu would think he'd totally lost his mind.

"Maybe you should lie down?" Zacharu answered, which didn't surprise the man. "We've had a rough couple of days, and I think you definitely need your rest."

"I think you may be right," the man agreed. He wanted Zacharu to believe he was resting so he could continue the conversation with the mystery voice.

"Creature," the man called out to the being once again in his mind, "what did you mean when you said we must work together before it's too late?"

As the man waited for the creature to answer his question, he felt the slightly familiar sensation in his head that he'd felt the day before. The buzzing sound became very intense and he closed his eyes. It did not cause him pain, but it was definitely one of the strangest sensations he'd ever felt. He put his hands over his eyes as if trying to block the feeling from being in his head. It didn't help, and, just as suddenly as it came, it was gone.

"Can I trust you, human?" the creature asked.

"Yes," the man said, hoping the creature would believe him.

"Do you have a family?" the creature implored.

"Yes, a wife and three children," the man answered in his mind. He wondered where these questions were leading.

"You love your family," the creature added, as if it were telling the man how he felt instead of asking.

"Yes, very much," the man answered. After a few seconds, he added, "Why do you ask?"

"You have a family and you love them… and I take it you would like to see them again?" the creature asked, ignoring his question.

"Yes, why do you ask?" the man yelled out loud. He didn't realize he'd done it until he heard the sound of his voice echoing through the passageways of the prison.

"Human?" Zacharu asked, now quite concerned.

The man sighed, took a deep breath, and said, "Yes, Zacharu,

I'm okay. Bear with me a few minutes… please?"

"Should we call Orob back down? I'm worried about you," Zacharu said.

"No! I'm all right! Trust me on this," the man answered quickly. His concentration turned back to the other creature.

"Please tell me what you want from me?" the man pleaded. "Yes, I love my family. Yes, I miss my family. Yes, I want to see them again, as soon as possible!

"What does that have to do with helping you?"

The creature was silent for a moment, then said, "I have been a prisoner here at this castle longer than you have, human. I, like you, was taken from my family against my will and was brought here, for no apparent reason, but that has changed over time. I've come to understand why I am here, and I believe that you, too, are coming to and understanding as to why you are here.

"I am a creature that has been sought after, not for what I have, but for what I will have. I come from a strong and proud bloodline, which I cannot alter.

"Once I have matured, many things will change. The good of the kingdom, the light of our world… yes, many things will change. If things happen as I've heard they may, evil could rule our world, and life as we know it will not be the same.

"I've done what I can to stop my body from growing, but being held captive has weakened me, both mentally and physically. Because of this, when my body begins to mature again, I will not be strong enough to stop it. I need to escape from here before that happens. It is imperative that I escape from here before that happens," the mysterious voice explained.

"I don't understand how I can help you," the man said.

"You must help me escape, before I begin to grow again. If you fail, the world as we know it may quickly be ruled by one of the most evil beings that has ever lived," the creature said.

The man stood up and grabbed the metal bars of his cell tightly in his hands as he struggled to believe he was communicating with the creature he suspected he was.

"Creature, what is your name?" the man asked excitedly.

After a moment of silence, the creature answered quietly.

"I am the one they call… 'Little Draco'."

Jeane

One

"Why aren't the children home yet?" Jeane thought as she sat next to Andar at the table. The meal she had prepared for their dinner was cold and completely forgotten.

Her worry and apprehension grew more with each passing second as slowly as an alia snail. If something happened to the children, she didn't know what she would do. The pain and sadness from the loss of her husband last year were still too fresh in both her heart and her mind.

"Jeane, do you have any idea where they might be?" Andar asked.

He knew his cousin well enough to know that, although her face showed almost no emotion, she was undoubtedly worried by the fact that the children had not returned home by the time she had asked them to.

Jeane tried to think back to the previous evening, when Nicho came to her saying they were going hunting. What did he say they would be hunting for?

A mountain bear? No... that was not it. A cave rat? No, that was not it either. She shook her head, unable to remember this one part of their conversation.

Andar rested a warm, gentle hand on her arm. He could see the obvious torment in her eyes as she tried to remember the events from the previous evening. He watched as her expression changed and a smile lit across her face.

"What is it?" Andar asked.

"They were going to go hunting for valley pheasants!" Jeane

217

said with sudden, clear recollection.

He startled her as he immediately stood up and grabbed his coat.

"Where are you going?" she asked.

"To round up some villagers for a search party. It hasn't been dark very long… if we get out there now with our torches, the children will be sure to see us and find their way back if they're lost," Andar said, glad to be doing something besides sitting and waiting. He would go find some people to help him search for the children, and soon they would all be home safe and warm.

It had occurred to Andar for a brief moment that, perhaps, Jeane was over-reacting, but after the past year, he couldn't really blame her.

"I'll go over and talk to Diam's parents and see if they've heard from them," Jeane said.

"The children could be there, but I doubt it. They know how hard the last year has been without their father, and I'm sure the last thing they would do is forget to come home on time," Andar replied. He could tell Jeane was trying her best to hide the fact that she was becoming more worried by the second. As he walked towards the door, he turned back and looked at his cousin.

"Good thinking, Cousin, but try not to worry. We'll find them," he said confidently.

Jeane watched as Andar opened the door. Her brow was furrowed a cloud of worry that darkened her soul.

"I'll meet you back here shortly," he said as he walked outside, closing the door quietly behind him.

Jeane nodded, and then donned her own coat before heading over to Diam's house. When she got there, she found just what she'd been expecting… no children. She explained the situation to Diam's parents and Nivek, Diam's father, immediately went out to find Andar and join the search party. Diam's mother, Ennyl, picked up Jole and followed Jeane back to her house.

Shortly after they got there, villagers began arriving to help with the search, and many had their own torches. In a short period of time, they were soon combing the nearby valley, calling out to the missing youngsters. After a few hours of unsuccessful calling and searching, they returned to the village.

That night, Andar stayed with Jeane and held her as she cried. Everyone in the village knew that Jeane and her family had shed many, many tears over the past year. This night proved to be no different, and neither of the cousins slept much.

At the first sign of dawn the following morning, they both got up and prepared to resume their search. With the assistance of daylight and a little bit of rest the previous night, they each packed a bag with necessities and headed out.

As they made their way through the village, they could see some of the other villagers were also preparing to help in the search. Jeane's heart swelled at the sight, remembering not so long ago when these same people, her extended family of sorts, went through the same motions to help her search for her missing husband.

"Why don't we search the woods today, Jeane?" Andar suggested. "We didn't find much last night in the valley, and I'm sure many of the other villagers will search there again today."

Jeane nodded her head just as they reached Diam's house. She wanted to make doubly sure that the children were not here before venturing back out. Ennyl met them at the door and confirmed their suspicions... the children were still missing. Andar noticed that Ennyl and Nivek were packing as well.

"Where are you going?" he asked them curiously.

"We're going to go to Nana's village, to recruit more people for the search. I have a feeling we'll need all the help we can get," Ennyl explained.

"Do you think you'll return by nightfall?" Jeane asked her.

"It takes a half a day to get there and a half a day to return. After going around the village to recruit people, it's likely we won't be able to return tonight. We should be back by tomorrow evening at the latest."

Jeane hugged them both as she said goodbye.

"Travel safely," she said as a tear of worry slipped from the corner of her eye. It rolled partially down her cheek before she managed to wipe it off. No other words were necessary.

With that, Jeane and Andar headed into the nearby forest to search for the children as a knot that felt as big as a pia seed settled in the pit of Jeane's stomach.

219

TWO

Jeane and Andar made their way through the forest, looking for any signs of the children. Andar had spent many hours wandering through these woods during his lifetime and was very good at tracking many of the creatures who lived here. Jeane followed him, trusting both her cousin's knowledge and instincts.

They had been walking for a short time down one narrow path in particular when Andar's face broke out with a smile.

"Jeane, look at this!" he said excitedly. She joined him where he was kneeling in the leaves that littered the ground, evidently happy with his find.

"Flowers," he said quietly. He picked one up and handed it to her.

Looking at the forest floor around them, she could see a large pile of small, browning flowers that had been scattered close to a chickleberry bush. She bent down and picked up a handful of the crumpled, broken flowers, smelling them as she did so. They had a slight fragrance, but didn't offer much more to her sensitive nose.

As Andar knelt next to his cousin, she asked quietly, "Why would they feel they needed to have so many flowers?" Before he could answer, she added, "Berries."

Andar looked at her quizzically.

"Huh?" he asked.

"These must be the chickleberry bushes where they picked their berries for me," she explained.

220

They looked around the bush and could see a few bruised berries and wrinkled, partially dead chickleberry bush leaves on the ground at their feet.

"This is a good sign. Come on, we need to keep moving," said Andar.

Jeane agreed. They each picked a handful of berries for themselves to snack on before resuming their search. After a while, they decided to sit and rest for a few minutes. Andar walked over to a fallen tree and sat down on the trunk. Jeane joined him as she took her pia bottle out of her bag.

"Flowers," Jeane said, more to herself than to her cousin. She still couldn't understand why the children had picked them. More intriguing than that, however, was why had they felt the need to have so many?

They sat on the tree trunk for a few minutes, enjoying the break, when Andar suddenly jumped up and walked over to the nearby rock wall.

"What is it?" Jeane asked him as she put her bottle back in her bag.

As she joined him near the rocks, she could now see what he was looking at.

A stick was wedged in between two of the rocks in the wall. It was close to a large clump of moss that hung off the side of the wall. As she got closer, Jeane could clearly see that the stick had pieces of jagged moss hanging from it. At the same time they both understood what they were looking at.

Andar reached out, grabbed a clump of the moss, and pulled it towards the stick. As he did so, a hidden entrance to a cave was revealed.

"Andar," Jeane whispered, almost as though she was trying to keep a secret. "Do you think this is where they went?"

He nodded quietly as he propped the moss back away from the cave entrance with the stick, wedging it once again between the rocks. It appeared to hold for now. He then pulled his bag off of his back and set it on the ground. From it, he removed two torches and a set of rock sparkers.

They worked together to light the torches. Neither of them ever questioned the unspoken fact that they were going to continue

221

on into the cave. Once the torches flickered brightly with fire and their bags were back on their backs, Andar held his torch into the cave entrance to have a quick look around.

As soon as he saw the dirt and rock covered floor inside the cave entrance, he knew they were on the right track. The abundance of footprints seen here and there were a sure sign they were on the right track. As he looked closer, Andar could also see pieces of broken flowers.

As Jeane looked on from outside of the cave, she smiled. Now she understood why the children had had so many of the pieces of flora. They had learned well! She could only hope they continued to show them this. Andar climbed into the cave as Jeane followed close behind. Like the children earlier, they both had a small sword sheathed at their side. As she followed her cousin into the depths of the cave, Jeane made sure that she kept one hand on the handle of her weapon, ready for the unknown.

THREE

They walked quietly through the cave as they looked for other signs of the children. For a while, they followed the crumpled and browning flowers scattered here and there along the path, but, after a time, there were no more to be seen.

They found a small cavern and took one of the two tunnels that branched off of it. It soon led to a dead end. They returned back to the cavern and took the other tunnel. This one led to yet another cavern, and here they found another clue.

Jeane knelt down, picked it up, and looked at it for a moment before showing it to Andar. He took it from her and lifted it to his nose.

"An alia leaf," he said, and then added, "it smells like some kind of meat."

He held it out to Jeane for her to smell it as well. She nodded.

"It's good to know they brought food with them," she said, a little less worried.

They made their way deeper into the cave and soon found a beautiful, cooling waterfall. They decided to refill their pia bottles before continuing on. This done, they walked on in silence. Words between them were not necessary… they could both feel the urgent need to find the missing children.

Andar followed the footprints on the path as best he could, but sometimes he would lose them in the dusty and rocky floor. When that happened, he used pure instinct. Deeper in the cave, they found a larger cavern, which was littered with large rocks. After exploring, they soon found an opening in one of the walls that took them into a smaller cavern. Here, they split up as they looked for more clues.

Once again, it was Jeane who found something.

"Andar, come look at this!" she called out quietly. Andar joined her where she stood looking over a pile of rocks.

A skeleton lay in the dirt, surrounded by the rock enclosure.

Andar quickly climbed over the barrier. Careful not to step on it, he examined the odd remnants of the dry and lifeless body.

"What kind of creature is that, Andar?" Jeane asked him quietly. "It's definitely not human."

"I don't know," he answered as he shook his head. "I've never seen anything like this."

He poked and prodded around the creature for a few seconds before climbing back over the rocks. From the footprints he could see in the dirt near the skeleton, it appeared as though the children had been here as well. He pointed this out to Jeane and she nodded. Seeing nothing else of interest in the small cavern, they headed back through the crack between the rocks and continued on in their search.

Back in the larger cavern again, they separated as they made their way along the rock wall. Andar did his best to follow the footprints he saw here and there along the dusty tunnel.

At the far end of the cavern, they found another small opening that appeared to lead further into the cave. Not wanting to surprise anything that might be on the other side of the rock wall, they carefully looked around the corner. What they found, instead, was another clue. Andar immediately walked over and picked an object up out of the dust.

"One of my arrows," he said as he held it out for Jeane to see.

"When Micah came looking for weapons, I also gave him some arrows. This is definitely one of them." He tucked the arrow into his shirt and they continued on. As they turned the corner they nearly walked into a very ragged spider web that hung only partially from the ceiling. It was obvious that no creature called the broken gossamer home now. They skirted around the web silently, and soon found themselves inside one of the largest caverns yet.

"Stay alert," Andar whispered to Jeane as they made their

way through the spacious area. As he continued to watch for signs of the children, Andar realized he hadn't seen any of the scattered flowers for a while. He stopped and knelt down for a closer look at the dirt-covered floor, silently questioning whether or not they were still going in the right direction. In his heart, he felt they were, so he stood up and they continued on. After a short time, they found a few tunnels that branched off the cavern into the darkness. Without flowers or footsteps to guide them, they found themselves unsure of which one to take.

"Which way should we go?" Jeane asked her cousin. After a brief hesitation, he chose one of the middle passageways.

They walked through tunnel after tunnel, winding this way and that, as they looked for signs of the children. Before they knew it, they found themselves in another large cavern that looked somewhat familiar.

"Were we just here a little while ago?" she asked.

"I'm not sure, but it just might be," he answered. With a shrug, they continued on.

They re-entered the tunnels and walked on without finding much of anything, when their path suddenly opened up into a small room that held little else than a small, motionless body of water.

As they explored the area, it didn't take long for Andar to find what he was looking for. He knelt down and looked closely at what appeared to be a cornucopia of scattered shoeprints in the dirt.

As he examined them, he noticed something else he'd never seen before. There, mixed in the dirt with the many footprints, were quite a few unidentifiable, large, wavy lines.

"What is it?" Jeane asked quietly.

"It looks like some kind of snake tracks," Andar answered. He glanced up at Jeane, and she couldn't help but see the worried look on his face.

"Andar?" she asked as she waited for an explanation.

He stood up and sighed as he looked at his cousin. "I've seen many snake tracks in my day," he explained, "but I've never seen anything like these. The snake that made these had to be at least the length of three men. That's an incredibly large snake.

"If I hadn't seen these tracks myself, I don't think I would have ever believed that a snake this size was possible."

"Three men!" Jeane gasped. Andar watched as her eyes began to fill with tears.

"What if...?" she began, but before she could finish, Andar took her into his arms and gave her a tight hug of encouragement.

"Shhh, Jeane, don't think thoughts like that!" he admonished her. "Your children have been raised well by both the family and the entire village! You must not give up hope that they are alive and well. Until we find something that tells us otherwise, we must stay confident!"

Jeane hugged him back. Her love for her cousin swelled in her heart. He was a good man, and she would always be grateful to him for standing by her during times like these.

After pulling herself together, Jeane followed Andar over to the other side of the pond. The water was as still as glass. She looked down into it curiously, but could see nothing but her own reflection in the torchlight.

"Come on," Andar said quietly as he led the way back into another tunnel. "We need to keep moving." They walked on for a little while and soon found themselves inside of another large cavern.

"Look!" Andar exclaimed.

He knelt down and picked something up from the tunnel floor, then stood up and held it out for his cousin to see.

A single brown flower.

"It looks like they were dropping flowers again," he said quietly, seeing the trail of flowers leading off into the dark distance ahead of them.

"Why would they drop them for a while, and then stop, only to start dropping them again?" Jeane asked as she wondered what thoughts had been going through her children's heads.

"They definitely had a good idea to drop flowers in the beginning of the cave. If they're like most children, they probably forgot about dropping them after awhile," Andar suggested. He had no way of knowing just how close he was to the truth.

On and on they walked, and soon ended back in the tunnels on the other side of the large cavern. When their tunnel widened, they stopped, unable to believe what they now saw directly in front of them.

A large, dark, gaping hole took up most of the floor before them. As they looked around, they could see many footprints everywhere in the dirt around the black hole.

"The children were definitely here," Andar said quietly. He also thought he could make out telltale signs of the children having slept here the previous evening.

"Nicho?" Jeane called out quietly, afraid of being too loud. "Micah? Tonia?"

The only answer she received were the sounds of her voice echoing back at her from the darkness of the cave around them.

Looking across the room, she could see something in a heap by the far wall. Cautiously, she walked over to it. Could it be something the children had brought with them into the cave? Something they forgot along the way? She fervently hoped it was something that would tell her how or where her children were.

When she reached it, she was immediately disappointed.

It was not at all what she'd hoped it would be. It was another creature, and she couldn't tell if it was hurt or sleeping. She knelt down cautiously to get a closer look at it.

It appeared to be a fairly common cave snake, the kind that sometimes makes it out into the valley. She knew cave snakes were not deadly poisonous, but some of the species did have powerful sleeping venom. She found a large stick lying in the dirt near the snake. Carefully, she prodded the reptile, but because the snake had not stirred since she'd seen it, Jeane had the feeling that the small creature was no longer alive. After poking it with the stick for a few seconds, she got no reaction from it. In fact, the small serpent's skin no longer felt pliable.

It was undoubtedly dead.

She knelt down and carefully touched it. The snake's body was cold, unmoving, and as stiff as a rock. It had been dead for a while, but had not yet begun to decompose.

"Andar, come look at this," she called out to her cousin.

As she turned to look for him, she realized with a start that he was directly behind her.

"Oh!" she cried out, surprised. "I didn't hear you walk up

227

behind me."

She smiled sheepishly.

"It looked like you found something interesting, and I wanted to see what it was," Andar responded with a smile. When he realized what it was, however, the smile faded from his face.

Jeane had picked up the snake and stood up with it to show Andar. Its scaled body was very rigid. As they examined it, they couldn't help but notice the peaceful look on its face.

"I don't think it's been dead very long because it's still completely intact," she said. "I wonder how it died. There doesn't really look like there's anything wrong with it."

"Could be anything... maybe old age," Andar suggested as his attention was drawn back to the dark hole in the tunnel floor.

"The children were definitely here." Jeane gently laid the snake back down where she'd found it, and then turned to join her cousin. They stood very close to the black hole and held their torches over it. As they looked over the edge, something on a rock just inside the hole caught Andar's attention.

He silently handed Jeane his torch and lay down on his belly. Carefully, he reached over the edge of the pit and ran his hand along the rocks until he found what he was looking for. He grabbed the item and scooted back. He then stood up and held the item out for Jeane to see.

"Nicho!" Jeane called out.

She took the torn piece of clothing from her cousin's hand.

"This is from Nicho's shirt!" she said excitedly. She leaned further over the hole with her torch, looking for her oldest son. The hole was deeper than the torchlight could penetrate, however, and she was unable to see anything but darkness beyond the radius of light. She leaned back away from the abyss and lifted the piece of material to her nose. She inhaled deeply. Andar watched as a smile suddenly played across her lips.

"My Nicho," she whispered as tears once again welled up in her eyes.

Andar's smile grew.

He knew now, without a doubt, that they were on the right track. He pulled his bag off of his back and began to rummage through it.

"What are you doing?" Jeane asked as a tear slipped down her cheek.

"I believe they somehow lowered themselves down into the hole," he said as he stared into the darkness of the pit. "I'm going to rig up a line for us to follow them."

Jeane tucked the scrap from Nicho's shirt into her pocket, and then rummaged through her own bag. In a few seconds, she pulled out some dried chicken bird wrapped in an alia leaf. She unwrapped the meat and held part of it out to Andar.

"Let's eat something first, Andar. We don't know what we're going to find once we get down there, and we may not have a chance to eat again for a while," Jeane said.

Andar had found some tarza vines in his bag and was busy tying them together. He stopped and took the dried meat Jeane offered him.

"Good thinking," he said as he smiled at her. "We'll find them, Jeane, I know we will." His words of encouragement comforted her.

After eating their snack in silence, Andar asked Jeane to toss her torch down into the black hole.

When she looked at him quizzically, he chuckled. He could just imagine the thoughts that were going through her mind. Some of the village people had often thought he was a little odd, which was something he knew and accepted. If his cousin began to think the same thing, especially now, it could be a difficult situation, indeed. Just as he expected, she asked, "Why?"

"We don't know how deep this pit is, right?" he asked, and she nodded silently.

"Okay, so in order for me to make a decent line to get us down there, I have to know how much of it I need." He saw understanding creep into her eyes, but it didn't last long before her face was masked by another question.

"But what if it's too deep? Sure, we'll then know how deep it is, but then I've also lost my torch," Jeane rationalized.

"I have a few more in my bag," Andar said.

Jeane smiled at him… she should have known.

"I may be an oddity in the village, but you must remember, cousin, that I've done this kind of thing before. I know how to prepare for just this type of… excursion," Andar said quietly.

As Jeane's smile faded, she said, "Oddity or not, you are my cousin and I will always love you. The fact that I question some of the things you do is only because I want to learn, not because I doubt you."

She took a step towards him and gave him a hug.

"Thank you, Jeane. That means a lot," Andar said. As she smiled at him, Jeane tossed her torch down into the black pit.

Careful of where they stepped, they both watched as the stick of fire descended into the depths of darkness. Within a few seconds, it landed in the dirt at the bottom with a soft thud. They waited for the dust to settle around it, and once it did, they were surprised to see the flame still flickering. From above, they could just barely make out more footprints in the sand near the fallen torch. After making sure he had a long enough length of tarza vine, Andar asked Jeane to stand up. He then securely tied one end of the tarza vine around her waist before he helped her put her bag back on her back.

Speaking quietly, he said, "I'm going to lower you down into the pit. As I do, I want you to be very careful and try to watch the area below you. If you sense anything bad or unsafe at all, you yell up to me right away and I'll pull you back up."

Jeane nodded and he continued.

"Keep your sword out and ready. I don't know about you, but I sense something very evil in this part of the cave," Andar said.

"Yeah, I do too," Jeane agreed with a whisper. With a hesitant glance at her cousin, she grasped the tarza vine tightly in her left hand, then unsheathed her sword and held it in her right. After one final nervous look down into the pit below, she nodded at Andar. With a return nod, Andar slowly lowered Jeane down into the gloomy abyss.

FOUR

Once Jeane stood safely at the bottom of the pit, she quickly untied the tarza vine from around her waist. She pulled on it twice then watched as Andar pulled it back up to the top of the hole. While holding her sword out in front of her, Jeane quickly retrieved her torch from the dirt. The light grew as the torch regained its original glow. As she looked more closely at her surrounding area, she first noticed the many bones that were scattered here and there near the rocky walls. She wasn't sure what kind they were, but, then again, she wasn't sure she wanted to know. The one thing she was absolutely sure of, however, was that she did not want to find a body down here. She was immensely relieved there were none in sight… yet.

As she continued to look around, something in the dust a few steps away caught her eye. Curious, she walked over to it and bent down to get a closer look. She smiled. The children had definitely been here. In the dirt near one of the walls, she found some chickleberries. One or two were still whole, but most of them had been squashed. She set her torch down on a nearby rock and picked some up. They appeared to be only a day or two old.

Yes, the children had definitely been here.

"Jeane, I'm going to toss my torch down to you," Andar called down to her.

"Okay," she answered.

She stood back up and got as close to the wall as she could. Once he knew she was out of the way, Andar dropped the second lit torch into the pit. It landed in the dirt a few feet away from Jeane with another soft thud. After waiting a few seconds for the dust to clear again, Jeane set the berries down and quickly picked up Andar's torch. Then she watched patiently as he slowly made his way down into the pit.

When he reached bottom, he stepped into the dust near her. She handed him his torch then picked up the berries.

"Look at what I found, Andar. The children were here," she whispered with a smile as she held out the small handful of fruit for him to see.

Andar nodded and couldn't help but notice the glimmer of hope that now shone on Jeane's face. He undoubtedly felt it too, but he was more cautious. His thoughts drifted back to the odd tracks he had seen in the dusty tunnel above them.

Jeane tossed the smashed berries aside before picking up her own torch off the rock. They carefully inspected the area for other clues, finding only a conglomeration of footprints.

They looked at each other, knowing they now only had two options about which way to go. They could both go back up the vine and return to the upper level of the cave, or they could follow the only tunnel that branched off of the abyss.

Andar suggested they follow the tunnel and Jeane silently agreed. He took the lead as he whispered to her that they must be extremely careful.

They made their way through the tunnel as it wound this way and that, and along the way they found many more unidentifiable skeletons. Some were definitely small animals, mostly intact, but they also passed many places where single bones had been scattered haphazardly throughout the underground passageway. Jeane was relieved that they didn't find any fresh carcasses because the smell would be horrendous.

As they continued on, the tunnel itself was barely tall enough to accommodate them. They were lucky that, up to this point, they hadn't had too much trouble maneuvering through it.

The further they traveled, the more nervous Andar became. Some kind of snake had definitely made the tracks in the dirt above the pit, and by the size of them, the reptile was a big one. If they happened across this snake while down here, they could be in for some real trouble… especially if it was cranky. He knew most snakes were harmless, but just the sheer size of this serpent, harmless or not, made Andar very uncomfortable. If it was as large as he believed it was, it could have easily eaten the children and not left any trace, whatsoever.

He didn't want to upset his cousin, so he kept these thoughts to himself. Jeane definitely had enough heartache during the past year, and she didn't need anything more to worry about. For now, they would continue to search for the children until they had a reason not to. After a while, they began to hear an odd noise. Andar halted them as he listened, trying to determine what it was. His hand remained defensively on his sword.

"Stay alert," he whispered to Jeane once again. The unfamiliar pulsing sound was like nothing either of them had ever heard before.

Slowly they made their way through the tunnel as they continued to head towards the noise. Their path soon led them to a u-shaped corner, and as they walked through it, they were both surprised to see an array of colors shining on the tunnel wall in front of them.

They stopped for a moment and quietly watched the colors as they shimmered beautifully in the darkness.

"Where do you think that light is coming from?" Jeane asked Andar quietly.

"I don't know, but be ready for anything," Andar cautioned again as they slowly continued on.

When they reached the end of the tunnel, closer now to the source of the shimmering light, Andar peered cautiously around the corner. Seeing no evident danger, he stepped into another small cavern and cautiously approached the source of the vibrant colors.

Jeane followed close behind her cousin and gasped in surprise when she saw the source of the glowing light.

In the small, dusty cavern they saw five stones arranged in a less-than-perfect circle in the center of the floor. Each of the stones emitted a different colored aura… green, blue, purple, yellow and red. The noise they heard earlier was much louder now and appeared to be coming from these stones.

Jeane looked at Andar, bewildered. He looked back at her quietly for a moment, his mind spinning with questions.

Long ago he heard a tale, which he had always believed was just that – a tale.

It was an interesting story about a set of glowing stones, located deep in the heart of a mysterious cave. The story claimed that if these stones were used correctly, they would create a portal to a fantastic place, a mysterious entryway leading into another world! This world, the tale went on to say, was filled with much danger and evil. The most interesting part, to him at least, was that it existed in a land filled with dragons.

Common sense told him that this was just a story… one of the many tales told around one of the frequent village campfires. It was a story that was told as entertainment… not as a history lesson.

Andar sat down on one of the nearby rocks, unable to believe the possibility that the oddity before could be the magic portal from the story.

It was just a tale… or was it?

"Andar, what is it?" Jeane asked him quietly. She knew him well enough to know he had something important going through his mind. She had been almost afraid to ask, but silence had never been one of her fortes. When Andar appeared to not hear her, Jeane lightly touched his arm.

"What is it, Andar?" she asked him once again. He shook his head. As he brought himself out of his thoughts and memories, he looked at Jeane. He felt bad when he saw the look on her face, because her worry was now unmistakable.

"I'm okay, Jeane," he said, unsure of how to explain this to her.

She watched him silently. She knew there was something he wasn't telling her, but she respected him enough to give him time to get his thoughts together. After a moment, Andar continued.

"Do you remember the stories around the campfire we used to hear when we were children?" he asked her. She looked at him with an odd expression on her face. Her eyebrows furled slightly, in confusion, as she answered him.

"Yes, of course. Why do you ask?"

"Do you remember the one tale about the mysterious cave with the magical stones that were shaped into a magical circle? The stones that were hidden deep within a cave that no one could find… yet there supposedly was one?" he continued.

Remembering suddenly lit up Jeane's face as she smiled.

"Yes! Yes, I do remember, but…"

Her words faded away as she looked at Andar. The look of remembrance was replaced by seriousness in the flash of a firebug.

"Andar, this can't be!" she whispered in disbelief. "You can't seriously think this is THAT cave, can you?"

"What else could it be?" Andar asked her.

"Well…" Jeane started.

She fell silent when she realized she had nothing else to add to her argument. She had no other explanation for the stones that were glowing in the dirt right in front of them.

"The story I remember said something about, if you knew what to do with the stones, you could use them to go into another world," Andar said.

"Whoa, whoa, whoa," Jeane said.

She held up her hand in a stopping gesture and placed it firmly on his chest. It looked as though she was trying to quiet his pounding heart. She rolled her eyes at him.

"What are you talking about? Why would we want to know what to do with the stones, even if there really was another world?" she asked, her voice deadly serious. Andar grabbed Jeane's hand on his chest and squeezed it gently before stepping away from her.

"Look at this," he said as he walked closer to the stones.

Confused, Jeane followed him.

"Do you see that?" he asked as he pointed towards the dirty cavern floor near the glowing stones. He hadn't wanted to talk to her about this, but now felt as though he didn't have a choice. He had to somehow convince her that they had to do this.

"I see dirt, Andar," Jeane said in exasperation. "What does that have to do with the tales we used to hear?" Jeane asked, still confused.

Andar looked at his cousin seriously; ready now to share the thoughts that were coursing through his mind. "Jeane," he said, "The patterns in the dirt inside the circle of glowing lights are just like the ones I saw a while ago, in the upper cavern."

"I don't understand..." Jeane interrupted, but Andar quickly held a hand up and looked at her seriously.

"I know that, cousin, but listen to me for a moment as I try to explain it to you."

With a sigh of confusion, she nodded.

"I didn't want to tell you this because I don't want you to worry, but the fact is, you just may have cause to worry," Andar said.

"The pattern here in the dirt is just like the pattern we saw earlier, before we climbed down here," he said. He paused a moment before he continued. "We know the children were here, at least one of them was down here, because we found the smashed chickleberries, right?" he asked her.

She nodded yet remained silent.

"Okay, this is what I believe."

He took a deep breath before he continued.

"First of all, I believe the pattern was created by a snake. That, in and of itself, doesn't worry me, but the size of the snake does. It is common sense that a snake that large must eat, and we've seen for ourselves that this cave does not appear to have an abundant food supply."

"Andar," Jeane said, but he held his hand up once again, silencing her before she could continue her sentence.

"Jeane, I didn't want to give you reason to worry, but I think you need to consider the different options that we're looking at here. It's possible the children got into some kind of trouble with this snake, can you see that?"

As tears began to well in her eyes, Jeane nodded. This time she didn't try to interrupt him.

"I'm sorry, Jeane, but it's obvious to me that this large snake was in both the upper cavern and down here. Either the same snake, or many snakes."

He looked at her sadly before he continued. "We also believe that at least one of the children was down here. I firmly believe that if we follow whatever creature was down here, it just might lead to one or all of the children," Andar said.

As her silent tears continued, he wrapped his arms around her and embraced her in a tight hug. When he let her go, he said, "That's why we need to try to go to wherever these glowing stones will take us. Do you see that?"

"But what if the snake didn't go there, or what if the children never went there," she asked.

Andar knew she was having flashbacks to when her husband disappeared the previous year. "This is the decision that we are faced with, cousin. If there's a chance that the children are wherever this circle goes to, then we must go there.

"There is no other option," Andar said firmly.

After a few seconds of careful consideration, Jeane nodded her head as she wiped the wet tear trails from her face.

"We step into it together," she said to Andar, letting him know her terms.

"Absolutely," Andar said. "Let's do it."

He gently took Jeane's hand in his own as he led them toward the glowing stones. Neither of them were surprised when the humming noise became both higher pitched and louder.

Jeane held his hand tightly as they took another careful step toward the circle. With the next step, the pitch changed again, this time growing even louder and higher than before.

As they watched, horizontal lines gradually became visible in between the stones. The left half of each line took on the color of the stone that lay to its left. The right half of the line did the same, but instead took on the color of the stone that lay to its right. An invisible barrier divided these lines, which was the center-point of each line. With a tight squeeze of Andar's hand, Jeane nodded to her cousin. He glanced back at her, and without further hesitation, they both took the final step into the circle of stones. As they did, the lines separating the stones glowed with their dual colors as brilliantly as the sun shines in a cloudless, mid-day sky.

Still in unison, they each placed one foot into the circle. As their second foot crossed the barrier and came to rest in the dirt within the circle, a major change began to occur. The high-pitched noise created by the stones was suddenly deafening! The light created by the stones, which was already quite bright, suddenly became unbearable and almost blinding.

With Jeane's left hand held tightly in Andar's right, they both closed their eyes. They were both frightened, but knew it was too late to turn back. In their spare hands, they held onto their torches tightly, yet without much thought. While their eyes were closed, neither of them noticed when both torches suddenly darkened.

They didn't understand what was happening to them, but they knew without a doubt that they were experiencing something they never had before. The air around them suddenly became much colder, and as they helplessly transported to a place unknown, something else transported to the world they were leaving.

FIVE

"Hold onto me tight, Jeane," Andar yelled to his cousin, but it barely sounded like a whisper. She responded by squeezing his hand with hers as tightly as she could. As they traveled, the only things they knew were the intense light, the cool air surrounding them as it gently caressed their skin, and the incredible feeling of weightlessness.

A sudden blast of cold air rushed past them from somewhere ahead. As quickly as it appeared, it was gone, and they both shivered without being aware of it.

Before they knew it, their feet were once again on solid ground. Andar opened his eyes, relieved that the intensely bright light was gone. As he released his grasp on Jeane's hand, she opened her eyes as well.

"Where are we?" she whispered.

"I don't know," he answered quietly.

Once their eyes adjusted, they could see that they were inside some sort of enclosure that was built out of stones and mud. It was covered with a partial roof, and what was left of it appeared to be ready to fall in on itself. It also had a few windows, but little else.

As he glanced through one of the windows, Andar guessed it was the end of the day here, wherever 'here' may be. He smiled as he looked at the clouds on the horizon. They were just turning pink with an apparent sunset.

Looking around, he was disappointed to find no recent signs of life other than their own footprints in the dirt covered, dusty

239

floor. The enclosure appeared to be completely abandoned. When he looked behind them, Andar was surprised to see no evidence of whatever method of transportation brought them here.

"I think we should stay here for the night, cousin," Andar said.

"We can eat and rest ourselves, so that we will be better prepared for whatever tomorrow brings. The sun has almost finished its daily journey across the sky, and since we have no idea where we are…" He paused, looking at her. He knew she understood his reasoning behind wanting to rest for a while, but these were her children they were looking for. He, better than most, knew just how difficult this whole ordeal was for her. "I just think we should stay here for the night," he finished.

She lowered her head for a moment, and when she raised it, he could see where tears had again welled in her eyes.

He knew she was trying to be strong. "No woman should have to go through the things that she has gone through this past year," he thought angrily. He didn't want to upset her even more, so he consciously suppressed his anger.

Jeane nodded slightly, almost as if reading his thoughts.

"Okay," she said.

With that, they prepared for the long night ahead.

Six

Just like the previous morning, the cousins were up before the sunrise. After a long night of little sleep, the new day would undoubtedly be long and exhausting for both of them.

They sat quietly as they shared small portions of dried chickenbird meat and water. When they finished breakfast, they packed up what few things they had brought into this strange world.

As the sun began to rise in the east, they were on their way.

Jeane walked out the door first, with Andar close behind. Before he got to the door, however, his eyes were mysteriously drawn to the dirty floor in the far corner of the room. Something about it seemed strange. He took a few steps towards the corner and, as he got closer, he stopped, not happy with what he saw. There, in the dirt, were large, scattered swirls. It looked almost as though someone had used the upper part of a tree as they moved the branches this way and that, creating mysterious swirls in the dirt. It reminded him of the village children drawing in the dirt with sticks, laughing as they tried to see who could make the most zigzagging lines. Andar was sure, however, these lines were not drawn by a child. They looked eerily similar to the pattern he had seen in the cave. This one was similar to the one left by whatever creature lived in the abyss.

He shook his head in worry, and turned to follow Jeane.

He decided not to tell her about the swirls for the time being. He didn't want to add more to her worries. He did, however, make a mental note to remain on guard during their upcoming travels.

Andar stepped through the doorway into the cool morning air, and he was able to catch a quick glimpse of his cousin standing a few steps away before he had to squint in the new day's sunlight. He covered his eyes to shield them from the glare.

As they took a moment to enjoy the beautiful morning, they couldn't help but notice the white pillows of fluffiness that were innocently converging on the eastern horizon. The sunrise was beautiful, with pale hues of orange, pink, and yellow. It was going to be a beautiful day.

Andar smiled at Jeane and said, "Ready?"

"Yes," she answered, and without another word, they began walking in the direction of the sunrise. As they made their way, Andar was surprised at how dry and rocky the terrain was here compared to another forest that he knew very well… the Orneo Forest just outside of Uncava.

He had done much tracking and hunting in his days through the mountains and valley close to the village they called home. The ground they walked on here, however, was quite different from that of his homeland. In fact, it was much different than any type of landscape he had ever seen before.

The conditions here didn't appear to be ideal for much plant-life. Other than scattered cacti and some brown, leafless trees they began to pass, few green trees or bushes were visible anywhere around them or on the horizon.

He tossed a worried glanced back at Jeane. They were both glad they had rested the previous night. The enclosure they'd slept in had not been much to speak of, but it had provided at least some shelter. Although neither of them had slept well, Andar was grateful for whatever sleep they did manage to get. He guessed they would be thankful later on for what little rest they did get, especially after being subjected to the heat of the day that now lay in front of them.

They walked on and on without talking much as they tried to conserve their energy. Luckily, they had brought extra pia bottles with them, which they'd filled with fresh water from the stream in the cave. As the day wore on, they stopped frequently for breaks, only sipping at the precious liquid as they did so.

Andar continued to look for clues to the children as they walked eastward. Since he had not been able to find any signs, whatsoever, of the children's whereabouts, he fervently and silently hoped they were going in the right direction. They stopped for lunch, another quick snack of chickenbird meat, and continued on. Soon, the sun was at their backs as it slowly began its downward descent into the western sky. The sky above, which had been mostly clear and blue for the better part of the day, became littered with many small, white, puffy clouds. Although the air was still warm, Jeane and Andar were both thankful for the relief from the hot sun.

For a while, they were busy watching the ground in front of them as they walked wordlessly with their heads down. Neither paid much attention to the horizon. When Andar happened to glance up, however, he stopped abruptly, which immediately got Jeane's attention.

"What's wrong?" she asked. She wiped the sweat from her brow and looked at him curiously.

"Look," he said quietly.

She looked in the direction where he pointed and smiled. There, on the not-so-distant horizon, was a thin line of trees.

"Shade!" she said happily.

They both looked forward to an extended break from the relentlessly hot sun that had been bearing down on them from overhead, and walked on with a renewed briskness in their step towards the trees.

"Andar, I know you don't want me to worry, but you know that I will, regardless..." Jeane said seriously, striking up a conversation.

"Yes, Jeane, I know," he answered. He waited patiently for her to go on like he knew she would, like she usually did.

"Please talk to me," she said. She stopped suddenly and grabbed his arm.

He stopped and waited for her to continue, but she remained silent.

"Talk to you about...?" Andar asked, but he thought he had an idea about what she was asking. He had hoped she would wait a bit before she began with her questions. They needed time

243

to search more… it was too soon. Yes, he had known it was just a matter of time before she began to ask for answers to questions that he simply didn't have the answers to.

It appeared he wouldn't have the luxury of time. Jeane looked down at her feet for a few seconds before her gaze turned towards the horizon. After traveling the entire morning without any breeze at all, out of nowhere, a sudden gust of wind blew her long, brown, curly hair across her face, hiding it for a moment. Although he couldn't see her face, he knew the expression she would be wearing there. When she looked back at him, brushing her hair away from her face, Andar was not surprised to see tears pooling in her blue eyes once again. Without a word, he reached out and pulled her to him as he tried his best to comfort her, and she began to cry softly. He waited, not saying anything. He hoped with all his being that his quiet strength would be enough for now to help her get past this steep mountain that life was throwing across her path yet again.

After a few moments, she regained her composure and pulled away from him. She wiped her eyes with the heel of her hand and looked at him sadly.

"I know you're worried about your children," Andar began.

She nodded silently, afraid that if she tried to say anything, she would not be able to stop the tears that were sure to flow again.

"If there's one thing you must know, Jeane, more than anything you've ever known, please know this," he said. He cupped her chin in his strong, callused hand, and forced her to look up at him.

"You know I've spent many years of my life tracking both people and animals, and you know how good I am at it," he said.

She silently nodded, her chin still resting gently in his hand.

"Know, then, that I will do everything in my power to find your children. If it comes down to sacrificing my life in order to spare theirs, I will do it in a heartbeat. Their lives are just beginning, and they deserve a chance to experience every bit that life has to offer."

With that, he released her chin and pulled her close to him once again. He could feel her shaking in his arms. She remained silent, still struggling to control her emotions. After a moment, she squeezed him tightly for a few seconds before she pulled away. She stood tall with squared her shoulders and took a few deep breaths. When she felt that she'd composed herself enough, she looked at him, prepared now to ask him the question she had originally intended to ask.

"Tell me this then, cousin..." she said with a sniffle. "Have you seen any signs of them? Any signs at all since we left the enclosure?" she asked. She was afraid to hear his answer, but in both her heart and her mind, she needed to know.

He watched her silently as he considered her delicate questions. After a slight hesitation, he answered her with the answer he knew she didn't want to hear, but there was no other way.

"No."

Jeane did not fall apart as he'd feared she would. Instead, she nodded her head slightly and quietly acknowledged his answer. She took a deep breath as she looked this time into the western horizon.

Without further hesitation, she said, "Let's get moving then."

She tried to smile at him, but it was a poor attempt. He smiled a small, encouraging smile in return before they both turned eastward.

They walked silently toward the line of tall fir trees, close enough now that they could both unmistakably smell their fragrance.

Once they reached the tree line, they could see exactly what it was they had been walking towards. The trees were clustered and would indeed provide some shade from the hot sun, but they wouldn't shade them as much as they'd originally hoped.

The cluster of trees consisted of some firs, but those were outnumbered by other trees which had surely provided magnificent shading once upon a time. Andar looked at the trees closely as he tried to determine what kind they had once been.

Redwoods?

He just wasn't sure. In today's here and now, these tall trees were nothing more than the dark and lifeless skeletons of the beautiful trees they once were. Their trunks were very wide, wider than a few men standing side by side, and the trunks themselves were knotted and gnarled. Most of these had large, black holes in them that had likely provided homes to some of the larger night owls, he thought. The tops of the dead trees were what really caught his attention, however. Some of them extended far up into the sky, their branches narrowing as they extended upward. It almost looked as though they were comically reaching for the stars.

With other trees, however, their top halves were mysteriously missing. These oddities seemed to be clustered together.

"Strange," Andar thought. "Why would the top half of only some of the trees be missing?"

He inspected the ground near these trees as he scratched his head. He had expected to see that their tops had fallen, perhaps in a storm or with a strong gust of wind, and landed in a heap at the base of the tree. He was surprised, however, that there were none. Of course, there were small branches scattered here and there on the ground, but the upper halves of the trees were nowhere to be seen.

"What's wrong?" Jeane asked him.

He pointed the trees out to her and expressed his wonder at the missing treetops. She shook her head, agreeing that it was odd, indeed.

As they made their way further into the trees they could see some that had large, dark, jagged holes carved out of their trunks. The farther they made their way into the band of trees, the more common the holes became, and some of the larger trees had more than one.

Andar wondered silently how some of the trees managed to stay upright?

"I wonder what or who would have done this?" he quietly asked Jeane.

She could only shrug, as she did not have an answer for him.

They found a small cluster of fir trees in the midst of the dead trees, and beyond that it looked like open, barren, rocky terrain on the horizon. The sun was nearly at the end of its daily journey across the sky once again, so they decided to stop for the night under the shelter of the trees. Tomorrow, they would continue heading east in search of the children.

Muscala

One

As the sleeping venom wore off, Muscala struggled to regain his balance, and slowly his mind cleared. As it did, intense anger began to build deep within him, a result of the betrayal that had just occurred.

"Aaarrrrrrrgh!" he cried as the sound echoed through the dark tunnels of the cave. Those thieving brats had lied to him! They'd had the amulet with them but said they didn't…

They lied to him!!!

"Aaaaaargggh!" he roared angrily, once again. His body was quickly overcome with an incredibly deep hatred that flowed from the tip of his long, muscular tail, to the tip of his serpent's nose! The all-consuming anger filled his entire body… his mind, his heart, his very being! When he found them, he would eat them one at a time, savoring every last bite. Oh, yesss… First, however, he would be sure to frighten them more than they had ever been frightened before. He knew from experience that the more the prey is frightened, the more delectable they were to eat.

Mmmmmmmm…

Yes, he would enjoy that immensely. His mouth began to water with the thought of fresh meat…

A sound in the distance captured his attention.

As he listened, Muscala could faintly hear an intense humming noise which was created by the joining of the stones; he could FEEL their power as it slowly washed over his entire body, his mind, and his heart. The Dragon's Blood amulet… ahhhhh, yes… calling out to him and him alone! Calling to him, Muscala, Lord of the Darkness, telling him to come, come, come… to find it and return it to its rightful owner.

Yes, soon, very soon, he would be next to his King! Lotor, the mighty sorcerer of Euqinom, ruler of the world of the mightiest dragons of all time!

Without further hesitation, the serpent began the chase. He slithered through the dark tunnels as fast as he could, becoming more focused with each passing second as the last remnants of sleeping venom cleared from his head. He followed both the scent of the children and the soft humming sounds through the dark tunnels, heading towards the other side of the cave.

As he neared the entrances to the various tunnels on the opposite side of the large cavern, he was just able to make out the glow from the stones in one of the tunnels as it became brighter… first blue, then purple. He slowed down a bit. It would do him no good to rush through the cave and end up making a mistake because he was too excited and anxious to catch the little thieves. He forced himself slow down and focus on where he was going, not on what waited for him at the end of his path. Very soon now he would finally… FINALLY… have possession of the amulet! The gem he had been in search of for so very long!

The serpent watched the glow in the tunnel before him and smiled. He reveled in the thought that his personal quest, which had spanned over many, many moons, was nearing its end.

He continued to slither through the cave in hot pursuit of his gem. He knew he was getting close now… he could feel it. He could feel victory dangling like a spider in its web right in front of his piercing, red eyes. Without warning, the glow of the stones was snuffed out and the humming noise accompanying it disappeared. The only sounds he could hear now were his rapidly beating reptilian heart and the slithering sounds his body made as it moved through the dusty and dirty tunnels.

The disappearance of the light from the stones disturbed him, yet he was unwilling to give up. He continued his chase without hesitation, following the unmistakable scent of the troublesome creatures. As abruptly as it had ended, the humming sound began again in earnest, louder this time than before. The amulet, HIS amulet, was calling to him, like a beacon in the night, reaching out to him, wanting to be found.

It was very close now. In the darkness, he smiled victoriously.

"Aahhhh, yessss! I can sssmell you! I can almost hear your heartsss beating in terrified unison! "Yesss!! I will find you, you little thieves! And when I do, you... **will... PAY!!!**" he taunted them. He would reach them in just a matter of seconds! His heart beat faster in anticipation.

Rainbow light suddenly filled the tunnel in front of him and he could hear voices talking. Yes, he was very, very close...

"Go!" he heard one of them say.

Muscala's mouth watered more now – so much so that he was practically drooling.

He slowed slightly as he neared the end of the tunnel, which glowed with a bright rainbow aura. The amulet continued calling out to him, stronger now, vibrating deep within his head. With the humming sound in the cave and the vibrations he felt in his body, it was difficult for the snake to concentrate on where he was going. In spite of all the added stimulation, Muscala was very aware that the amulet would be in his possession in just a few short moments.

Even this was not enough to make him stop... oh no! Almost as if in a trance, he slithered through the mouth of the tunnel and into the small cavern where the light was being generated. The humming sound became almost unbearable as he got closer to the light. When he entered the cavern at the end of the tunnel, he stopped dead in his tracks, confused with what he saw in front of him.

Only one figure stood before the motionless body of water known as Still Water, not five. Where were the others? He slowly brought himself back to reality, away from the unending, oppressive humming. Once he accepted the fact that there was only one figure here, his attention immediately turned to the glowing stones. Both anger and lust filled his heart as Muscala stared at the most beautiful sight he had ever seen. The lone figure before him held the stones in its hand, a shimmering pool of vibrant colors.

The serpent stood frozen for a moment, mesmerized by the light display, his previously angry and lustful thoughts suddenly gone from his frenzied mind. The spell was broken as Micah, standing off to the side of the rainbow pool, turned and looked at the giant snake.

Muscala came out of his trance, immediately overwhelmed by feelings of extreme relief and exultation when he saw Micah standing alone with the amulet. The magical gem rested next to the other stones in the boy's opened palm. The snake wasn't surprised to see that the glow emanating from the amulet was much stronger in comparison to that of the other magical orbs.

"What are you doing?" the giant snake demanded quietly as he looked from Micah to the bright colors in the shimmering pool of water.

"Where are the othersss?"

Muscala glared at Micah with lust-filled eyes as the boy answered him.

"Safe and away from you!" Micah said proudly. Confused, Muscala watched as the boy took a step toward the shimmering rainbow of light that used to be known as 'Still Water'.

Understanding suddenly filled the serpent's eyes as he realized where the others had gone.

Muscala hissed at him angrily.

"Give me my amulet, boy!" Muscala hissed again. He smiled at Micah widely as his eyes became transfixed on the red stone.

When Micah didn't do as he asked, Muscala began inching his way towards him.

"Give it to meeeeeee!" the snake growled angrily.

"Pardon me," Micah said, breaking the spell.

Muscala stopped and looked at him angrily. He fervently hoped the boy's confidence would crumble and he would do as Muscala demanded… relinquish the amulet.

"You were a most gracious host," Micah said with obvious sarcasm in his voice, surprising the snake, "but our wonderful stay has come to an end."

As Muscala looked at him quizzically, Micah continued.

"I'm sorry, but I must be going now." Muscala watched as the boy closed his fingers over the glowing stones that rested gently in his hand. Without hesitation and before Muscala could comprehend his words, Micah joined the others as he stepped into the rainbow. As soon as he disappeared, the rainbow also disappeared, leaving only darkness and a motionless body of water in front of the flabbergasted snake.

"Noooo!" Muscala yelled as the shock of what just happened hit him.

"No! No! No! No!" he cried repeatedly in disbelief. His cries quickly escalated to shouts of anger. "Arrrrrgh!" he shouted. His eyes widened with distress and his heart filled with hatred.

He was Muscala! The King of the Cave! The Ruler of Darkness!

No creatures, large or small, had EVER outsmarted him!

This was the way it was after living for years in this cave. Now, impossibly, he had been outsmarted… not once, but twice! And by the same thieving, menial group of creatures, no less!

Oh, how he would make them pay!

"Arrrrrgh!" he shouted again angrily. He turned quickly and headed back to his home, maneuvering expertly through the tunnels and the darkness. When he reached the abyss, he descended quickly down the hole, going beyond the place where Nicho had fallen and continuing further into the depths of his home.

Once he arrived deep within the heart of the abyss, he stopped for a moment to collect his thoughts, and plan his next move. Angry blood still coursed like a burning torch through his veins as he thought again about how they had gotten away with the amulet… HIS amulet. Once again, his blood began to boil and anger quickly consumed him, and he knew he would have to calm down in order to think clearly. He remained where he was for a moment and closed his eyes, concentrating on his goal… the amulet.

After a few moments, his pulse stabilized. Ready to continue, he followed one of the tunnels even deeper into the cave. He knew exactly where he needed to go, and before he knew it, he was there.

Before him were five small rocks, which glowed softly in the darkness of the tiny, underground cavern. Their colors were familiar – red, yellow, green, blue and purple – and they formed an uneven circle in the center of the tunnel floor.

He hesitated slightly.

It had been quite some time since he had been on the other side. Once he got over there, his life, and his very existence, could be in grave danger.

Right now, however, he didn't care about that. His only concern was to find and take possession of the gem that had caused so many problems and so much heartache in his life.

The stones before him began humming in anticipation, beckoning him to move forward. He barely heard this, because his mind was filled with finding and taking possession of the amulet.

Without another thought, Muscala slithered into the circle of light before him and disappeared.

Two

Muscala transported through the portal silently, unable to help the way his body gyrated through the air as it whipped him this way and that. Having traveled through this very same portal a few times before, he knew what to expect. That didn't seem to matter right now, because he still found it difficult to control the way his muscular body writhed as it moved through the portal wind. With closed eyes, he waited patiently the few seconds it took for him to complete his journey. Before he knew it, he was back in the land he used to know so well, once upon a time... the land he had done everything in his power to leave.

Yesss, it had been quite some time ago. Muscala opened his eyes and found himself in the old outbuilding on the far side of the valley of stones. From the way the sunlight shone on the building's floor, he decided it must be close to mid-afternoon.

As he cautiously glanced around, he noticed that the interior of the building didn't really look much different. Enough time had passed since he'd been here last, and he had expected things would have noticeably changed. It seemed very odd that they hadn't.

Muscala recalled that Nivri had once mentioned something about wanting to convert this building to a spell house. The sorcerer had believed that the rocky terrain outside would serve as a wonderful conductor for some of his spells.

Muscala decided not to worry about the building – it didn't really matter to him whether or not the crazy sorcerer decided to make it a spell house. Right now, it looked abandoned, and that was just fine with him. He had other things to worry about besides the dirty, run-down building he now found himself in.

Yes...

He closed his eyes for a moment. His tongue flicked wildly as he looked for signs of recent activity in the outbuilding.

He needed to be sure about whether or not the children had been here... if the one that carried his amulet had been here...

Flick... Flick... Flick.

Nothing.

There was no trace of any of them. Exasperated, he opened his eyes.

Of course, they had gone through a totally different portal, and that didn't mean they would necessarily end up here. Muscala knew it did not matter which portal one traveled through. Only a special spell could get you to an exact destination.

No... they would end up in the same world, but not necessarily in the same location.

Yesss...

As he thought about the predicament that the children had likely found themselves in, he smiled. The chances were good that, as they traveled through the portal, each instance of travel had ended up in a different location. This meant the chances were also good that the boy who carried the magical stones and his amulet was not with the rest of the thieves.

Muscala smiled again as he thought of an even better possibility.

The chance that the boy... what was his name? Millek... no. Marta... no. Minah? No...

Micah! Yes, that was it!

He paused for a moment, hissing quietly as he looked around the room. He still felt the need to ensure that he was indeed alone.

Yesss, even though the reptile was certain that the boy was not here, there was a definite possibility that Micah had come through the cave portal to some location close to here.

The boy with hisss amulet... the boy he would love to find!

If Micah had come through the portal to some place nearby, Muscala was confident that he would find him...

Oh, yes!

He would find him and stalk him… he would frighten him and make him PAY for taking that which did not belong to him!

The amulet was his! Not theirs!

Then, once he finally tired of toying with the boy, he would end his miserable life before taking back his gem! And once the business with the boy was completed, Muscala could then attend to his other unfinished business…

The business from long ago…

His thoughts drifted back to Nivri. He had listened to the sorcerer gloat time after time about being Lotor's apprentice. Of course, that had been long ago, when Nivri was young and immature…

The snake silently wondered if the sorcerer still lived in the Castle Defigo. He was sure that he did. It was in a convenient location and was really quite a large castle for someone who was merely an apprentice. Nivri had not lived in the castle for very long when Muscala last departed from this world. The young sorcerer felt very comfortable in his new home.

Yes, Muscala assumed that Nivri still lived in the castle. The only other castle even remotely close to Defigo was Immolo, but that was Lotor's mansion, and no fool would try to overtake that castle! Only if Lotor died would anyone take it over, and that, in and of itself, would be quite an undertaking. If something happened to the mighty sorcerer, his castle would not be handed down to just anyone. Any apprentice who might be interested in taking Immolo to be their own home would have to participate in a grueling competition where they would have to demonstrate their magical capabilities. Then, only the winner of this competition would be worthy enough to take over the most powerful sorcerer's castle.

Muscala shook his head slightly as if he were coming out of a daydream. He knew he had to put aside all other thoughts and memories of his prior life in this world…

For now.

Right now, he knew he must focus on finding the boy and reclaiming his amulet. Once that was accomplished, his nerves could settle down and he could deal with other things.

The amulet… he must find the amulet. Once he found it, he

could return to Nivri and make all the past wrongs right. If he could do this, there would be no need for him to go back to his most recent home, the dark, stuffy cave. Instead, he could remain here and get back to the life he so abruptly left behind. If he could only bring the amulet back to Nivri, the sorcerer could then work his magic once again and return Muscala back to...

A large bird flew over the outbuilding where the roof had fallen in, startling Muscala out of his thoughts. He shook his head as he tried to try to clear his thoughts. He desperately needed to focus on the task at hand. He closed his eyes and took a few deep breaths. After a moment, he was ready to head out. With a final glance at the interior of the building, Muscala slithered out the door. He immediately turned towards the east, heading toward Defigo.

The children would be heading in the same direction... of this he was sure. They would head toward the castle in search of the unknown.

Muscala had an advantage over them, however...

He knew exactly where he was going, and could make it there very quickly if he really wanted to.

No, not yet.

He would make it to the castle in due time. Nivri would just have to wait.

Muscala had other plans.

His priority right now was to find the boy. When he found the boy, he would find the amulet. His amulet.

He had no doubts that, much like the rest of the pesky thieves, the boy would head east.

And if Muscala was lucky, he would be somewhere along the way, waiting for him.

Still smiling, Muscala slithered over the rocks as he continued the chase.

About The Author

MJ Allaire grew up in South Florida and after graduating high school, she joined the Navy and ended up in Pearl Harbor, Hawaii. Three children and ten years later, she moved to Connecticut. In her late 30's, she stumbled into her dream — not just writing and creating a world for both young and old, but visiting schools where she promotes both reading and writing.

This series began as nothing more than a single story for her children to read, but has turned into something much more. One story has evolved into a series, filled with magic, adventure, dragons, and of course, good versus evil.

For more information, please visit any or all of her websites below:

www.mjallaire.com
www.denicalisdragonchronicles.com
www.grizlegirlproductions.com
www.getkidstoread.org
www.booksbyteenauthors.com

Other books in this series are:

Dragon's Blood:
Denicalis Dragon Chronicles - Book One

Dragon's Tear:
Denicalis Dragon Chronicles - Book Three

Dragon's Breath:
Denicalis Dragon Chronicles - Book Four

Please visit us at:
www.denicalisdragonchronicles.com
www.mjallaire.com